Totally Bound Publishing books by Aurelia T. Evans

Single Books
Red Queen
Intervention

Arcanium
Fortune
Carousel
Aerial
Ringmaster
Contortion
Spider
Funhouse
Haunted
Skeletons
Silk
Illusion

Meridian
Stone & Chains
Fever & Fray
Strange & Familiar

Collections
Frostbite: Gravedigger

Meridian

STRANGE & FAMILIAR

AURELIA T. EVANS

Strange & Familiar
ISBN # 978-1-80250-590-0

Interior text design by Claire Siemaszkiewicz
Totally Bound Publishing

Published in 2024 by Totally Bound Publishing, United Kingdom.

Totally Bound Publishing is an imprint of Totally Entwined Group Limited.

STRANGE & FAMILIAR

Chapter One

She didn't like the way that man was looking at Angel.

The perpetual designated driver, Katelyn nursed her Diet Coke at the bar. She wouldn't be able to hear what the people next to her were saying unless they yelled in her direction, but Katelyn didn't need to hear that man to have all she needed to know to be uncomfortable.

He stared into Angel's eyes when she looked at him—attentive, sensitive, so much so that even Katelyn would have been deceived—but as soon as Angel looked away, his gaze wandered over her like a butcher inspecting meat. He wasn't leering. His burning attention—impersonal, clinical—seared Angel's neck along the waterfall of blonde hair that she'd spent an hour curling just right while wishing aloud for a personal stylist, down to her ass moving to the palpable beat jolting through the floors and chairs.

All that wasn't really enough to justify Katelyn's suspicions. When Angel broke away from him to talk with Maria and Aly for a few minutes, he didn't follow or offer to hold her drink. She kept her eyes peeled for powders or pills, but the man did nothing but stare when he wasn't aware he was being watched.

Katelyn kept telling herself that she was being the paranoid mother hen who always ruined the party. Maria, Aly and Angel told her she needed to loosen up and stop expecting the worst of people, but she couldn't shake her bad feelings when she had them. And Angel was such a small girl, although Katelyn knew firsthand that short people could be dangerous in their own right, on the level with the most vulnerable part of a man's anatomy.

This man, however, was a giant. Katelyn couldn't place him as a University of Texas-Meridian football or basketball player, and she would know. Delta Tau was a big fan of both programs, unofficial cheerleaders and often fawning groupies. He could have been from one of the Dallas schools, or he could have even been a Cowboy or a Maverick, but really, why would a professional athlete travel several hours to Meridian to pay to dance and pay more to drink? Sure, Meridian nightlife had a decent reputation, but Dallas wasn't exactly a ghost town after ten.

So he probably wasn't a professional athlete, and he looked a little old to be in college, a little young to be a retired pro.

Maybe a boxer or an MMA fighter. Katelyn sipped her drink again and traced the contours of his muscles with her gaze. His skin was almost shadow, even under the neon lights, but he was so big that she could discern each individual muscle group from a distance in the dark. Some kind of athlete—that much she knew. Perhaps a bodybuilder as well, naturally big but bulked up on top of that. His arms strained the limits of the sleeves that contained them, and his chest pushed against the front of his shirt. His jeans weren't of the skinny variety, but they clung to him from ass to calves by virtue of his size.

He was the kind of guy a girl didn't mind ogling, but he wasn't exactly the kind of guy a girl wanted to be unsure about.

When Angel continued talking with Aly and Maria, the man wandered off. Katelyn finally caught him chatting up another blonde, this one even smaller and more delicate, but they spoke with the same straightforwardness as Aly and Maria with Angel—like friends. The plus-one for entry, perhaps, since girls could usually get into 360° just fine. Even Katelyn could get in when Aly, Maria and Angel trailed her along with them—the perks of association. The only problem was when guys hit on her trying to get to them—or because they'd already struck out with the drunk hotties and thought they'd get a little coyote ugly for their troubles.

Katelyn didn't think she was that bad, which was why she never hesitated to give trolls a one-finger salute if they didn't get the first five hints, but she'd faced facts a long time ago. She'd been initiated into Delta Tau because she was smart, because she cleaned up well and because she was a legacy. She evened out the pictures and—like Maria, who dyed her hair blonde but kept her last name—kept the sorority from getting too much attention from the diversity police.

It hadn't escaped her notice that her friends—and they *were* friends, no snark—were talking with each other on the dance floor while she played house mother at the bar, making sure her chicks didn't get hurt while they had their fun. Even so, people-watching was fun, too.

Big Guy was still talking to Tinkerbell, but Tinkerbell had turned her attention to the laughing, talking, dancing trio. Now, both of them were staring.

Katelyn's mind did its worst-case scenario party trick, with images of cages and auctions. She closed her eyes and shook her head, laughing at herself. Jumping to conclusions had its evolutionary purpose, but God, she felt so ridiculous once she realized what she was doing. Odds were, Big Guy was a creep and Tinkerbell was just a creepette, glaring at the girl Big Guy was creeping on—or maybe she was giving him wing-woman pointers.

Big Guy and Tinkerbell split into the crowd, and Katelyn lost them.

Maria, Aly and Angel stumbled off the dance floor, giggling like mad, and surrounded Katelyn in a mob.

"Hey, girl, come on. Aren't going to do anything except watch?" After Maria's fourth drink, she was well over the decibel level needed to be heard.

"We don't bring you along just as a taxi, you know." Aly ruffled Katelyn's hair. Katelyn quickly used the condensation from her Coke glass to smooth it back down. She hadn't spent an hour on her hair like Angel had, but she didn't want to have to take her braid down to fix whatever mess Aly would make of it while high—just E, but it meant she didn't always know when to stop.

"Come on. Join us." Maria pulled on Katelyn's wrists. "You can't just sit up here all night. We have a reputation to maintain."

"I'm here. I'm partying. I'm good," Katelyn said.

"We got to get you laid, lady," Aly said. "We got to find you a hot guy. You have at least two hours before we leave to get it on in the car."

"I have condoms in my purse. What?" Maria said when other people around them looked at her strangely. "If they only knew how many times a guy whips his dick out and says he forgot to bring protection, but he'll just pull out when he gets there. Hell no."

"I don't want to get laid," Katelyn protested.

Once her friends decided they wanted her on the dance floor grinding the nearest meat sack they could find, it was hard to dissuade them, but a club was the last place Katelyn wanted to hook up. At this time of night, everyone but her was drunk, and that made for some interesting ideas of what was sexy.

Still, dancing probably wouldn't hurt, just to get the girls off her back. Besides, she could keep a better eye on them while dancing with them than watching from a distance.

"Good girl," Angel said, coming up from behind and dancing against her for the delight of the guys around them.

"Do you know that guy?" Katelyn asked.

"Which one?"

"The one you were dancing with before."

"Gotta narrow it down, Kate."

"The big Black guy."

"Oh! Yeah, no, I don't know him. Hot, though, isn't he? I bet he can pump it all night long."

"I don't know," Katelyn said. "You know what 'roids do."

Angel laughed, pulling Katelyn's braid. "Still, 'd be nice for a test ride. He felt big enough when we were dancing like this."

"I feel big enough, too," Katelyn said, grinding back to Angel's giggles. Angel spanked her before dancing around and rubbing their asses together, riding

Katelyn's skirt up. Katelyn couldn't help her own giggles. She ground back through the end of the song, when Angel slung her arm around Katelyn's shoulder and kissed her cheek before moving on.

Katelyn let herself be roped into two more songs. Aly did her usual offering of the pills she kept in her bra, trying to get Katelyn to have a better time, but she never took it personally when Katelyn turned her down, just shrugged and closed her eyes, rubbing her willowy self against whoever came up against her. Katelyn envied her abandon—ecstasy or no ecstasy. And her figure… Aly still took dance, but her professional hopes had been dashed by height the way some dancers' dreams had been shattered by an ass, like Katelyn's. Katelyn's more mature body certainly couldn't do what it used to do when she'd taken classes with Aly back in middle school, before she'd grown from a size four to a size eight in a year, bloomed from an A cup to a D almost overnight, then continued to grow all through high school.

All that mattered here, though, was the beat. Nothing like a good beat to take the mystery out of movement, and nothing like friends to keep her from being too self-conscious. She was what she was. She'd known what she was going to become based on what her mother looked like, and hell, it hadn't gotten in her way yet. So why not be okay with it, cellulite and all?

She'd caught herself in the mirror before leaving—red dress, low-cut to let her boobs jiggle all a horny freshman would want, swishy skirt, cute flats, serviceable Katniss braid in her natural ginger. There was nothing to be ashamed of just because she couldn't compare with Maria's sequins and sass, Angel's Jessica Rabbit figure and Aly's modeling side hustle. She'd made it, basic bitches. So she wasn't the party girl her friends wanted her to be, but she could dance her ass off with the best of them.

The next time Katelyn looked up, Maria, Aly and Angel had gradually shifted away. She found Aly first, because Aly was taller than most of the girls around her. Katelyn did a double-take when she saw that Aly's dancing partner was Tinkerbell, their ashy-blonde hair almost identical, although that and their waif-like thinness were the only things they had in common.

A little bit of closeness wasn't surprising on this kind of dance floor, but Tinkerbell stroked over Aly's arms, and Aly seemed lost, her eyes glazed as their bodies undulated against each other—not in a 'this is so much fun, be a part of my fun' way, but in a 'God, fuck, yes, that's sexy' way.

Katelyn felt dirty just noticing. Abrupt bisexuality like that was kind of verboten in Delta Tau, unless there were Alpha Mus around. The sorority could wave a rainbow flag during Pride, but God forbid anyone sleep under a rainbow blanket. Katelyn didn't have a problem with it, but word got around, even if the person in question wouldn't remember much more than a fuzzy Polaroid in the morning.

Katelyn looked around for Angel and Maria to help her rescue Aly. It was only midnight, but Katelyn thought it was time to get Aly home to sleep it off.

Maria was a few feet away, one arm around the man in front of her and the other around the guy behind her. She was holding her sixth drink. Katelyn was pretty sure the man in front of her was gay, but that wasn't any of her business. Even when Maria was stumbling, a quickie in a bathroom was about all Katelyn had to worry about from her.

Katelyn scanned the tops of everyone's heads, searching, increasingly frantic, for Angel's particular blonde, which was a bit like trying to look for a drunk person in a bar—every other freaking person was blonde in here.

Her heart jerked in her chest when she finally saw Angel's lavender top pressed against one of the black-painted columns as she clung to the giant form of the muscled man she'd been talking to earlier. She wasn't talking now. They were connected at the mouth, tongues passing between their open lips as though neither could get enough of the other. Angel's hand was pale against his bald head. She was wild, lost, her eyes as glazed as Aly's. She didn't usually take any of Aly's E, but Katelyn couldn't dismiss it—and that just worried her more.

Her stomach twisted in sickly circles. If any of her girls decided to go home with a strange guy—or girl—was there really anything Katelyn could do about it? Was there anything she was *supposed* to do about it? She didn't mind spending the night in the library when one of the girls decided to entertain, although usually everyone was considerate enough to do it at their guys' dormitories or in the privacy of a car or an abandoned room somewhere on campus. Strangers at the club were another thing, especially when Katelyn was the only ride home.

Big Guy reluctantly parted from Angel, who panted and clutched at him to bring him closer. He stroked the length of her neck, down until his thumb caressed the peak of her breast, which pressed hard and teasing against her thin top. It wasn't like she could wear a bra underneath.

Katelyn couldn't help how intensely she blushed. She wasn't completely inexperienced, but she knew better than to ever use the V-word around her friends and frenemies at DT. She wasn't waiting for someone special. She just didn't want to get it over with to get it over with—and that meant she wasn't willing to settle for some mouth-breather and a Walk of Shame in the morning, hoping no one would notice a bloodstain on the sheets.

Bumping, grinding and twerking on the dance floor was nothing. Seeing Big Guy's large hands so deft over Angel made Katelyn too uncomfortably aware of her own body. She couldn't wear flimsy tops like her friends, because not wearing a bra was akin to inviting an assault and battery charge from her boobs punching someone in the face, and her ass could never fit in compact parking. But she suddenly wanted hands like those—not necessarily *his*, but *something* like his—on her like that. Preferably somewhere more private, but at that moment, Katelyn's yearning was so strong, she couldn't blame Angel for biting her lip and arching into Big Guy's touch.

Then Big Guy slipped his giant hand under her shirt, groping her firmly and sensuously with no regard for the people around them, and Angel didn't slap him the way she or Maria always did if a guy got too fresh too fast. Instead, she looked like he had a direct line to her G-spot with the power of his stare.

Katelyn glanced at Aly. The similarities between Aly's and Angel's expressions hit her immediately. Angel had had only one drink, Aly two plus enhancements, and Angel was with a man with godlike arms while Aly was with a fairy-like woman—complete strangers—but they'd both been hit hard with the same something.

Still playing with Angel's breast, Big Guy glanced across the crowded dance floor, directly at Tinkerbell. They both nodded.

Just a dip of the head, but Katelyn abruptly stopped dancing, leaving the people around her without someone soft to press against, and wove through the throng to Maria.

"Hey!" Katelyn shouted over the music. "We need to get Aly and Angel home. Something's wrong."

"Relax, killjoy. You're just jealous because they're getting some tonight and you're not."

"I'm not being paranoid. I think they're being tag-teamed by people who put something in both of their drinks. Something is very wrong. We need to get them home."

"Oh, whatever." But Maria extricated herself from the man-wich she'd been enjoying.

Katelyn tended to think of all the ways that things *could* go wrong, sometimes to an outrageous degree, but she also had an uncanny ability to figure out the ways that things were already going wrong. DT could talk about how Katelyn was the buzzkill, the good girl, the surrogate mother, all they wanted, but when Katelyn insisted, the girls knew to listen. She'd saved at least three girls from roofies and five from being taken advantage of during house parties.

"You get Aly," Katelyn said. "I'll get Angel."

Maria rolled her eyes in annoyance, but Tinkerbell had her mouth at Aly's ear, lips brushing the shell, and Aly was nodding. Katelyn gave Maria a little shove as Tinkerbell led Aly toward the back exit. If Maria grumbled about not being anyone's babysitter, she didn't do it where Katelyn could hear, and she worked her way through the crowd fast enough. As soon as Maria started bickering with a belligerent and visibly confused Aly, Katelyn turned to rescue Angel.

A determined glare and refusal to stop got people out of her way in a hurry. As long as she didn't spill anyone's drink, people filled up the space she left behind like water flowing around a stone and went back to the business of having a good time.

Up close, Big Guy seemed even bigger, and his groping seemed that much obscener, yet arousing. He whispered in Angel's ear much as Tinkerbell had with Aly, but it seemed so much more sinister when it came from a man who towered over the object of his attention instead of vice versa.

"Hey, girl." Katelyn nudged Angel's shoulder with as little awkwardness as possible. "Maria and I aren't feeling so hot. It's time to go."

"No." Angel flopped back against the column and pouted up at the man. "I'll find my own way home."

"You'll find your way to a hangover and regret. How many drinks have you had?"

"Just two." Angel stared at her empty hands. "Maybe three."

"Yeah, we're taking you home." Katelyn tried to extricate Angel from Big Guy with all the diplomacy she could when hands were touching intimate places. "Sorry, man. Find someone else."

"We weren't finished." He even rumbled like a giant. Next thing, he was going to threaten to grind her bones to make his bread.

"There're plenty of options out there, but we need to go," Katelyn said, hoping he didn't decide he'd prefer her as a Hulk-smashed blob of jelly on the floor. Those arms were bigger around than her head. Being right next to them like this was more than a little intimidating.

And Angel was still doing nothing to help separate herself from the man. "He invited me to a party. Exclusive. Hard-fucking-core. Wanna come with?"

"Yes," the man said. When Katelyn would extricate him from one place, he'd find another. At least now he was over Angel's clothing instead of under. Still awfully handsy. "You and your friends are all invited."

"So you're not a perv. You're recruiting." Katelyn abandoned all attempts to contain the situation and instead yanked Angel behind her.

Now the guy was starting to look pissed off, but also...intrigued—and not in a good way.

At this point, Katelyn's stomach decided it really wanted to be empty—yeah, empty. She swallowed back bile. They needed to leave. *Now.*

Katelyn backed them both away. "Maria's going to blow chunks all over someone else's dress if we don't go." She glanced at the bar and the entrance. The bartender was checking on her, making sure nothing escalated. *Good.*

Now that Big Guy had completely turned his attention from Angel to her, she experienced the full force of his gaze.

What are his eyes made of, magnets? Is he so big he literally has greater gravitational force?

"I don't think it's your friend who feels sick," he said. "Our party can fix that."

"A party isn't the cure for what ails me."

He stepped forward every time she stepped back, and his stride was greater. Soon they'd be walking into people on the dance floor. It didn't help that Angel kept trying to get back around Katelyn.

He held out his hands for both girls, glancing again in the direction of Tinkerbell. "You'd be surprised."

Katelyn slapped Angel's hand before she could take one, then hooked her arm through Angel's to whirl her away. The longer she stayed and argued, the more likely she'd agree to that party of his—and not because of any grand argument. *Those eyes.* Those eyes that made her pulse race in her ears off-rhythm to the music.

His hand weighed heavy on her shoulder. "Stay," he whispered in her ear, sending shivers through her. If it hadn't been for Angel stumbling from the turnabout, Katelyn might have just let the man have his way.

"No," she said firmly. "We're going. Good night."

He could part a crowd faster than she did, but Katelyn could maneuver better. She yanked Angel along, despite her slurring protests.

Three drinks, my ass. The guy must have given her another one, plus extras.

She met up with Maria, who was keeping a similarly sloshed Aly away from Tinkerbell. After a brief look at Big Guy, Tinkerbell fixed her attention on Katelyn as well.

Definitely some kind of conspiracy, and Katelyn didn't want to know.

She clamped her hand around Maria's wrist and dragged all three girls to the front. She didn't even try pretending everything was okay as she paused at the bar.

"Hey, Ben, those two—the blonde in the metallic dress and the big guy over there—something's up. I think they're drugging girls and inviting them to some private party."

"Your friends okay?" the bartender asked.

"More or less."

"Those two are regulars around here, but I'll have them looked into," Ben said. "Sorry if they were really bothering you girls."

"All good."

"Night. Get home safe."

"He'd totally hit that, *chica.* Man, she is *wasted,*" Maria said, supporting Aly as well as she could when she wasn't exactly 'walk a straight line' material herself.

"Just need to get to the car." Katelyn checked behind them. Tinkerbell and Big Guy had disappeared once more into the crowd, and that actually scared her even more, because a giant and a fairy shouldn't have been inconspicuous.

"Hey, can you keep an eye on us till we get in our car?" Katelyn asked one of the bouncers. "I think someone's following us."

The bouncer—big, but only his neck was thicker than Big Guy's—nodded.

That made her feel a little better as she led the three girls to her car and helped Angel into the front passenger seat.

"Wanted to go to the party," Angel murmured. She tucked her heels up and leaned against the window. That would do until they got home.

Katelyn climbed into the driver's seat and made sure at least Maria was fastened in. Aly's head was in Maria's lap. Maria finally looked troubled.

"Geez, what'd these crazy kids take?"

"No idea," Katelyn said, "and I'm not staying to find out."

* * * *

Something was dripping, and all Katelyn initially thought was that she'd been so careful not to drink anything, much less drink and drive.

She opened her eyes against a splitting headache. The world was upside-down, flashing, red, dark. Very dark. Dark-alley dark. Why the hell would she be driving upside-down in dark alleys in the middle of the night?

It took her more than a few groggy moments fighting blurry vision and the squeezing vise that encased her whole head to figure out where she was.

She hung in the sling of her seatbelt. Blood dripped down her face from a split welt on her head and from her mouth where the airbag had caught her lip on her teeth. None of her teeth felt loose or missing, though, and after a quick inventory, she concluded that none of her limbs were broken. Based on the blur of her vision, however, she might have a concussion.

She had no idea how long she'd been like this. Was she alone? *Please, God, let me be alone. Let me have gone out for a late-night coffee run to caffeinate before a post-clubbing study session.* She didn't remember dropping the girls off, but she also didn't remember anything after leaving 360°.

It hurt to turn her head. *Whiplash.* But she managed to creak her stiff muscles enough.

Angel hung much as Katelyn did in her seatbelt harness. Her legs had smashed against the glove compartment at an awkward angle. Glass from the broken passenger window glittered red like stars over a forest fire in her mane of hair, which was stained dark in streaks, but Katelyn couldn't tell where the blood was coming from or if Angel's chest moved.

"Aly? Maria?" Katelyn groaned.

She didn't think she could turn her head all the way to see them, so she checked the rearview mirror when she heard a noise beyond the ringing in her ears. Aly had collapsed in an upright seated position in the upside-down car, her body splayed and at bad angles like a broken doll. Her neck was wrong, her head too loose at the apex of her spine. She'd been lying down in Maria's lap…not strapped in.

Maria wasn't in the car at all.

That sound again. Not anything she'd associate with a car crash, unless something was leaking heavily.

Thick and fluid. Almost like a blow job, except that wasn't right either.

Aly's body shifted in the mirror, the head adjusting itself and the hair pushing itself away. Aly's neck was broken. She shouldn't have been moving at all.

Katelyn whipped around, whimpering as her own neck screamed in protest.

A woman was draped over Aly, her face buried in Aly's neck. She pulled up at Katelyn's cry of pain.

Blood, black in the darkness, dripped from long ivory teeth, welled over lips, a cup runneth over. More blood flowed from the open, wicked gash in Aly's neck.

Tinkerbell ran the back of her hand over her mouth. "You're alive. Jude will be so pleased he gets to kill you."

Chapter Two

Traffic cones. A flashing detour sign. She'd been suspicious the moment she'd driven into the alley, and she'd tried to back up. No one had been behind her when she'd checked, but when she'd looked out of the front again, Big Guy was there at the hood. It should have been impossible. She hadn't been followed. How could they have known where Katelyn was going *and* gotten there first?

Regardless of how, Big Guy had been there anyway, Tinkerbell a glittering, grinning apparition behind him. He'd taken hold of the front of the car and lifted it from the ground.

"No way," Maria had muttered.

Then he'd flipped the car over, front end over back, as though it were nothing more than a card table.

Based on their present position, he might have done it more than once after Katelyn had blacked out. Or maybe he'd had enough momentum from the one flip to roll them over multiple times. *Impossible.* All of it was impossible, yet it was happening. Men who could flip cars, women who couldn't be seen in mirrors... This was happening. Katelyn couldn't think hard enough to refute it, not even to consider it a dream.

"What—? Who—? What—?" There wasn't any phrasing to make any kind of sense of what was going on. She groaned against the increased pressure and pangs in her head, the way the world seemed to sway.

"Very articulate." Tinkerbell shook her head, then plunged her teeth back into Aly's neck.

"No. No." Katelyn's protests sounded more like the car creaking every time Tinkerbell moved, unconcerned about the broken glass and compromised integrity of the vehicle.

"Do keep trying," Tinkerbell murmured with her mouth full.

The driver's side window shattered. Katelyn screamed and kept screaming as a pair of gigantic hands tore through her seatbelt as though it were beef jerky. He caught her before she hit the roof of the car, pulled her out, then set her down on her feet. Her screams transformed into shouts as the blood flow and reorientation made her already unbearable headache like hammers pounding her skull.

"You, my dear, have made my night far more complicated than it needed to be," Big Guy said. *Jude*, Tinkerbell had called him. "Oh, you can stand. You can do it. Here we go, love."

He tucked his arm around her waist and braced her against his body. Though his words suggested impatience or frustration, his expression leaned more to the considering intrigue of before, the kind that made Katelyn struggle to get away, but pushing against him was like wrestling a mountain.

"No, no, I'm afraid it's too late for that. You have to understand, it's nothing personal. We bear your friends no ill will. They were convenient, and we were hungry. An unfortunate coincidence. But you posed quite an obstacle, and now you have my attention, for better or worse. How did you know? We've been trolling 360° for years, among other clubs and bars. Sometimes hunters notice, and we have to avoid a watering hole for a while, but you're no hunter—not so much as a stake in your purse or misguided cross around your neck. So tell me— How did you know?"

"How did I know *what*?" She winced as she buried her head in her hands, which rested against his chest, but the world was on full tilt, and she had nothing else around to lean against.

"How did you know both your friends were targets? How could you tell we wanted more than harmless flings?"

"Seriously, no one ever notices? You couldn't have been more fucking obvious."

"We've been operating here for ten years. Not a single hunter detected more than a suggestion. What did you see? Once you saw it, your entire demeanor changed, and we weren't even after you."

"You're not going to let me go, are you?"

He stroked her hair. After the accident, she wasn't worried about her half-destroyed braid anymore. He didn't seem to mind, either. "I can't."

"You're going to kill me?"

"Maybe."

"Why?" She tried to look up at him, but another set of iron nails plunged into her skull, and she shouted again, desperately holding her head together to keep brain matter from leaking out of her ears.

"Shhh, shhh." For a cold-blooded, murderous giant, he was surprisingly gentle. "It'll all be over soon. Like I said, it isn't personal. The only problem…" He drew his brows together and brushed his fingers over the bump on her head, gathering drops of blood on his fingertips. "I've fed. Tinsel has fed. Your other friend is already bound and wrapped for Cara. So that leaves you the odd girl out."

"This isn't real," Katelyn muttered. In a few minutes, she was going to wake up in her own bed with a sympathetic hangover, and the people she'd rescued her friends from weren't hardened psychopaths on bath salts.

"The nightmare is real, love."

That wet sound from the car was now just above her head. When she chanced a look, she caught him sinking his fingers, stained with her blood, into his mouth.

"Oh God." These people were sick, sadistic, his gentleness not sensitivity but posturing.

"There are worse things than a nightmare. The only question now is how I show you that. I should kill you, drain you dry while your last words are to beg me for *more, harder, harder, more*."

"Sick creep-fuck," she muttered, trying again to push away, but he swept her off her feet like a groom with his bride. A quiet part of her jostled brain couldn't help but relish the feeling that so few men could give her, as effortless as he made it seem.

"Not a single vessel disappoints, and though I've fed, I can always take more. But it would pain me to let you go to the grave with your secret." He gazed between the bump on her head and her swollen mouth, both still bloody as hell. "Perhaps you may yet be of some use—to me, to us. The next time I ask how, you'll be in a much more confessional state of mind. And if you're lucky, love, I might just give you the gift they all seek, the diamond in the darkness—an eternity to live and die in these bloody pleasures. But for now, for now…I think I'll have a taste but pour you the wine."

"No…no…" she whispered as he lowered his head, his gaze fixed upon her mouth with terrible hunger. Fear lanced through her, briefly overriding pain, and she writhed and twisted in his arms. But though she held up her hands to push at his face, claw at his eyes, all he did was kneel on one knee, propping her upper half up with his other leg. He curled his hand around her neck, threatening to squeeze.

When he smiled, two wicked, sharp teeth plunged down from above his eyeteeth to slot over his lower lip. "Don't worry. They're not for you. Calm down. Don't struggle. I don't understand *why* you're struggling. So many things to ask, but you're in no state to answer." He kissed her forehead. "I smell the inflammation. My communion can help that, too."

He gazed down at her with somewhat bemused affection as Katelyn continued her fruitless efforts to fight her way out of his arms.

"Tomorrow should be interesting," he mused. "You'll tell me everything I want to know. Once I get what I need, perhaps I'll kill you then. Either way," he whispered into her bloody hair, smearing his lips over the wound, "I'll make it good. Trust me."

"You killed… You'll kill…"

"We are what we are." Jude licked his lips, then nearly dropped her, grunting with effort Katelyn didn't understand. "*God,* that's good."

"Please let me go."

"I can't do that," he replied as he gathered his composure once again. "But I promise, in a little while, you won't want me to."

"No. No, no, no, no, no." Tinkerbell stormed around the totaled car. Big Guy had called her *Tinsel,* but

Katelyn was pretty sure she'd misheard. Who named their kid Tinsel? Who named *themselves* Tinsel? "We agreed, Jude. Eliminate the threat. That's all. We don't need any additional responsibility, between our needs and our obligation to Cara."

"*Your* obligation to Cara."

"She's *our* family. We don't need the one who messed up this whole night staying with us twenty-four-seven. I don't care if she gets familiar or gets fangs, Jude. We're not taking her in."

"It's not your decision."

"It's *my* home," she snapped.

"It's *our* home. It's *my* decision. I chose the confrontation, so I choose the conclusion."

"Everyone thinks they want to sire or they want a familiar until reality sets in after no one can take it back."

"I'm flattered," Jude said.

"You're usually an exception, but right now, you're a fucking pain in my ass. Would you stop looking at her like you've adopted a bedraggled kitten?"

"But she's mine." He held her as though Katelyn wasn't trying to get away at all. And Katelyn was losing steam, pain catching up to panic.

Tinsel crossed her arms, scowling. "You're going to regret it, just like I regret ever being soft with you."

"You were never soft with me," Jude said quietly. "And I won't be soft with her."

"Then do what you were going to do and get it over with. We have to give that other girl to Cara soon, and the more your girl struggles, the more likely she'll get someone else to notice."

"I'm not going to rush this. I'm not going to rush *her*."

"All she needs is a drop. One drop and she's yours. Or we can just fucking go, and you can turn her at home. Then I don't have to choke on my own vomit watching you coo over your new dove."

"Sounds romantic." And for some reason, he didn't sound like he was kidding.

"You guys are pecan pie with walnut and peanut butter icing," Katelyn said through gritted teeth. The harder she tried to escape Jude's arms, the less she seemed able to move.

"She's putting together coherent epithetical metaphors," Tinsel said. "Shall I get the duct tape? I'd love to tape her pretty little mouth—and cover those eyes, whatever they saw in us."

"We'll know soon enough. Mouth, not eyes, Tinsel. Don't be cruel."

"'*Don't be cruel.*' As though he doesn't know the first thing about who we are. What we are."

Tinsel ran into the alley and came back with a roll of duct tape much faster than she should have been able to.

Katelyn was weakening, her limbs shaking and her headache pulsing almost like a vibration, her blurry vision swaying, exhaustion sinking over her like a hot, wet blanket. She barely slapped Tinsel's hands away while she bound Katelyn's wrists and ankles. As soon as Katelyn tried to scream for help, Tinsel gleefully smashed the tape over her mouth, sticking the adhesive to her teeth, tongue and swollen lip. Tinsel put several more layers over the first…just in case.

Jude raised an eyebrow but apparently decided not to comment and instead stood with Katelyn still in his arms. He carried her away from the scene of the accident—not so much an accident—and deeper into the alley, where a black Cadillac SUV waited. He settled her into the back seat, deliberately strapping her in with a glint of amusement in his eyes.

Those are my friends you killed, Katelyn thought. *Don't you dare make them a joke.*

A thump behind her made Katelyn jump.

"It's just your friend," Jude said before closing the back door.

She's in the trunk and I'm in the back seat?

She's in the trunk, and she's still alive*?*

Katelyn's screams were muffled through the layers of duct tape, even to herself.

"Seriously, you couldn't have killed her or at least dripped her? Now we have to listen to that all the way home," Tinsel said as Jude ducked into the driver's seat.

He twisted around in his seat. "I need you to stay quiet. I have to live with this woman, and so will you. Now, be a good girl and let the concussion pull you under. There's nothing terrible in that darkness. It's where you want to be. The only way to wake up from the nightmare is to fall asleep. There we go. That's my girl."

The more he spoke, the more his words wrapped around her head like velvet, taking over from the vise. Soft fingers drew her consciousness down. She couldn't keep her eyes open.

I shouldn't sleep. I have a concussion.

"When you wake, I'll heal you—one way or the other," he said, almost a whisper, gentle as warm blankets and soft mattresses, white-noise music. She sank deeper and deeper into the leather seat, listing to the side against the seatbelt, and again, it was he who caught her, his arms surrounding her, his voice leading her into the dark.

* * * *

Had she been asleep? She didn't know, couldn't remember so much as a sliver of a dream. She was in darkness one moment, her eyes open the next. There was no longer duct tape on her mouth.

Unconsciousness—or whatever it had been—hadn't done anything for her headache, and being bound made the stiffness of her shaken body even worse.

"I know. I know it hurts—but only for a little while longer." Jude stood from the threadbare settee and knelt beside where she lay on a gray quilted coverlet in a perfectly ordinary bed, as far as she could tell. The room itself was oddly industrial, metal panel walls, thick girded door, no windows, but its accoutrements were those of a home.

Katelyn didn't struggle. She hadn't been able to fight him off without duct tape. With it, she was a trussed-up partridge.

Jude seemed even more out of place than the walls, but in the light, the unfettered warmth in his gaze surprised and disarmed her. He physically looked like he could crush a tank, but his countenance, his whole demeanor, was far from menacing.

That was the danger of him. She wasn't fooled, but the panic his presence induced was nowhere near where it had been, no matter how much she tried to convince herself to fear him more.

Now wasn't the time, however, to fight—not without a rocket launcher. She needed to plan her escape, for whenever she got the chance.

Sometime between the car and this room, he'd unbraided her hair. He arranged it behind her shoulders now. "I'm sorry things had to go this way. If you'd let us have your two friends, you and your other friend might have avoided this fate entirely. In trying to save all, I'm afraid you failed to save any."

"You're *sorry*? There are places for people like you," Katelyn said, "with rubber rooms, cattle prods and sedatives."

"We're not crazy."

"No, you're worse. You're calculating, methodical, deliberate and strong. Add violent and delusional, and we have a dangerous problem."

He smiled. "You've known me for less than a cumulative hour and you've already narrowed me down to a science—accurate, if limiting. I suppose I seem quite the villain to you, don't I? It's hard to see us through the eyes of our victims anymore. We've been what we are for so long. We're not villains, though."

"That's right. You're just misunderstood. Spoken like a true villain."

"You're too old to couch adversaries in terms of hero and villain. Not all predators are evil."

"I'm pretty sure human ones are."

"Unless you're vegetarian, you can't possibly believe that, and hypocrisy doesn't become you. Even so, love, I'm *not* human."

"Now we're back to delusional."

"I thought you realized. I thought you saw." Jude drew his lips back as fangs sliced from his gums once again.

In bright light, they were so much harder to deny as a concussion-induced hallucination. She saw those long teeth—*fangs, they're called fangs, and you know it*—but her brain seemed to erase them from her vision, unable to process what their existence meant.

Nothing else in her life justified this kind of revelation. She'd gone to church on Sundays for most of her youth, with nary a miracle to be found. She'd joined friends in visiting a fortune teller, but it had been nothing that couldn't be explained by standard astrology vagueness and cold reading. She'd never had any reason to believe in ghosts, psychics, mediums, religion or things that go bump in the night. She'd slept in the dark in security and safety, content in the knowledge that the only thing to fear was human, well-cowed by sharp or blunt objects wielded by unyielding hands.

None of this could be real. Unpleasant. Terrifying. Awful. Painful. *Not* real.

"Perhaps you understood but have not yet accepted." As though those black eyes could pierce right into her thoughts. "With the mind that discerned our danger but not *what* danger."

"Can you *not* for about five seconds, you pretentious bastard?" Katelyn rolled onto her back. No exit that direction, either—just the one door. *No escape.*

"I won't shuffle about hissing and crying *bloooood* like a mindless zombie to assuage your denial." Jude raised himself to sit on the edge of the bed. The springs creaked harshly at his weight, and she rolled back toward him against her will, her mouth meeting his thigh. Katelyn hadn't known a person could be so hard all over. His grin widened when she jerked away, wincing again at the sudden movement.

"I could have killed you. According to Tinsel, I should have. But I didn't, and I don't intend to, and although I could, I'm not going to turn you. That would just reward your interference. I suppose I could keep you as a donor, but I have no interest in tasting you in sips. Best not to taste too often, and never with my teeth, after the sample I've had, or I might never let go. So all that's left is changing you a little instead of a lot.

Become mine, love." He caressed her cheek. "Become familiar. Choose me. It'll make this so much easier."

"No. And stop calling me 'love'. You don't know me, you sadistic fucker. You don't love me." She still wasn't struggling, but she flinched from his touch when he tried to stroke her lips.

"That wasn't a request. It was a command." Jude slid his palm under her chin, engulfing her neck with his hand. Their disparate sizes and his inhuman strength—*which doesn't mean he isn't human,* she told herself—meant he could snap her neck like a twig. She froze. "The time will come when you obey my commands like you swallow."

"You wish, perv," Katelyn shot back. She stiffened when he briefly squeezed her neck—nothing more than a veiled threat.

"This should be interesting." Jude raised his chin as he inspected her. "You have spirit, love, but it's your will and your mind that interest me. How will they react to buckling beneath me, I wonder? Will they lose their luster once you give in without such a fight? I've never done this before. We're a small Family, no need for familiars, but I'm almost certain you'll be useful to me…to us."

She just glared.

"Decisions, decisions," he said, as though just to hear himself talk. "I could coax you into a more compliant mood, have you take my blood and my body willingly, but I have the rest of your life to make you compliant. I can't help but wish to take advantage of a good fight, boiling the blood for both of us. Conquering you will make victory all the sweeter, and I'll trust your capitulation much more when you finally get your own taste."

Katelyn fought against his soothing timbre. The man was a natural mesmerist. That, at least, was real, and therefore a real threat. She wouldn't make it easy for him to render her calmer by the sheer power of a good baritone.

"Yes. I think I'm itching for a good fight." He abruptly removed his hand from her neck and rent the tape from her hands in a single pull. He tossed the tape to the side, heedless of where it landed. He presented his back to her as he did the same to the tape around her ankles.

She abandoned all her reasons for not struggling, every fiber of her body and mind straining and screaming and pumping with adrenaline as the meaning of his words sunk in—as much as she could rationally process.

As soon as her hands were free, she pounded at the broad expanse of his back. He moved like a tiger—pound for pound as flexible and free as he was powerful—when he whipped around and grabbed her wrists to pin her to the bed. The world tilted, whirled, swayed then stilled. He straddled her, his body a gigantic shadow limned with fluorescence that did nothing to diminish his awesome size and shape.

"Keep trying, love." Those strange and beautiful teeth glinted in his smile. "You amuse me. Can you feel your heart beating? I can hear it. I can *smell* it. Do try again."

He freed her wrists, bracing his fists on either side of her head, and laughed as she scratched at his face, going straight for his eyes, but he somehow managed to evade her nails every time. She caught skin yet couldn't tear it, like trying to scratch the metal walls with pieces of chalk.

His amusement was still warm, as though she were only a kitten trying to bite his hands and scratch his face in play, but there was a diabolic edge now, sensitivity receding in favor of the sinister.

She didn't have a knife or a gun to her head. Her life was in danger, but from him alone, the prodigious strength of his hands, the flex of his muscles—his *teeth*. He didn't need a gun. But without one, Katelyn felt like she had an obligation to fight, even though she already knew she couldn't win. Her friends called—*had* called—her a pessimist, but she wasn't. The universe simply tended toward chaos.

The man above her *was* chaos.

He was too solid to deny, yet ephemeral above her blows, as difficult to harness as hurricane-force winds. He evaded her yet was everywhere. She tried to buck him off her hips, but he was immovable, and doing so brought her closer to him, widening his grin more. She tried to knee his groin, but he didn't give her enough room or leverage.

His chuckle thundered down upon her. "You're stronger than you think, little girl. You'd fell a lesser man. And watching you struggle— You have no idea how fierce you look trying."

She shrieked, then squeezed her eyes shut against the tear-inducing pain from the sound of her own scream and her futile, body-protesting efforts to escape and take a piece of him with her.

He finally lowered himself to nuzzle her hair above her ear. "It's a shame we can't know what it would be like if your strength equaled mine. Enough of this. Submit to me. Taste me. Become familiar."

Her anger and fear combined in hot tears down her temples. He pressed his chest against her breasts, and every time she struggled, she rolled her hips against his. He tenderly kissed her ear as though she weren't squirming like a desperate eel, nipped lightly at the lobe before kissing along her jaw. He kissed like a lover, not a rapist, and although she attempted to recoil into the pillows, she couldn't deny the shivers of heat and desire that seemed to trail from his cool lips.

"*Yes,*" he hissed. "Perhaps now you understand why your friend gave in on the dance floor. I could have had her against that column for everyone to see, and she would have screamed her ecstasy for the crowd's delight. Our privacy will lower your inhibitions, though, so know that the only one who sees you writhe in pleasure is me."

She shook her head. "No. No. Get off me."

"Not much longer now." He stroked the hair from her forehead. "Kiss me, and I'll make it quick."

She spat in his face.

That, he clearly didn't see coming. As her saliva dripped down his cheek, his mouth turned down in displeasure and distaste.

"Oh, I promise, you will regret that in the sweetest way." He pushed himself upright, pinning her hips even more firmly to the mattress, and wiped his cheek with the back of his hand. Then he brought the palm to his mouth.

He sank his teeth—*fangs*—into his palm with an unbearably wet tearing sound. When he pulled them out again, blood trickled in thin rivers down his fingers. The blood was darker and thicker than it ought to have been, but that was the least of her concerns as he brought those fingers to her mouth, dripping on her chest along the way.

"No, no, no..." She shook her head to avoid his fingers.

Unhygienic. Wrong blood type. Blood-borne disease. STDs.

"My blood will take away your pain," he said quietly, all amusement gone. "My blood will heal your wounds. My blood will change you into something 'wondrous strange', beautiful, dark, *mine*. I like the sound of that. I've never had someone who was mine before. Take my blood, love. Take it into you."

"I'm not your—"

He plunged his fingers in, dominating her mouth and curling his fingers against her palate as though to ground himself inside her.

She was prepared to sink her teeth all the way to bone as his fingers passed her lips.

Then his blood spread over her tongue, coated her cheeks and teeth and every last crevice, dripped down her throat like thick hot chocolate, and all thoughts of stopping this, stopping *him*, ceased.

"There's my girl." After sinking his fingers all the way into her mouth, he pulled them back, then pushed them in again, caressing her tongue with each new coating of his blood as it continued to run down his hand and into her open mouth. His mouth parted, gleaming behind his fangs. "You would take all my blood and more if you could, but although all good things must end, that's only so new good things can begin. Drink my blood, the way I wish I could drink yours. *Drink*."

With each swallow, each pass of his fingers in and out of her mouth, she wanted more. She licked at his fingers, curled her tongue around them, moaned every time he almost pulled out to let more blood gather. She held his wrist, his forearm, stroking cord upon cord of muscle all the way up to his massive biceps, as though coaxing the blood down faster into his hand. He was smooth, firm, cool but not alarmingly so, and though his fingers were implacable, he was once again gentle, attentive—quite attentive—and otherwise unmoving over her.

Then he dragged his fingers from her mouth to her mewing protests, smearing his blood this time over her skin, then lowered his head to lick himself off her, into her.

Her displeasure at losing his blood shifted to irresistible desire as he slid his tongue over the places he'd given her his blood. He possessed her, conquered her, left her hot and melting beneath him, her body on fire, even as his stayed cool. Tears dripped down her face for another reason altogether. Sparks of his touch on her and around her, she absorbed the electricity of his blood, cementing their connection, as though it bound their very souls.

Does he have a soul? Do I, anymore?

She let that thought drift like an untethered kite. The man was real. His kiss was real. His blood was real. Jude was all and every, moon and stars in shadow, and everywhere was white light, dark body and red—so much red inside.

He dipped down to where he had dripped onto her chest and lapped up his blood to offer it to her. She sucked it down gladly, drawing her lips over his tongue to take every last drop. Again and again he did this, his licks turning to kisses as he reached the soft, yielding flesh of her breast, groaning as he plumped it above the low neckline and ran his fangs over her, denting the skin before kissing her breast again.

She couldn't catch her breath, her heart pounding—and this time she could hear it, smell it, rising from beneath her skin with her heat. Sweet and savory at the same time. Delicious. It was no wonder he couldn't keep his mouth off her. As he availed himself of the bounty that was her breasts, shoving the fabric of her dress aside as well as her bra to free them, she found the places that his bleeding hand had wandered since. She brought her own fingers to her mouth this time. The more and more she tasted, the more the scent that came from him—from *his* blood—seemed even more attractive than her own. She could never have enough.

Her head was remarkably clear but simplified, as though his blood was rewriting her from a blank page. What he recreated was so much like what she had been, it was hard to determine the difference, but only because she couldn't spare the brain cells to look—not when there was more of him to taste.

Sometime during his kisses and caresses, he'd settled between her legs rather than over her, the bulk of his weight supported by the bed instead of crushing her. Her skirt rode up over her hips, his thighs strong between hers, and she whimpered as he rocked his undeniable erection against her, grinding like a teenager, although he did nothing more, nothing to free himself from the undoubtedly uncomfortable confines of the soft jeans stretched over his legs. He contented himself with the taste of her flesh and the rhythm of his desire, each soft moan that his canting hips inspired.

"I can't." He pulled back with gritted teeth, panting heavily and harshly. His eyes burned through the black, his teeth like those of a saber-toothed tiger above her. He shook his head to emphasize his resistance. Slowly, but surely, the fangs drew back into their sheaths. "I can't have you," he repeated, as though to instruct himself rather than deny her.

"Have me," Katelyn pleaded. "God, have me."

"Jude will suffice." He smiled wryly and propped himself on his elbows over her, contemplative as he breathed in her scent, seeming to test his resolve. It remained solid, like the rest of him. His teeth were all human, as though the fangs had never been there. But now she didn't bother to deny. Trying to reconcile his fangs with her previous reality no longer had any relevance.

"If I have you, I'll taste you. If I taste you, I'll bite you. With my blood inside you, if I bite, you'll turn," he said. "But there's no reason I cannot give you the pleasure you seek. I want to pleasure you."

"No…" She tried to pull him down, but she made as much of an impact as when she'd tried to push him away.

Jude ran his fingers through her hair, catching on the tacky streaks from her blood, not his. "I'll give you what I can, little girl. I'll give you all my blood you can stand. Take it. Take *me*."

Without warning, he lifted her from the bed as he rolled onto his back. The broadness of his body was even more pronounced when she straddled him, her thighs practically parallel to the bed.

The change in position also brought her flush against his erection. She bit her lip, much less swollen now than it had been mere minutes ago, but her reduced headache, whiplash and various car-related wounds barely registered—not when he brought his self-inflicted wound back to her mouth, covering half her face as though smothering her. She probed the wound with her tongue to counter whatever limited healing had occurred. He hissed and pushed his cock up against her in involuntary need.

She couldn't help grinding down, either, meeting his repressed desire with her own uninhibited lust. She didn't even know who she was anymore, and she didn't care. She'd become a creature of sheer carnal sensation. Nothing mattered but pumping blood and skin on skin, life flowing within and without. Everything else outside their connected bodies—friends, family, victims, exes—none of them meant anything. Blood was life, and that was all.

He couldn't look away from her, from her mouth buried in his bloody palm, her blood-soaked tousled hair, her dress in disarray. Her breasts were bare and peaked above the forcefully displaced bra and dress, swinging and shifting as she continued to rock her heated, soft cunt over him. He brought his other hand to one breast—not squeezing and hurting her the way some fumbling freshmen had done, thinking that because they were big and soft, harder was better. He stayed tender but persistent, wetting his fingers and making her nipple glisten as it puckered under his firm circling strokes.

In some ways, she wished he would go harder, painful or not. She'd always been a cynical romantic, wanting but suspicious of the sweetness that men offered. But with his blood in her mouth, all she wanted was more, more, more, harder, more, *harder*...just like he'd promised. She wanted him to clamp down on her breasts, twist and tug at her nipples, make her scream in pain and drown her in blood, then do it all over again and again. She'd never had sex, never been more than half-naked with a man, but now she wanted him to tear off her panties and plunge in, tearing into her as he did the same with his teeth in her neck. Images, wishes, fantasies she'd never had before reeled through her mind, but when she tried to spur him forward, he only became gentler.

And still, his blood poured into her, as though she'd become the well to his spring, a slow but never-ending flow of *him* entering in. She moaned into his palm, pressing his hand closer to dig the wound deeper with her teeth, to have a fountain of it in her mouth, in her body. She was wild and writhing above him, feverish with need, climbing higher and higher and higher from the littlest things until she filled to the brim and burst. Blood poured over her, inside her mind, clouding her vision, until every sense turned to taste, and it all craved blood and life and death in one glorious, extended orgasm that quaked her to her blood-drenched soul.

She slid to the side, gasping against the pleasure and the craving entwined together like dysfunctional lovers. Her chest heaved as she struggled now for air, control, some kind of foundation that continued to slip away from her in a torrential red landslide.

"You'll live." He licked his blood from around her mouth and along her lips. He looked pained when he withdrew once more, his jaw tight. "My blood joins with yours. Now you will come when I call, exact my will, protect me and my interests at the expense of your own life. And I will take care of you. My blood will give you life for as long as I live. You'll never want for any need. You will protect me in the daytime, and you will have nothing to fear in the night. Rest, love. Your transformation is nearly complete."

She whimpered, her breathing shallow and harsh.

He kissed her lips lightly. "Shhh. When you wake up, this will all seem like a bad dream, but you'll know better soon enough. So rest while you can. Close your eyes, little girl. Sleep now in my communion. Sleep."

Chapter Three

She woke up upside-down again. The lights now flashed red and blue, but consistent white hurt her eyes. Dawn tinged the dark sky outside her web-shattered window. No headache, no whiplash. Her dress was disheveled but more or less in place, although her hair was unbraided. The rubber band was surrounded by tiny glass shards on the roof of the car, as though it had snapped after impact.

Impact with what?

Everything that had happened before was as vivid as everything happening now, yet she questioned her own memory as she moved against her seatbelt, groaning from the heaviness in her head.

She still tasted his blood on her tongue, a memory so powerful she thought she could swallow it. Had it only been a dream, like when she woke up from one of those awful teeth-crunching nightmares with her jaw aching?

An intense sex dream after a car accident that had left her without a scratch? Unlikely—but unlikely didn't mean impossible.

What she *remembered* was impossible. Vampires belonged in books, movies and television, to be considered only as long as a bucket of popcorn lasted. But they didn't exist. Vampires in the real world were nothing more than disillusioned, delusional or ill people. Superstitions served no one.

Yet she remembered Jude's teeth on her breast and his fingers in her mouth.

Katelyn supposed fantasies based off a weird dream weren't anything to be afraid of. Sexual dreams rarely made sense when she had them.

But she was still stuck upside-down in a totaled vehicle, and that was a *real* problem.

Two people crunched over the concrete gravel and glass—a woman and a man, based on the size of their practical shoes.

The man crouched down in front of the passenger's side, the woman in back. A flash of gold reflected from the man's belt, partially obscured by his leather coat.

"Two dead." The woman lowered her eyes in disappointment and respect.

Katelyn strained to see the man's face, groaning. "Help me. Stuck..."

"Mike was right. We've got a live one here." The man jumped to his feet and hurried around to her side of the car. The woman took his place on the passenger's side, peering in with disbelief.

"Ma'am, my name is Detective Dunn," the man said. "We were in the neighborhood when the call came in. An ambulance is on its way. Are you hurt?"

"I don't think so." She should have had the world's worst headache, not to mention bruising and possibly fractures from the seatbelt. Even if she hadn't gotten a concussion from knocking her head on the steering wheel or the air bag hitting her too hard—the details on that were still fuzzy – she still should have been one big Advil commercial.

The man tried to open the crushed driver's-side door, but it wouldn't budge. "All right, ma'am. I can't come in through your door, so you're going to have to go with Detective Black. She's going to try to meet you halfway. If we can't get you out, the firefighters will be here in minutes. Can you undo your seatbelt? Careful. You don't want to fall on your head. That's probably had enough abuse tonight."

Katelyn brushed glass away from her side of the car and braced her weight on the roof as she fumbled with the torn but somehow still-harnessed seatbelt.

He tore the seatbelt as though it were jerky.

She could see where he'd torn it. The material had supposedly snagged on the armrest, the buckle on the parking brake, a series of unlikely coincidences to keep her harnessed. Sometimes coincidences happened, though. The buckle mechanism didn't work at first, but after some creative angles and a little luck, the seatbelt gave. Holding herself up by her hand on the roof and her feet hooked under the dash, she eased herself down, crawling to keep from somersaulting into an ungainly sprawl.

"There you go. Now Detective Black will help you out. Slowly. Take your time. Try not to look," Detective Dunn said.

Katelyn raised her head and was immediately confronted by the very large gash in Angel's throat, from one side to the other.

That wasn't there before. But she couldn't know that for sure if her memory were faulty, if the accident had caused a temporary glitch that couldn't tell reality from dreams.

Actually, she wasn't so sure it was temporary. She wasn't even certain whether these police detectives were really there and not something she would wake up from. If she couldn't trust her memories from after she left the club, could she trust them now? Ever again?

But with easy-shatter glass digging into her palms, Detective Black's hand on hers in encouragement and her friend's mutilated corpse mere inches from Katelyn's face, it all felt too real, and she had no choice but to proceed as though it was.

Which meant that her friend's ripped-open throat was very real. It shone darkly in the flashing lights, the viscera beneath the torn skin exposed…captivating. The buzz of flies droned in her ears, lured by the siren song of decay to lay their eggs. Perhaps some had already hatched. She'd never taken a forensic course. All she remembered was that flies only lived for about twenty-four hours, and she wasn't sure whether that was true or just common myth.

Maggots, emerging from the flesh to eat the dead… In earlier times, maggots cleaned dead flesh from a rotting wound, because they didn't eat the living.

Her friends were dead. Yet the scent of their life captivated her.

"Ma'am? Are you all right?"

If she just leaned in and…

What the ever-loving hell am I doing?

She had been this close to licking Angel's insides just to…what?

To taste the blood.

Katelyn shook her head, violently shaking.

"Ma'am?" Detective Black patted her hand to remind Katelyn that she was still there to help her.

"Sorry… It's just so…" Katelyn left what she really thought out of her comment and let Detective Black fill in the blank with something more acceptable than *delicious*, especially since Katelyn didn't actually think her friends' slit throats were delicious. Not at all. She was devastated, confused, scared, angry. Really, she was.

But that didn't stop her stomach from growling loudly enough for Detective Black to hear as she ducked around Angel's suspended body. The detective probably thought it was just an ordinary involuntary reaction—maybe Katelyn was hungry because she hadn't eaten dinner or maybe that sound wasn't hunger but indigestion. There were any number of explanations that a reasonable person could come up with. She'd come up with those two right there, and she clung to them like handholds on a cliff.

With Detective Black's help, she managed to squeeze through the window and extricate herself from the car. Her only wounds were from the jagged edges tearing at her dress and skin.

"They don't look deep," Detective Black said. "It's a miracle, really. We didn't believe Mike when he said someone didn't have a scratch on them, but he thought you were dead."

"You're amazingly lucky," Detective Dunn added, standing from where he'd been inspecting the two girls in the back seat.

"I guess you could say that," Katelyn said.

"Oh. I'm sorry. I didn't think that through. Were they friends of yours?"

"Sisters. Same sorority," Katelyn said. "The decal's on the back of the car."

"I smelled alcohol." Detective Dunn's expression remained innocuous, but Katelyn didn't miss the acuity underneath. He was a tall, well-built, all-American, white-bread man—probably used his aw-shucks good looks to conceal the instincts that had brought him to plainclothes detective.

"You're going to give me a test," Katelyn said. "I know the game. I hope not being able to walk a straight line right now won't be held against me, although I think I could."

"I'll get the breathalyzer," Detective Dunn said. "Andrea, if you could keep an eye on her and make sure she's okay..."

Detective Black nodded. "Standard procedure," she said to Katelyn, almost apologetically.

"I know. But of course it smells like alcohol in there. We went to Club 360°," Katelyn said as Detective Dunn returned. "My friends all had drinks, and in the interest of full disclosure, Aly—the one on the...on the roof with a broken neck—probably has some ecstasy. It's none of my business, and it's not what killed her, so spare me the lecture. That's their life, not mine. I had a Diet Coke. I'm sober."

"You don't have to justify it to us." Detective Black took the machine from Detective Dunn, who neither commented nor put up a fuss. Detective Black had a better rapport. Like Katelyn had said, she knew the game. "We're not going to charge you with possession on someone else's person. We just want to make sure you were driving sober."

Katelyn obediently took the nozzle in her mouth and blew into it.

"You're taking all of this remarkably well," Detective Dunn said when Detective Black turned to check the machine's results.

"If numbness and legs made of jelly are doing well," Katelyn said. "I just can't...wrap my head around it. They were dancing a few hours ago. Was it a few hours? What time is it?"

Detective Dunn checked his watched. "Five in the morning."

They'd been in that wreck for almost five hours? No one had found a horrendous accident *all night*? She found that hard to believe, and yet… "How long was I out?"

"Breathalyzer's clean," Detective Black said. "She's more sober than a Baptist preacher on Sunday."

"And if we took a drug test?" Detective Dunn asked Katelyn.

"Do I look buzzed to you? I'm stunned, not drugged."

"You keep saying that, but you seem awfully clear-headed. Makes me wonder if you're not as stunned and shaken as you say."

"Then have the EMTs test my blood. I don't give a shit, sir," Katelyn said. "The only pills I take are vitamin supplements. I've got nothing to hide. I'm… Is it tomorrow? Or did I dream this whole day?"

"I'm afraid I don't follow," Detective Dunn said.

"Neither do I. I'm confused, man. I don't know what happened."

Detective Dunn must have finally caught the trembling in her fingers as she ran them through her hair, tugging at the roots, because he reeled in the bad-cop routine a bit.

"If the EMTs clear you, would you be up to giving a statement at the precinct and answering a few questions—just to clear a few things up?"

Katelyn was no fool. She'd been told a thousand times that cops did their jobs by pushing, and citizens were supposed to let lawyers push from the other end. She knew she should call her parents, who would call their lawyer to tell the police to back the fuck off. But she just wanted this over with. She didn't know how much of what she remembered had actually happened, but she knew she had nothing to do with the accident, and although she'd briefly considered burying her face in Angel's open wound, she had nothing to do with the mutilations. She hadn't done anything wrong but trust a detour sign.

So even though she knew that nothing she said or wrote would be acceptable in the eyes of someone who already regarded her with suspicion, she didn't call her parents. She just nodded, control unraveling further from her fingers, as though reality itself had started to fray.

* * * *

Detective Dunn set a small Styrofoam cup of coffee with the two creams and two sugars she'd asked for in front of her. It was department coffee, so Katelyn didn't have high hopes, but it would perform its function.

"Your statement, while thorough, still leaves a lot of questions, Ms. Dillon. Wouldn't you agree?"

He sat across from her in the small, cramped office he and his partner had squeezed themselves into. On the door, the two detectives had their own little nameplate. An orange sticky note underneath read, *The Q Division.* Detective Black was nowhere to be seen. The door to the office was slightly open—not quite an interrogation yet.

But Katelyn knew that she'd provided far more questions than answers. Even her facts were fuzzy.

The club scene—two alleged predators, nothing concrete, just a bad feeling, leaving after interacting with the bartender and the bouncer, who could verify that Katelyn had talked with them. At least, Katelyn hoped the bouncer would remember. She was sure Ben would.

Driving until the detour—although she couldn't explain how the two alleged predators had known where they were going, much less how they'd arrived there before she had. Waking up when the police got there.

The rest were undefined recollections that she couldn't be sure of—the man in the alley flipping them over, waking up while the alleged predator bothered the other girls.

She certainly wasn't going to tell this detective that she'd come her brains out while drinking the blood of the man who had killed her friends. Not only was that just plain wrong, but Detective Dunn was already scrutinizing her like a particularly difficult puzzle. She didn't need him to scrutinize any closer or suspect her any more, especially when she wasn't positive he was wrong.

Katelyn laced her fingers together, her knuckles white. "I'm afraid I'm not very helpful. All I *know* is what happened at the bar. But the only other people who can confirm what happened in the car aren't available anymore."

Detective Dunn leaned back in his chair. "What I'd like for you to do, Ms. Dillon, is tell me *everything* you remember, even if it's nonsense. Even if you think it was a dream."

"Method in madness?"

"Something like that."

"It's all pretty unbelievable," she said.

"Try me."

Katelyn didn't look up, didn't show any signs of being startled by his warmer timbre.

The Q Division. He'd said he and his partner had been in the neighborhood, but Katelyn had only been awake for a few minutes. What if they hadn't been in the neighborhood? What if the officer who'd found the accident had called them, specifically?

What if Detective Dunn bringing her to his office instead of an interrogation room wasn't because he wasn't interrogating her but because the nature of the interrogation was the sort of thing people didn't want recorded—the weird, the arcane, the unlikely, the unreal? What if…?

Katelyn shook her head slightly. *Knock it off.* She could play what-if conspiracy games all day. So what if the Meridian Police Department had an unofficial *X-Files* section? That didn't mean this detective was going to take her seriously.

Even worse if he does. A chill trickled down her neck.

"Look… Whatever you tell me is not going to leave this room, except in a report that no one but a few officers are going to see," Detective Dunn said. "Your breathalyzer was clean. You're not shaking anymore. You're a little pale, which isn't surprising after what happened, but your color is otherwise good. I'm waiting on a tox screen to clear you, but I don't think you were high. I don't think you totaled your car, slashed your friends' throats, then tied yourself back into the driver's seat."

"That's exactly what he thinks."

Katelyn's extremities stiffened into petrified wood, and her stomach turned to lava.

This wasn't one of the many voices that her brain created to represent her thoughts—not one of hers at all. This was a completely independent voice.

And it sounded like *him.*

"Obfuscate. Don't say a word about me after the club. Protect me, and I will protect you."

"He'll know I'm lying," she thought, although she didn't know whether she was thinking it at anything or anyone.

"Make him believe it, love. I have faith in you."

"Seems a stupid way to kill someone." She started slowly, shaken, but the words eventually came to her, each one more natural than the last, until she almost believed herself. "They were my friends. All I *know* happened was something flipped my car, probably some texting asshole. What I remember after that is a traumatized-brain dream. I remember waking up once to lights from a detour sign. I thought I saw some people—a man and a woman, like you and your partner. One of them might have climbed into the car, but even without hitting my head, I still went ass over teakettle. My brain's a little scrambled. They could have been the other people involved in the accident. They could have been figments of my imagination. They could have been voyeurs wanting to see an accident victim up close—or they could have been serial ax murderers, for all I know. They could have been *you*."

When Katelyn stood, her hands and legs were trembling again, and her hips and legs stung where the window glass had scratched them. "Now, I've had a really long night, my car is a wreck, my friends are fucking murdered and all I want to do is go back to the house, take a hot shower and sleep until Tuesday. And I'm going to have to call their fucking parents and offer them the exact same lack of explanation I have for you. Are you going to charge me with anything, like being a secret slasher villain, or can I go home? Either way, I'm not saying another word with you looking at me like that, not without a lawyer present to talk me off a ledge."

"You're not under arrest," Detective Dunn replied. "You're just giving a statement."

"Then I can leave."

He sighed, standing as well. "Yes. You can leave. You're a student at UTM, yes?"

"Yes."

"Undergrad?"

"Yes."

"What's your area of study?"

"Social psych. Why?"

"Just curious," he said. "And you live on campus?"

"I'm not leaving town, if that's what you're asking."

"Good. In that case, if you could just sign your statement and the accident report, you'll be able to leave. Is there anyone you want to call? I assume you'll need a ride."

"My phone still works. I can call our house mother. She'll be able to help me with the families." She lowered her head again, weight pressing against her shoulders at the thought of having to call Angel's, Aly's and Maria's parents.

"We handle the notifications," Detective Dunn said, a little more kindly. "I'm sure they'll want to call you or your house mother after we've contacted them, but I think it would be best for all involved if we give them the facts."

"You're not going to prejudice them into thinking I did it, are you?"

"Why would I do that?"

"Because you think I did."

"What makes you think that?"

"I don't think it. I know," Katelyn said. "But it doesn't matter what you think, as long as you eventually realize that the *facts* fit my side of the story in the end. *Fact* is, those girls' families know me, and they're not going to believe it, either. *Fact* is, they have enough they're going to have to deal with without being told the responsible one is a crazed maniac. Wait until you have the *facts* before you tell them it was anything but an accident."

Detective Dunn pushed the completed statement across the desk toward her and handed her a pen. "Then you don't think it was just an accident, either."

Damn it.

"You're doing just fine, love. You know how to get out of this. It's not a trap, just a chance to clarify."

"Of course I don't." Nothing of her fear or the conversation in her head showed themselves in her expression—at least she dearly hoped not. "The wreck could be an accident, but no accident is going to slash anyone's throats. *That's* the crazed maniac."

"You're very perceptive for someone with a jostled brain."

"You should see me when I've got all my wits instead of just a few. I think you already have a theory about whodunit, but that theory has nothing to do with me. You're just trying to figure out where I fit into it, because I'm uninjured and unmurdered."

"Do you have any idea why this so-called crazed maniac would have gone after your friends but left you alone?" Detective Dunn asked.

"You tell me."

"I just want to know your thoughts."

Katelyn passed the papers and pen back to Detective Dunn. "I have no idea. Maybe the guy or guys had a thing for drunk girls, and I didn't fit the profile. Maybe he—or she—had a thing for thin, pretty, blonde girls, and I didn't fit *that* profile. I have no fucking clue about the motivations of obsessives, man."

Detective Dunn nodded, taking the papers and shuffling them into one pile. "All right. I have your phone number if I need to call you."

"At which point I'll give you my lawyer's number."

"That's your right as a free citizen of the United States, Ms. Dillon. I'm sorry about your friends—and what happened to you."

"So am I."

Katelyn collapsed back into her chair again. Detective Dunn stepped around the desk and picked up her purse. She accepted it graciously. On the floor, it had been just too far for her to pick it up for her phone.

"Take whatever time you need."

His entire body language had changed, less business-like, more casual, more compassionate. Detective Dunn didn't believe it was her anymore. Had she really gotten away with it with rational but totally bogus speculation?

"I am pleased."

Katelyn shuddered again, but she hid it by hunching over her purse as she searched for her phone to call her house mother Debbie to pick her up.

* * * *

There was one bath in the sorority house, and it was on the second floor. Debbie had taped a sign on the bathroom door saying no one was to disturb Katelyn.

The house mother had immediately diagnosed Katelyn's straightforwardness as numbed grief, and Katelyn had a feeling she was right. A coping mechanism—a survival mechanism, really. As long as she had logic, she had control.

But when she'd entered the bedroom she shared with Angel, Aly and Maria, she hadn't been able to get out of there fast enough. She'd been unconscious for heaven knew how long—which wasn't the same as sleep, so she was exhausted as hell—but one look at Angel's disheveled bed, Aly's writing desk and all the little accessories of their personalities and Katelyn couldn't stay there any longer without seeing the bloodstained gash of Angel's throat and Aly's broken neck. She'd gathered pajamas and toiletries and hurried out of the bedroom, even though she'd known she would have to come back eventually. She could try to sleep in the common rooms, of course, but she couldn't lock anyone out of asking her questions down there.

There were no locks on the bathroom. Debbie's sign and a doorstop would have to suffice as a deterrent against the incurably curious.

Katelyn set her pajamas and toiletries next to the tub, then removed her shoes and her dress. There was a mirror over the sink and a full-length mirror by the bath. Katelyn checked the scratches from the car window, then over her head for where the blood that streaked her hair might have come from. No gash or bump that she could see. Detective Black had taken samples from her hair and hands and under her nails and had stood with the EMT while he'd inspected her for any wounds worth taking care of. He'd cleaned the scratches, but otherwise she was fine. *'Nothing you wouldn't get from a playground fall,'* he'd said.

Katelyn was confident they wouldn't find anything in any of their tests, and despite Detective Dunn's suspicions, she didn't think Detective Black believed she'd done anything. She was a mystery, yes, but she had never been a suspect in Detective Black's eyes.

Staring in the mirror, she traced the worst of the glass-scratch lines. Her nails scraped along the early healing, breaking through thin flakes of coagulation. New blood welled up in tiny drops.

Katelyn's lips parted in a nearly silent moan, and her mouth watered at the scent—just a hint of what she'd smelled in Angel's neck, perfume that had permeated the entire car after the wreck.

Before she fully realized what she intended, she ran her finger over the wounds and brought the bloody tips to her mouth.

Sweet. Sweet like ginger. Sweet like vanilla. Sweet like dark chocolate. Just a little sweet, but it filled her mouth, coating it there and all the way down her throat. Savory like soup and stew and fresh, cooked meat nearly raw. Raw and red, with life still practically tangible in its preserved death.

The next thing she knew, she'd taken four fingers deep in her mouth, and her hips and thighs were smeared with blood from where she'd scratched herself to claw it back to the surface.

What the hell am I doing?

Katelyn's eyes widened, and she yanked her fingers out of her mouth, staggering from the mirror and falling to the tiled floor. Her stomach twisted and growled, threatening to disgorge what little was left inside at the same time it demanded more.

No. This was not happening. How long had she been out of her mind? How long had she been hurting herself just for a...

Taste.

"Oh God, oh God..." She closed her eyes, resting her forehead against the bathtub porcelain. "What's going on? What's happening to me?"

She huddled against the bathtub in only her bra and panties, the scent of her blood like a burning candle in the room.

"This is ridiculous." After running the back of her hand over her mouth, she licked her lips. Then she shuddered, because a scrim of blood had transferred from her hand to her lips.

Katelyn clamped her will down upon whatever was making her fall apart. She clutched the lip of the tub and pulled herself to standing. Motion by motion, she unhooked her bra, threw it on top of her dress, removed her panties, turned on the hot water and put the plug in the drain.

While she waited for the tub to fill, she toed her clothes to the side of the room in a pile. As she climbed into the bath, she inhaled sharply when her cuts hit the water, but the longer she stayed under, the more she adjusted to the sting.

Katelyn rested her head against the rim of the bathtub and forced herself to relax, starting with her toes and moving up her body. With the aid of the heat, she slowly loosened, her limbs turning boneless in the water. When she reached her crown, she let herself sink all the way under, her hair swaying around her face. Little bubbles escaped her nose, but otherwise she just lay there under the water until it became hard to breathe. Then she surfaced just enough to take another deep breath and go under once again.

Finally, she emerged, slicking her hair back.

Her fingers caught in the places she was still bloody. Sighing, she turned her head to the side to work the dried blood out of her hair, trying desperately to ignore the scent steaming from the bathtub as she tinged the water pink.

There was something in her hair.

She sat up and probed the bumps at the back of her head. No bruises or goose eggs. Something was really *in* her hair.

They wriggled against her fingertip, and she jumped. The bath water rocked back and forth, almost spilling over the side. Her cry echoed across the tile and mirrors.

Katelyn picked out the cluster of what had been trapped in her hair and opened her palm.

Three maggots, squirming, searching blindly. Katelyn stared at them in disbelief. These hadn't come from her. There was nothing for them to have come from except the only dead things she'd been close to in the last few hours. She'd brushed against Angel. Maybe a few had fallen from her friend and gotten stuck in her hair. Maybe there was something in the blood streaks for them to feed on.

Feed. She couldn't mistake her own voice in her head this time, but it was unrecognizable, and stronger than the urge to take her own blood. After all, drinking her own blood was nice, but it was just recycling what was already there.

This would be new.

She couldn't stop herself in that split moment of hunger so strong, the pangs nearly doubled her over. She tipped the maggots into her mouth, burst them with her teeth and swallowed them down in a matter of seconds.

Katelyn stared at her now-empty palm. If she hadn't already been sitting down, she might have fallen, but she felt like she was falling anyway.

She reached for her soap and loofah. She jerked the plug out of the drain, then turned on the faucet. While the water replaced itself, she scrubbed furiously at her palm, then ducked her head under the pouring faucet, raking through her hair and over her scalp to get anything left out. Tears gathered under her closed lids. She squeezed them shut, but her face twisted, and the sobs forced themselves out. She knelt there, water pounding her head, crying like she'd never stop.

"What's happening to me?"

Chapter Four

Wearing her pajamas and wrapped in a fluffy robe, her skin scrubbed nearly raw, Katelyn finally entered her bedroom again, this time with the intention of staying. She locked the door and stared at Angel's bed, the bunk right above hers.

All this had started because she'd wanted to save Angel. Maybe Angel wouldn't have made it through the night either way, but Katelyn couldn't know that, not really. She only knew that her friend—the girl who could have made Katelyn's life in Delta Tau torture and instead had been one of the first to welcome her into the fold—was dead.

She hadn't been all sugar and spice, but that was the case with anyone and everyone. So she'd cheated off of Katelyn's work in some of the classes they'd shared. So she'd been a little shallow. The most she or Aly or Maria had deserved was a couple of Cs in their classes and a harmless prank or two. Horrible death wasn't even close.

Had she killed Angel and the others? She couldn't bear to think it, but there was something wrong with her—and not just scrambled brains. What if whatever was going on with her was related to the murders? What if, after all the people she'd protected her sisters from, she was the one she'd never seen coming?

"No, little one. You have nothing to fear. Go to your bed. Sleep. You'll wake up feeling refreshed and renewed, your transformation complete. Rest. Wake. Feed."

Feed.

She clapped her hands to her ears, as though that would shut out the intruding voice and the sound of her own stomach growling. The voice went silent on its own. Her stomach didn't.

She'd cried herself out in the bathtub. She couldn't handle any more tears. Katelyn staggered to the bed, barely pulling the sheets back before crawling in. Still wrapped in her robe, she covered herself with a haven of terrycloth and jersey. Her skin and the blood pumping beneath it were overlain with vanilla and cocoa butter, the strongest scents in her collection.

It made falling asleep much easier.

* * * *

When Katelyn awoke again, she wasn't refreshed and renewed like the voice had said. Under the blankets and the robe, she'd overheated. She held her head against the dehydration headache pounding behind her eyes as she sat up.

The bathroom at the end of her hall was communal, and she didn't want to cross anyone's path. She could only imagine how they would stare at her—with pity that she'd lost her best friends, with curiosity for what she'd gone through, with suspicion that she'd been involved and hostility, whether conscious or unintentional, that she had survived when the other three had not.

Katelyn opted to text Debbie to ask if she could bring some water upstairs. The house mother brought a small case of bottled water as well as five different fast-food appetizers.

"I didn't know what you'd be in the mood for," Debbie said sheepishly.

Katelyn wasn't up to explaining why she wasn't hungry. After gratefully accepting the paper bag of food, she closed the door with a brief but genuine goodbye, ignoring the glances from two other sisters down the hall.

She tossed the bag onto her desk and focused her attention on opening a water bottle and downing half the contents. Once she determined it would stay down, she finished the rest of the bottle.

Her phone blinked with text and voice messages, but she couldn't bring herself to answer them. She was in no state to handle any older adults, despite her nonchalance at the police station. No, she wasn't okay, and no, neither were her friends. She was barely up to handling solid foods. She hardly thought other people's grief would do any good for her nerves—or theirs.

A few people knocked at her door, but unless Debbie told Katelyn it was just her, she didn't get up. She stayed out of the way of the windows, even with the blinds drawn, and drank bottle after bottle of water. She didn't look up any news about the incident. She ate a little of what Debbie had brought, but although her stomach accepted it, she wasn't enthused for fast food, so she had to stop at some point.

Streaming and food delivery were all well and good, but she'd eventually have to leave the dormitory, not the least because she had classes on Monday.

Only when the light on the blinds had dimmed, cloaking the bedroom in heavy shadow, did Katelyn's appetite partially return. She ate cold French fries, cold tater tots, cold chicken and cold stuffed jalapeños, but not all at once and certainly not the whole servings provided. It had been sitting in the bag for a while and tasted lifeless and bland. Salty was good, but even the spice of the jalapeño wasn't enough to interest her.

"Come to me."

Katelyn covered her ears. "I'm not hearing this. I'm not hearing anything. It was a dream. A vivid hallucination. Some kind of way for my brain to process trauma. This isn't happening. I don't believe it."

"Come to me."

"I don't even have a car. It's totaled. I can't come, even if I wanted to." She pretended she was only talking to herself. Talking to oneself was healthy, a sign of intelligence. Once a person started replying to voices that weren't their own, that wasn't healthy at all.

"You will come to me. You will find a way. You will always find a way. You will cross oceans if I need you to. Katelyn, my own, my familiar… Come to me."

"No," she whispered.

"I need you. I want you. I can satisfy you. Come to me."

She rested her head on her desk, still holding her hands fruitlessly over her ears. Nothing she did could drown him out. He filled her mind the way the taste of her blood had filled her mouth, as though a fine mist suffused the brain matter from wall to wall of her skull.

"Now."

Katelyn shed her robe and pajamas to dress herself in a long-sleeve lavender tunic, gray leggings, boots. She twisted her hair up into a messy bun, dumped the contents of her clubbing purse into more practical black leather one, then unlocked her door and walked out as though she hadn't been avoiding her sisters all day.

There were stares. There were whispers. But her stride must have convinced them that she had somewhere to be.

Katelyn's insides felt as though someone had used her guts to play cat's cradle, because she was doing all these things, registering them in her conscious mind, yet whenever she tried to shift direction—head to the common rooms to talk with someone, stop by Debbie's room, go to the kitchens to see if something else could spark her appetite—she didn't move from her original trajectory. She wanted to, but she didn't. Her whole being seemed fixed upon the need to leave the house and get to wherever she was going. She didn't even know where that was. She just knew that if she kept moving, she would find it.

"Katelyn! Is it true?" Anamaria, a sophomore, ran up to her. "I thought it was just a joke, but everyone's talking about it. Are Aly, Angel and Maria really dead? It's like *Scream* or something."

"I need to go, Anamaria." Katelyn's voice shook—and not just from the rhythm of her quick gait.

Anamaria grabbed her arm. "I just want to know if—Ow!"

Katelyn froze, holding up her hand in disbelief. The slap had been as loud as a crack of close thunder, and Anamaria had hit the wall from the force of the open-handed blow.

"I'm— I'm sorry. I don't know what— I just really need to go. I need to go *now.*"

Jennifer, a senior sister, ran over and put a protective arm around Anamaria. "Have you lost your mind, Dillon?"

It was true that living with a bunch of other competitive girls wasn't always a walk in the park, and trying to get into the sisterhood could be questionable. Once someone was in, though, that was when it got good. Maybe that wasn't true for other sororities, but it was in Delta Tau. You were supposed to protect your sisters.

I can't control myself. What if I couldn't control myself in the car, either? I'm hearing voices. I'm the right age.

There was no history of psychosis in her family. There was no *reason* for any of this to have happened, unless the car accident really had jostled her brains around. Everything that had happened after the car accident simply *couldn't* have happened. The fact that Jude's voice was the one in her head… Well, that wasn't coincidence, but it wasn't significant, either. It didn't mean that all the things in her memory from after the club had really happened, because they *couldn't* have.

"What's your problem?" Jennifer asked again.

"Sorry. I just need to go. I have a counseling session. Grief counseling."

Katelyn had always been mostly ambivalent about anything more than a white lie, but the big lies were coming more and more easily.

"I hope he does a lot more than grief counseling," Jennifer said. "Innocent until proven guilty, I guess."

"I didn't do anything. I just didn't sleep very well today, and I've been in a goddamn car accident slash triple homicide. I'm sorry." She couldn't apologize enough, but the knot in her stomach wasn't letting up any more the longer she stayed.

"Hence, your stuff will still be in your room when you get back. But get your shit together, Dillon. I hope you've got a damn good counselor—and a damn good lawyer."

"Can I go now? I was already interrogated once today."

"Yeah," Anamaria said. "Sorry for getting in your way. I should have thought—"

"It's not your fault," Jennifer interrupted, glaring at Katelyn. "You're lucky you're useful, Dillon, because most of the people who could speak for you are dead. You better wish on that lucky star of yours that we don't find out you're in any way responsible. I swear to God, if you did that to Aly, Maria and Angel, you're going to look *forward* to prison. Got it? And if you hurt another sister…"

Katelyn didn't stick around for more recriminations from the sorority's unofficial enforcer. She stopped, though, outside the house and stumbled into the bushes, where she unleashed everything that she'd eaten from the takeout bag. Katelyn coughed against the sourness burning her throat and spat out what was left in her mouth. Most of the bushes along the house had had their share of acidic fertilizer over the years.

She braced her hand against the white brick wall.

There was a spider web on one of the bushes. She searched all around it and inside and determined the original inhabitant was either good at hiding or no longer in residence before she realized she was doing it again. It was like driving on autopilot, knowing that she had gotten from point A to point B but with the line between more or less missing from her memory.

Katelyn stumbled from the bushes and lost herself instead in the dull click of her boots on the concrete. The voice in her head was right. If she had to cross a thousand miles to get to whatever was calling her, she would walk until the heels wore off and her feet were nothing but bleeding blisters. She hoped it wouldn't come to that.

It didn't feel like she was called across the country or an ocean. In her mind's eye, she saw a building in the industrial district, with a sign in the front windows like an old barber shop, but she couldn't read it, nor was she given street names or intersections. Just a general sense of location and an increasingly urgent need to reach it pulling her home like a pigeon to roost.

So she walked, striding through the campus among people who didn't know her well enough to recognize her.

A bicycle in one of the many racks available for students didn't have a lock on it. Without thinking, Katelyn added theft to the list of the many things she'd never done before but now simply happened.

The wind tugged at her hair and swept over the loose material of her shirt, which flowed around and behind her.

Her heart pounded as she erupted into traffic. Her calves hurt, her thighs burned and cold air raked in and out of her lungs. She had cycled in the on-campus gym plenty, but it was different on a real bicycle, and although there were sometimes bicycle lanes, neither the pedestrians nor the drivers wanted her on their piece of concrete when the bike lanes ended. It didn't help that she didn't know where she was going, only that she was more often than not heading in the right direction. The closer she came, the more certain she was that she was being lured, guided, as though her body were made of pulled strings.

She abruptly hit the hand brake so hard she almost flipped forward. The picture windows at the bottom of the rectangular building with tall, barred windows on the upper floors looked just the ones in her vision. The air around the building was pungent, sharp with smoke and flesh.

Old-fashioned writing on the windows read: *Butcher. Charcuterie. Local. Organic. Meat.*

The bicycle fell with a clatter. She left it behind. It had served its purpose.

A bell over the door announced her entrance.

The shop smelled like raw meat, and the display cases bore out the olfactory overload—section after section of red, pink, bone-in, bone-out, bloody, juicy meat. At the far end, charcuterie, with displays of more exotic preparation and delicatessen offerings. This wasn't just a mom-and-pop butcher shop. It looked like they took wholesale orders for restaurants as well as personal orders. There was even a menu for barbecued meats, which would account for the charry odor.

The wiry and delicate but well-defined man behind the counter wielded knives as though they weighed nothing, and the meat offered no resistance.

A male customer discussed an order with the young man. Two other customers, also men, one in a suit with his phone out and the other in more casual clothes, waited for their turn.

Katelyn felt very female when all four men turned to look at her. *One of these things is not like the other.*

Not only was she newly mad, but her madness didn't even have method. She was paralyzed under the fluorescent lights with uncertainty and fear—fear of the unfamiliar place she'd entered, fear of what had brought her here, fear of how she could get back...if she could get back at all. Fear that she would always be like this forever. Lost. Changed. Unable to return to what she had been—a neurotic but otherwise normal girl who'd more or less had a handle on her life and the lives of others. As Jennifer had said, she'd been useful, even to herself.

Now, her mouth watered so much from the scents around her that she had to keep swallowing, lest she literally start to drool. She'd suspect she was pregnant if she'd ever had sex before.

You do have whole hours unaccounted for.

But even in her hallucination, she hadn't had sex—procreative, anyway. She felt funky all over, but not like she'd been ridden hard and put away wet in a state of unconsciousness. She thought she'd know if she'd lost her official virginity—blood on her underwear, some kind of pain or discomfort—but there was none of that.

"I'm sorry." Katelyn slowly backed away from their alien gazes, gazes that said *you don't belong,* although there wasn't any malice or threat. "I'm sorry."

The doors from the main building into the shop swung open.

He came out in a butcher's shiny black apron, drying his hands.

The other men in the room gave a basis for comparison. He was twice the size of the second-largest man yet moved as though he were slender, with the grace of a much smaller person. His giant mitts dwarfed the hand towel he used. The same apron the young man wore to serve the customers provided much less coverage on the large man's body.

It was him.

Jude.

He was real. He was there. And when he looked over the counter, he met her eyes with immediate recognition.

She stopped backing away. He dropped his towel and strode around the display cases to the gate leading to the customer's side. She met him halfway. He slid his arms around her waist, and she wrapped her arms around his neck, standing on tiptoe as he bent down to kiss her.

He devoured her, devastated her in an assault of lips and tongue, possessed her and showed his complete possession to the complete strangers in the butcher shop. She whimpered helplessly as his low moan trembled through her. He crushed her against his torso as he shifted his arms to hold more of her, one broad hand sliding up between her shoulder blades and the other moving to caress her ass. She had more than handfuls to offer the average man, but he more than met the task.

Then he grabbed her by the back of her neck and jerked her away but held her near his mouth. Both of them panted, their breath mingling between them, hers warm and his cool.

"I knew you would be devoted to me," Jude whispered. "I just didn't expect the depth of my longing. No one told me it would be like this."

She wanted to say something, anything, but she shook from scalp to soul, and her mouth wanted his on hers again.

He glanced at the customers, who were still staring, although now for very different reasons.

"Let's take this somewhere more private," he said.

Chapter Five

"I'm pretty sure that constitutes about thirty-four health code violations," the wiry butcher said as Jude led Katelyn behind the counter and through the swinging metal door. "Just kidding, Mr. V."

"Cody's a good boy—part of our Family, though not of our line," Jude muttered as he guided her through a short hallway and another swinging door. It opened into a large room of hanging frozen meat, hard from the cold and most of the scent contained beneath frost, but not all.

Katelyn swayed as she stared at the expanse of vegan nightmare. Good thing she'd never been vegan, otherwise she'd be even more conflicted than she already was.

"It's all right," Jude said, smiling slightly. "If you can wait, though, I have something fresher for you to enjoy. Tinsel told me to anticipate your appetite. It doesn't quite reach the level of a new vampire, but it'll be quite strong to you. I know you've been distressed, and you'll need to adjust to many new things. I'll help you face them. I'll take care of you as no one has ever taken care of you before."

"As long as I take care of you." She made every effort to hold her breath as she passed through the rows out of the meat locker.

"Yes. The relationship between a vampire and familiar is a symbiotic one. We are both stronger yet more vulnerable for it."

"You can't be serious."

"Deadly serious."

Beyond the meat locker was a warehouse that had once housed working machinery. Now the machinery lay dormant, like forgotten twentieth-century idols that had lost their shine. They passed metal drums that dwarfed even Jude.

"I thought there would be more…butchery in a butcher shop," Katelyn said.

"This was once a meat-packing plant. We don't need the machines for what we do now. We have the meat lockers, we installed barbecue pits on the roof and there are some curing rooms. The rest are for the personal use of our little Family. Bedrooms. The Slaughterhouse. Do you know where we are?"

"It was all kind of a blur getting here."

"We're on the fashionable side of the industrial district, close enough to walk to the teeming, fragrant Meridian night life. It means we can overcharge for our meat and access all the blood we'll ever need. For a small Family that hasn't decided to incorporate, I think we're doing quite well for ourselves."

"Vampires. You seriously want me to believe that you and Tinkerbell are vampires who drink actual blood? God, is her name really Tinsel or do I keep mishearing it?"

The thunder of Jude's laughter echoed among the machinery. "Tinsel *is* her name. She thought about taking another when she turned—some of us do—but she decided to keep it."

He ducked under a low door into a huge kitchen, where Tinsel was putting together a catering order.

"We do just enough to justify our presence here and pay our rent," Jude continued. "But we're low-maintenance creatures, and we got the building for a song."

"Only took a little convincing," Tinsel said, closing an aluminum container. "You know what that's like, don't you, Katelyn?"

"You'll have to excuse her," Jude said. "She's still out of sorts over the effort my decision put her through. A great deal of subterfuge is necessary to hide our marks if we insist on allowing our victims to be discovered. We obscured our fingerprints and the dents from our hands, and we eliminated the punctures from our teeth."

"If we leave *anything* behind, that's a trail," Tinsel snapped. "If we leave a trail, someone can follow it. Because we left behind murder victims, we have Homicide on our asses and have to hope Forensics doesn't acknowledge the DNA of long-dead persons. This is not a good time to be sloppy."

"They think I did it," Katelyn said.

"Oh...good," Tinsel replied, with a fake but beautiful toothsome smile.

"They'll clear you. There's nothing but proximity tying you to their deaths," Jude said.

"Despite what the TV shows say, circumstantial evidence *does* matter," Katelyn said.

"They won't have enough. You're just another victim. At least, that's how law enforcement and the media will see you once you're cleared."

Katelyn didn't want to tell them, but it spilled from her mouth as though she'd been compelled to speak. "Homicide isn't investigating. Ever hear of the Q Division?"

Jude and Tinsel shared a significant, troubled look.

"Just one man and woman," Tinsel said. "Unlikely they have the resources to follow every lead."

"They'll have to punt it back to Homicide, and Homicide will be looking for a human being. They'll never come here," Jude said.

"And if they do, we have our ways of dealing with them. Homicide won't know to guard themselves against us. None of them ever know."

"Except Katelyn." Jude rested his hand on her shoulder.

"Thankfully, we don't get into this kind of mess often," Tinsel said. "Please, if you're going to give her a tour, give her a blood glass for Cara while you're at it. I'm busy with this at the moment, and she's been very uncooperative. Maybe a familiar's fresh vein would tempt her appetite."

"Only after my familiar's appetite has been tended to."

"Cara is *Family*." Tinsel threw a large fork down on the stainless-steel counter. Katelyn winced. "Your sister in blood gets precedence over your new little pet that's caused us nothing but trouble since the moment she set eyes on us."

"Cara is accustomed to hunger. Katelyn is not," Jude said, with far more patience. "Once I satisfy Katelyn, we can take care of Cara. Then I'll solve our little mysteries, sire of mine."

"Fine." Tinsel grabbed the fork as though prepared to stab Katelyn in the chest with it, but she kept her distance. Black anger like ink filled all the way to the edge of her irises. It was more apparent—and chilling—with Tinsel's coloring than Jude's. "Don't make me say 'I told you so,' Jude."

"I'll make you wish we'd had Katelyn with us sooner."

"I'm not… This is…" For the four hundredth time, Katelyn wanted to say 'crazy', but there was a point at which she couldn't be surprised by what she heard anymore.

Jude was real. Tinsel was real. And they were both continuing conversations about things she'd assumed hadn't happened or were just dreamed. Either she'd completely lost the plot and was living in a fantasy world inside her head, or the things she'd dismissed as dreams or hallucinations had really happened—just as this was really happening.

Tinsel's impatience was somewhat placated by Katelyn's loss for words. "The sooner you accept the supernatural, the sooner your brain will stop trying to eject you for your own safety like an overzealous train conductor. We've all been there. You think I was singing choruses after waking up in a morgue freezer? Even worse, I couldn't see my reflection as I pushed my way out. I thought I was a ghost punished with hunger I couldn't fulfill until someone else saw me and I satisfied that hunger upon him, poor soul. No one was there to tell me what I was or reassure me that I would eventually have control. I never did that with any of *my* blood babies."

"And for that, I thank you." Jude bent down, and Tinsel met him for a lingering kiss.

Something stabbed in Katelyn's chest at the sight. Closed though it was, no one could deny the depth of affection—the kiss of a long-married couple, not platonic.

Never had she reacted so viscerally to something as common and careless as a kiss. She couldn't remember being nearly this jealous about anything.

He made you his.

But a familiar was basically a servant—not an equal, not like Tinsel. Tinsel had made him equal to her by turning him into a vampire.

And in the club, he'd seduced another small, curvy but slender blonde girl.

Not Katelyn. Nothing like her. She'd just been in the way, and he'd thought she would be useful.

Her gut wrenched in her abdomen as though something clawed to get out. She clenched her hands into fists but said nothing. She wasn't the kind of girl to lose her head over a man. She'd never been that kind of girl. She'd never *liked* that kind of girl.

But she wasn't the same girl anymore, was she?

"You'd better feed her," Tinsel finally said, resuming her brisket-cutting. "She looks like she's going to scratch out of her skin."

Jude opened a restaurant-grade refrigerator and pulled out a glass milk bottle, full to the brim with something like dark red wine. But wine wouldn't be that thick. "It isn't as good for us, but some vampires buy it for their own familiars, and a handful of international dishes call for it. Where there is demand, we provide the supply. We'll always keep some on hand for you." Jude slid the bottle across the counter like a bartender with a beer stein. "You're still in school, yes?"

Katelyn wrinkled her nose at the bottle. "Yeah."

"Your presence would be missed if you quit?"

"If I dropped out, not only would people assume I was guilty, but my dad would have puppies. What is this?"

"I should think that was obvious," Tinsel said. "We're not wasting the human supply on another human, if that's what's got your panties in a twist. It's sow blood."

Katelyn pushed herself back from the counter. "I'm *not* drinking blood."

Jude stepped around the island and cradled Katelyn's head near the base of her neck. How easily he could squeeze through her skull, break her brain stem. She could barely comprehend his size, nor could she shake the rightness of his presence, as though the vibration in her body had attuned to his. His proximity practically hummed.

"I know what you did," he said quietly, twisting the bottle cap open. "I think you'll find this less distasteful than maggots and spiders. Tasting your own can dim a craving, but it will never satisfy. I know you can smell it. It's life that we offer you, Katelyn—life taken without crime or passion. If you eat meat without qualm, there is no reason to say no to blood of the same animal."

She took a step toward Jude, compelled forward by the blood. "It's disgusting."

Tinsel flipped over another slab of brisket to slice. "No more disgusting than anything else that you eat. You'll acclimate yourself to a familiar's appetite in time, and you can still eat the usual human food, although it won't have the same luster it once had. Sorry, girl. It's time to jump in the deep end and grow a pair."

"I have enough of a pair, thank you." Katelyn still shuffled forward like a zombie, the scent from the blood bottle enveloping her in fog.

"It won't hurt you, Katelyn. I promise." Jude held out the opened bottle to her.

"You have to stop holding her hand sometime," Tinsel said.

"It's only her first day."

Katelyn wrapped her hands around the neck and body of the bottle and eagerly lowered her head to the glass mouth. Jude grunted a little at how hard and intensely she drank and swallowed, drank and swallowed, her gulps loud in the metal room.

At the first slide of it down her throat, she knew cold blood, especially with preservatives, wasn't what she preferred. However, that was like saying she preferred hot chocolate to chocolate milk when she still loved both. She moaned in gourmand ecstasy, gulping and gulping until she'd reached the bottom and there was no more fragrant, filling life left.

She dropped the empty bottle and grabbed the next one Jude handed to her, heedless of the shattered glass skittering over the terracotta floor.

The blood seemed to hit her stomach and disappear. She didn't get full. Her heart raced as though she was running a half-marathon, but she hadn't moved from where she stood.

After he gave her the third bottle, she finally started to slow down. Jude stood behind her now, her back to his chest, and he parted his mouth near her exposed neck, the length of vulnerable blood vessels caressed by his harsh breath. As she threw back her head for the last drop, he dragged his mouth over her pulse, his grip on her arms bruising. The wet slide of his fangs emerging sounded like knives withdrawn from bloody flesh.

This time Katelyn didn't drop the bottle. She slammed it onto the island and reached back to stroke his bald head and pull him closer. Just as everything inside her had craved life in blood, everything inside her now desired nothing more than the death his teeth could deal. He'd been so close last night. Maybe now he would…

"Control yourself," Tinsel said, throwing an aluminum foil ball at his shoulder. "Your familiar is new to her change. You don't have that excuse. And she *is* your familiar, *not* your companion. Remember that."

"No," Katelyn protested as Jude retreated, careful around the broken glass.

He went for a broom without comment.

"Yes," Tinsel said. "It's part of the limbo of being a familiar, honey. It's being denied what your soul now craves even more than life. And if he knows what's good for him, he'll hold to our agreement. You're old enough for tough love, Jude, and you've been around long enough for self-control. We'll eat soon."

"It won't happen again," Jude said as he finished collecting most of the glass. Blood still stippled the floor and smeared where the broom had been. It was decidedly odd watching a giant sweep.

"Leave it," Tinsel said. "I'll clean the rest before it spoils. Go give Cara her human blood. The girl yesterday should have given her some color, but I don't know when next I can bleed someone for her and she'll agree to drink."

Somehow, although the sweeping had looked strange, a giant calmly doing as the tiny girl asked didn't seem out of place at all.

Jude retrieved another bottle from a different shelf in the fridge and beckoned Katelyn to follow him. She fell in step immediately, picking her way around the mess with cheeks hot in embarrassment, shame and satiation all at once. When Jude obeyed—or disobeyed—it was his will that drove him. When Katelyn obeyed, it was also his will. Now that she was close to him again, unshaken by fear or car wreckage, she recognized his influence like fingers digging into malleable dough.

Her whole being whispered in his grasp, *you are his*.

Jude led her from the kitchen into the main warehouse room, then up a flight of stairs. He directed her into a corridor that looked like it had been converted from meat storage into residential suites. "She's still not happy about keeping you alive."

"Yeah, I got that."

"But in the end, she's not the only one who can expand this Family, and you're already proving entertaining, at least. If you could have seen how she looked at you drinking that blood with your neck bared… And I still hold out hope you'll be tremendously valuable to our Family. I have a good feeling, love."

"I live to serve," Katelyn said dryly.

They reached a closed door bolted from the outside. Her heart skipped. The only reason to have a lock on the outside was to keep someone in.

Jude handed her the bottle. "Don't drink that." Then he grabbed the handle of the deadbolt at the top of the door and pulled. Even he had to exert some effort.

"Cara doesn't want to be a vampire, does she?"

Jude undid the chain lock as well, a pensive cast to his expression. "Then you accept we exist?"

She'd just drunk a bucket of blood that hadn't weighed her down in the slightest, and not only did the lingering taste and the droplets on her boots keep her salivating, but the bottle in her hand also posed a true temptation. She'd subdued her craving, but she wasn't anywhere near done.

She should have tossed her cookies after the first few swallows. The car accident *could* have rewired her brain, but what a strange way to do so. And the longer she spent time with Jude and Tinsel, the less she thought they were crazy, too. *She* had lost her goddamn mind, but Jude and Tinsel were solid, unflappable, real and unfazed by all the accoutrements of supernatural vampirism. She couldn't believe she was accepting this melodramatic crap, but she could only deny what was right in front of her for so long.

She didn't know whether she felt any better believing she wasn't responsible for her friends' deaths, if Jude and Tinsel were. Because here she was, following him like a puppy starved for affection, talking to him as though he wasn't a murderer by his very nature.

"Cara has resisted the transformation since Tinsel turned her six months ago," Jude said.

"She drank from Maria," Katelyn said quietly.

"Almost every drop, once Tinsel sliced a vein right in front of her. I won't sugarcoat this life, Katelyn, not least because I suspect you'd see right through the marzipan."

"It doesn't take a detective. You and Tinsel said it all. The locks just confirm it."

"And in the club? Tell me how you knew something was wrong."

She grasped the bottle so hard that he removed it from her grip before she could shatter it. It wasn't some big secret, but Katelyn still resisted the order, not entirely sure why this was something so important to withhold.

"If I didn't have Cara to attend to, I would press the question." He turned his solemn attention back to the heavy door. "When we have a moment to ourselves, then."

"It's just observation," Katelyn burst out. "That's all. People sometimes ask how I see things, but *I* don't understand how they're overlooked."

He paused with his hand on the doorknob. "Later," he finally said, then pushed open the door.

The room was dark except for a single lamp. Blankets covered the brushed metal walls—to hide the lack of reflection, Katelyn realized. Cara lay in the middle of her bed in a white nightgown. The room was too dark for Katelyn to read, but Cara didn't seem to have any trouble with her book.

She looked like any girl at all, propped up on her elbows, her bare feet in the air, like she was taking some alone time under a blanket fort during a sleepover. She was about Katelyn's age, maybe younger. Her brown hair framed her face in a long bob, and when she raised her head at their entrance, her eyes were as black as those of the other two vampires.

Her nostrils flared in Katelyn's direction. Cara froze like a rabbit in the sights of a wolf, although in that room, she was the wolf.

"She's mine," Jude said gently. "Not for you."

Cara's shoulders loosened, and she let out a quick exhalation, but Katelyn noticed she didn't inhale again.

"Why'd you bring her here?" Cara asked. "It's not safe."

"No, it's not safe for *you* to resist your hunger for so long." Jude handed her the bottle.

"This will suffice," she said, twisting the top off.

Katelyn stumbled back against the door, slamming it shut with her weight. If she'd thought resisting animal blood had been difficult, human blood—pure, if not fresh—assaulted her.

"Hard to resist, isn't it?" Cara held up the bottle in a toast before emptying its contents in a few brief swallows. She licked her lips involuntarily, then self-consciously. "But I do my best."

"I still don't understand why," Jude said.

"Because you think if it feels right, if it feels good, if it feels natural, it must be okay. But the body and what it screams for can't be trusted in anything, even less so after turning. You, new girl…you know I'm right."

"Katelyn," she replied. "And I don't completely agree, on principle."

"Oh, you want to give in to the blood cravings? Just itching for Jude to turn you so you can suck the life out of someone for a moment's unnecessary pleasure?" Cara crawled backward on her bed and reclined against the pillows like a tragic, tubercular romantic heroine. Even after the bottle, she didn't look well. Dark circles cradled her black eyes, and her pale lips were colored only by the leftover blood that she darted out her tongue to catch between comments.

Jude sat on the edge of the bed. "The pleasure is unnecessary. The pleasure is a gift. The feed, on the other hand…" he said, with all the weary patience of rehashing an old argument.

"We're immortal. If we don't feed, we still live."

"If you can call this living."

"Lead us not into temptation," Cara said grimly.

"We tell her that she doesn't have to stay with us if she resents the transformation," Jude explained for Katelyn's benefit, "but we cannot in good conscience let her leave. A starving vampire is a careless one. Setting her free is condemning her to death. You do yourself a disservice with this eating disorder, Cara."

"You bring in these girls, you slash their throats in front of me and all I can see after I'm done is their dead eyes. I'm haunted by each one. I don't understand why you can't just satisfy me with donor blood all the time. It's unethical to steal it from people who need it more, but not as immoral as murder."

"Donor blood is difficult to procure, for emergencies only, and those we might cultivate ourselves are risky to keep. We are well suited for disposing of, not sustaining bodies. If you want a willing donor, you must learn control. You can only learn control by keeping yourself fed and strong."

Cara turned onto her side away from Jude. "You and Tinsel are the ones who insist on keeping me alive." She leveled a dark stare at Katelyn. "Whatever they've done to you, kill yourself now or run. Resist them."

"I can't," Katelyn said.

Jude stroked her cheek. "Katelyn knows her place in this universe better than you do. She doesn't have the luxury of ignoring it. She couldn't, even if she wanted to."

"I have my mind, so I have my soul," Cara said. "I'll fight damnation every day I'm forced to stay undead.

Then maybe I won't be damned when a hunter finally puts me out of my misery. If you're a familiar, Katelyn, then I'm sorry for you. You don't have a choice. Pray that when you finally do, it's not as a demon like me, with so much blood on your hands that they may never be clean."

"Last night..." Katelyn began.

"A moment of weakness," Cara replied, "that they exploited."

"She was my friend."

Cara sat up, her eyes in their sockets like funnels in thunderclouds. "Then you understand. I'm sorry. But she's the fortunate one now."

Katelyn rubbed the gooseflesh on her arms as Jude bolted Cara back into her room. "I can't decide if she's the smartest or saddest person here."

Jude stroked the metal door as though to give Cara comfort through it. "No reason she can't be both."

"It doesn't seem smart to turn someone so obviously born-again. How did you expect her to react?"

"Tinsel cultivated her, but Cara didn't put up much of a fight until after the transformation. She showed none of this religious reluctance when she was making love to Tinsel before she knew Tinsel was a vampire."

"Nothing like dying for a come-to-Jesus moment."

"It's good to know you can't observe everything. I was beginning to wonder if you were psychic."

Katelyn rolled her eyes. "Why does everyone think something they can't explain must be magic?"

They continued down the corridor until they reached his room. She recognized the utilitarian style immediately.

"Surely you've realized that vampires aren't the only myths that aren't," Jude said. "It was a reasonable thought."

"Reason. A lot of that going on." Katelyn sank into the armchair and covered her face with her hands.

Jude sat on the end of his bed. His legs were parted, one hand behind him, bracing him. The other he outstretched. "Kneel before me, Katelyn. Come home."

Katelyn whimpered, the pull of his command practically dragging her from the chair, but she clutched the arms. She wasn't going to do this. She wasn't going to become his servant. *No, not servant. Servants can quit.*

After the blood, she felt more herself, less distracted by her own changes, but no matter how she struggled, she couldn't hold back. She slid from the seat onto her knees, then crawled toward him, despite concentrating with all her might on standing and backing away.

"You are in no danger, my familiar." He brushed her chin with his thumb, then wiped a tear of frustration from her cheek as she shuffled closer between his open legs. He brought her tear to her mouth.

Trembling, Katelyn took his thumb in, the memory of his first communion flooding her. He probed her mouth, offering the salt of her struggle over her tongue instead of blood. The black in his eyes seemed to heat, expand. He lifted her face to his by her mouth. Against her own wishes and will, she raised herself up to meet him, her body and mind traitors to her in every way. Their loyalties had shifted, if they had ever belonged to her in the first place.

Jude stopped before kissing her. He slipped his thumb out and anointed her forehead with something like affection. But that was all.

"You are bound to obey, but I've left you your will and self in all other things. I can take that away. Most vampires who have multiple familiars do. Would you prefer that? You wouldn't need to worry about being implicated or complicit in what I demand. No consequences. No pain. No distress or despair. I've been told it's actually quite pleasant, letting go of reality and simply living in here." He stroked her hair over the contour of her skull. "There would be none of these fights, none of your resistance. Is that what you want?"

"No," Katelyn said quickly. Nothing scared her more than the idea of losing herself entirely—even worse than this pervasive, invasive sense of madness.

"You can always change your mind."

"Is that what you really want from me?"

"I didn't turn you just to have an obedient servant. I much prefer keeping you present. But it *will* cause you more distress."

"I'll fight you," Katelyn said.

"I've noticed how tenderly you fight, love."

Katelyn pulled back her hand to slap him. He caught her wrist before she could swing it forward. He smiled, his teeth bright against his darker skin.

"Don't worry. Tinsel is right. I shouldn't take advantage of your compliant state. I apologize for my own weakness. There will be some lingering... reactions," he added with a glance at her lips, "but you needn't fear me. On your knees, on my bed, in yours, do not fear."

She lowered herself to her heels as he brought her wrist down. His words heated through her body, following all the places his blood had suffused. But she told herself the desire only came from him, part of the loyalty he had stolen with his communion.

"I only wanted to show you that my wish is your command. The days are yours. The nights, however, will be mine."

"I go to college," Katelyn said. "I'm part of a sorority. If I miss too many events, fail too many tests, people are going to notice. The sorority will kick me out. The university can kick me out, too. My parents will get involved. You can't take me away from that. You can't take my nights. I need to sleep, you know."

Jude sighed. "It is unfortunate that you're in school. Junior or senior year?"

"Junior."

"Even more unfortunate. I can make some accommodations, but not as many as you'd like. I have plans for you."

"I have plans, too," Katelyn shot back.

"Mine take precedence."

"You fucking bastard." She swallowed against her tightened throat and pushed herself to standing.

He grabbed her hand again before she could retreat. "I'll do my best to give you what I can, but our nights are short enough as it is. You must simply make room for my world. You might find you are less suited for your own than before, just as we are. Your priorities may change—and not just to mine." He tugged her closer him. "Biology might suit you better than whatever you're in now."

"Psychology suits me fine."

"That explains a bit." Jude stood and turned them around so that the backs of her knees hit his bed. "You'll want to sleep for what I have in store for you tonight."

"I have a fundraiser..." she started, but she fell in what seemed like slow motion through a cloud.

"You've been in an accident, your friends are dead and everyone thinks you're a suspect. They'll let you skip it. Sleep while you can. Then we'll see how useful you can be."

Chapter Six

She'd never been to this bar before—and for good reason. Its clientele was older—at least the men were. The women were mostly her age.

Humberto was the kind of place talked about plenty in sorority circles, especially after a professor was let go five years ago for frequenting the establishment. The whispers were usually laced with derision, but Katelyn had caught a glint or two in some sisters' eyes at the thought.

Attractive or rich older men—both, if lucky—roved with an eye for a piece of arm candy, a midlife-crisis enabler or just someone adventurous and energetic in bed, the kind of women these men assumed would or should flock to them. Not that the younger women were much different, leveraging their youth and attractiveness for a good meal, a diamond bracelet or hopefully a skilled and more experienced lover or future husband, depending on the girl.

Katelyn was wearing the same ensemble she'd ridden to the butcher shop in, but her hair was brushed and pulled back in a loose ponytail. Jude was wearing a suit, business turned evening with a dark blue shirt underneath his blazer, unbuttoned to show the hollow of his throat, and a fedora covering his bald head.

His suit and affected manner aged him, effective camouflage. Katelyn assumed the only reason she'd been allowed in was because she was with him. This bar was no stranger to a good curve, but Katelyn was self-conscious of the fact hers were probably the most generous. No one looked down their nose at her, but a person knew when she didn't belong—same as when she'd entered the butcher storefront.

Jude handed her a drink.

"What is it?" Katelyn asked.

"Whiskey. One swallow, love. I sense your anxiety, but there's nothing for you to worry about…yet."

Katelyn handed it back. "I don't drink."

"If you insist." Jude knocked back the shot himself.

"Can you do that?"

"I paid for it."

"You know what I meant."

"I know what you meant. It does nothing for me, but it doesn't hurt me, either. I won't expel a font of ashes or anything. I just didn't want it to go to waste."

"Why did you bring me here?" she asked.

He wove them through the small standing tables with couples and threesomes talking and laughing together. The whole room smelled of smooth alcohol, which was better than the beer miasma in some of the clubs, but she still wasn't a fan. She preferred the unmanufactured perfume underneath, what emanated from the warm, aroused skin of the people around her.

He helped her into one of the booths that was tucked into the wall. The booths themselves were circular, the easier for Jude to go in the other end and slide around next to her. His powerful thigh pressed against her ass as he oriented her toward the rest of the room, giving her a panoramic view of the bar, the seating tables, some of the booths and the small dance floor in the back, where the dancing wasn't necessarily pornographic, but Katelyn wouldn't describe it as romantic, either—and in this quieter bar, it was hard to blame the rubbing and grinding on the beat.

"What do you see?" Jude asked.

"A May-December relationship brochure?"

She could practically feel his smile on her neck. "I mean, when you look at these people, the individuals, what do you see? Describe them to me."

His request hadn't taken the tenor of command, so she was still free to evade. "You have eyes. In this light, you probably see better than I do."

"You're stalling."

"I don't know what you want."

"If we'd been doing our work right last night, only a hunter would have been able to pick us out from a crowd, because they'd know what to look for. And you're no hunter."

"You're asking me to share some special secret or esoteric skill. The fact is, two people making meaningful eye contact over a crowd while coincidentally targeting two of my friends just happened to trigger my suspicion, and I tend to be suspicious in general. If you or Tinsel had chosen only one of my friends, I might not have made the connection. Maybe I would have just let Aly or Angel go with you to make their own bad decisions without interference. One measured seduction would have been innocuous. Two was too obvious."

"We couldn't have met each other's eyes for more than a second. We sense each other's intentions the way I feel your emotions and hear your shallowest thoughts now."

"A second is enough."

"Do you think any of them would have noticed?" He nodded to the rest of the room.

"They wouldn't have been looking. I wish I had more to offer, but if I were super TV-detective observant, I would have driven a different way home last night. But it was just a case of boredom, looking after my friends and partner-predator behavior on your part."

Jude encircled her from behind, his arm possessive over her chest as he peered over her shoulder. "Try anyway."

Katelyn held up her hands in frustration. "I could make stuff up. It's not like you can verify anything I say."

"Katelyn, tell me what you see." This time his words carried gentle weight.

She sighed, closing her eyes. After a deep breath, she opened them, switching on whatever mechanism enabled her to see beyond the moment. It mostly functioned in her unconscious, but she could bring it to the surface if she chose, which wasn't often. This wasn't really a trick people asked her to take out at parties. Most people actually didn't like putting themselves under a microscope for the entertainment of all. Social media and reality shows were both carefully curated content.

But now she opened her eyes—really *opened* them.

Most of what she saw was hardly scandalous, considering the context. A few married men who had switched their wedding rings from one hand to the other or into their pockets. For some of them, there was a tan line on the fingers where the rings had been. Some of them kept touching the pocket they put it in, conscious of its monetary value, if not the value of the commitment it represented. Katelyn was sure at least two of the young women in the room were hiding engagement rings of their own, based on the rocks they sported on their right hand. Most people who cared about not having an affair knew to check the left hand, but they tended to overlook the right, for some reason.

She saw people drinking more than they should—deliberateness or awkwardness of step, flushed ears, slight sway, extra effort to speak. She saw pills that shouldn't mix with alcohol—prescription, not technically recreational. She saw a few black irises that made her question her own perceptiveness if she'd never noticed them before in other clubs.

On the dance floor, a couple now attempted to use the man's blazer to shield a surreptitious hand job. They made no attempt, however, to conceal their X-rated kissing, although they'd have done better at the former if they hadn't been occupied by the latter. She indicated the couple with a nod in their direction.

"He's new to his money. Serviceable department-store suit, scuffed shoes, *expensive* watch. The diamonds have to be real, because that thing is hideous. Probably bought it for himself with his first six-figure paycheck. Celebrating with a young hottie. He had his car valeted. The ticket is in his pocket, which, in this part of town, meant he wanted to show off. So, luxury vehicle, probably a sports car instead of a muscle car.

He likes flash, not nostalgia. Unmarried. Hopefully disease-free, considering."

"And her?" Jude asked.

"Jerking him off for a thrill, but she's into it. Red cheeks could be alcohol, but lips parted suggests otherwise. She's worn that top all day—easy to wear, versatile and it looks more lived in than the rest, which is still crisp. Public transportation—no car key in her clutch. Graduate student or young professional. If I had to hazard a guess, I'd say young professional over graduate student. Either that or she gets an allowance I don't even want to think about. Clothes are deceptively upscale. Stitching and fit never lie, and I recognize the pieces. I can't afford that shopping center. Her feet are killing her, though. Yes, definitely hoping disease-free, because that was not wrapped," Katelyn added as the young woman licked her hand with a coy smile.

"Interesting picture you paint, love. Impressive."

"There's no way to confirm any of this. I'm just making a series of educated guesses," she said, brought back to herself and acutely aware of Jude's presence.

His body practically curled around hers, his mouth so near her neck and ear, while the couple they'd been observing kissed again as though they were naked. Watching them and leaning closer to his massive, all-encompassing body tightened her nipples under her bra, so much so that they protruded against her shirt as though she wore nothing underneath. Jude brought his hand down to her leg, but though she half expected him to slip it between to caress her tingling labia, he just squeezed her thigh and raised himself upright again.

She reached for him the only way she thought would work. "When they're finished here, she won't take him back to her place. She'll let him drive her to his home, more modest than she expects because he hasn't had time to move to a fashionable condo or apartment, but his wine will impress her. She'll let him take her to bed. His excitement will make it less successful for her than she'd hoped. If she's lucky, he's courteous or teachable after his orgasm. I think he will be. He shares a kiss, doesn't keep his own rhythm and hope she keeps up. If she has to, she'll fake her orgasm because she likes him. One-night stand, maybe a little more if he wants to hook up again. But they're in it for the fun and the taboo, nothing more. That'll lead to some wall-banging for sure."

Jude couldn't stop staring at her lips, even though she hadn't put on a single bit of makeup before leaving the sorority house, and she hadn't done that since junior year in high school. She almost always wore foundation, lip gloss and mascara, if nothing else. Yet in a room full of lipstick and smoky eyes, he couldn't tear his gaze away from her.

"Please…" she whispered, unsure whether in warning or plea, but either way, he slid his hand along her cheek to angle her head as he met her with his own sensual, insistent mouth. He leaned in, forcing her to submit, to yield to his rhythm that she fell into without a fight. Despite his power over her, he was neither aggressive nor self-absorbed. She clutched at the lapel of his blazer, then at the first closed button of his shirt, as the tip of his tongue teased her lower lip with a caress for anyone to witness, like the couple *in flagrante delicto* on the dance floor.

"Naughty girl," he murmured against her lips. "You did that on purpose."

"You can't make me feel this way and not do anything about it. It wasn't my choice to want this as much as I… I've never…"

"You'll have your satisfaction." Jude brushed the front of his trousers as he reluctantly pushed himself away on the vinyl seat, forcing distance between them. The outline of his cock was unmistakable, much more pronounced in those trousers than in jeans. It was all Katelyn could do not to follow and wrap her hand around his erection through the material.

He nodded to the crowd. "Again. What do you see?"

"Care to narrow that down for me, Butch?" she asked, sulking as she turned back around.

"The woman with the scarf speaking to the man with a mustache."

"What do *you* see?" she retorted.

"A woman and a man I could seduce. I rarely need to know details. I don't need a legend or ruse if all it takes to convince them to give me their blood is my influence and my touch."

"Then why do you need me?"

"A lure. A lure that breaks our pattern. It makes the work so much easier for us if we don't trip a hunter's wire. Unless the will has been taken, a familiar is indistinguishable from an ordinary human, though my blood in you tells other vampires that you are marked for another."

She recoiled, although to the rest of the room, it would have seemed like she simply leaned back in her seat. "You want me to find victims."

"I want you to find victims that you know I'll like—not just for nourishment but enjoyment. My preference leans strongly female. Tinsel welcomes either, without discrimination. To know exactly what I like, though—

beyond the bare skeleton of desire—you have to know what to look for, a quality I cannot even describe."

It's easy enough for me. Small, young, blonde, a little perky—the kind of Teutonic ideal that's fucking sickening coming from you. I wonder if Tinsel was already your type before she turned you or turning you created the type.

"The couple you pointed out aren't your style, then," she said. "You'd want that girl at the bar, talking with the self-made millionaire. She's just his type, too—young, naïve, blinded by his money and shallow charm, although he doesn't acknowledge anyone below a certain tax bracket as human, much less worth more than a four-minute lay and a call for a taxi. He's a smarmy asshole who probably only keeps condoms in his back pocket to avoid child support payments. All you have to do is look at how he talks down to her and shows off the things he thinks will get the girl's panties off faster. She's a little less than vanilla, thinks she's more daring than she is, but her gaze is too guileless, her flirtation too obvious.

"She's not innocent, but she's in over her head, trying to catch a conceited millionaire, in a clearance-rack department-store dress. It's pretty on her, and I'm sure she's a lovely girl, but she's better off looking for someone with more character and sincerity. And he'd probably do better just calling an escort—fewer tears to navigate afterward. She's the kind you'd go after, though. You'd give her all the consideration a girl could want until she experienced your touch and fell under your spell, when you wouldn't have to be considerate anymore. Then comes the time to pay the price."

Jude said nothing as she plowed on, keeping her voice down but stream-of-consciousnessing every last bit she could glean from the people they saw—and from the man behind her, in the less than twenty-four hours that she'd spent with him so far. He hadn't contradicted her yet.

"Or how about that girl, with her skinny-rita and bronzer to show off the recent dye job? She covers her mouth *and* her nose when she laughs. She thinks her nose is bigger than it is and that her eyes are her best feature. She's a tall drink of water, and she knows she's attractive, although she doesn't know how much. She has accepted two drinks from men she's turned down, one from the man she's talking to now. He just feels starstruck that she chose him. He doesn't even care that he has to look up at her when she's wearing heels. Whenever she turns away, he does nothing but look at her ass, down her legs, and you know he's imagining her with her legs in the air and wearing only those shoes.

"That's the way you looked at Angel. She's the girl you killed, by the way. She was prone to getting drunk on the weekends, and she was sometimes a mean girl, but she was my friend, and you probably didn't even know her name when you slashed her throat and put her back in the car with me. All you saw when she wasn't looking at you was an expanse of neck and creamy chest, like a classic cover for a vampire novel. It's all so predictable—not hard to discern what you want at all. I can count four women in here that you'd love to sink your teeth into."

"I don't limit myself to blondes," Jude said, with a tinge of amusement.

"No, you don't limit yourself. But I'm willing to bet they catch your eye first."

"What are you willing to bet?"

"Nothing you can't just take whenever you feel like it."

His chuckle made the whole booth hum. "There is one woman in this bar that I would like to feast upon tonight, one I truly crave. If you guess right, I'll let you choose a man instead—one that would give you what you want as well as what I need." He slid close to her again, his breath disturbing her hair as he let his lips brush her neck. "It's not just blood that carries the life that you crave."

"Gross." But his hypnotic voice conjured images to the surface of her mind that continued to pluck at her bothered core. Her cunt fluttered around emptiness that felt uncharacteristically hollow, as though her torso had become a gutted tree stump.

"Like I said, you may find that your interests have changed," he murmured. "I can taste your lie."

"I'm not picking a victim, female or male."

Jude caressed the length of her arm. "'Victim' is hardly the word. Had you allowed us to take your friends conscious and alive, they would have gone happily into the dark night of their death. Maria did, in the end, even with one as out of control as Cara. We make last moments transcendent. Other death-dealers cannot promise so much."

"You didn't have to deal in death at all."

"If I wanted to argue food ethics, I wouldn't be a butcher. Death is a part of life, whether dealt by vampire, car accident, disease or old age. We're a part of this world. The sooner you get used to it, the sooner you can embrace your new position in the food chain. If you insist on viewing us through an outdated lens, however, I'm afraid this life is going to be quite joyless. And I wouldn't want that for you."

"If you didn't want that, you shouldn't have given it to me."

"Would you have rather joined your friends?"

She wanted to say yes. That was the kind of thing that heroines said when the villain forced them to choose between an easy path and the moral high ground. But the truth was, she wouldn't have wanted to become a murder victim along with her friends. She would have rather been with the rest of the Delta Taus at the Chocolate Festival fundraiser, manning a pudding booth. She would have rather her friends still be alive with her, with chocolate cookies and cakes to raffle off. Or if her friends had to be dead and she had to be transformed, she would have preferred if he'd taken her all the way, instead of with a foot in both worlds and belonging in neither.

"I didn't think so." His large hand swallowed hers. "I think you'll find that if you choose a man to seduce, you'll have a better time than you anticipate. You'll still have a reward from the woman I desire if you choose the wrong one, of course. You'd like a little human blood, wouldn't you, Katelyn? There is no shame in desiring life. We all want it in one form or another. You just crave a more literal form of it these days."

"Either way, you want me to decide who dies tonight. That's not something *I* have to do to feed. They're simply...cravings, wanting things that a vampire wants. You made me a poseur for the rest of my life. Thanks so much."

"What if I told you that no one has to die tonight?"

Katelyn had been planning a well-timed flounce, but the altered premise compelled her to consider. How many times was she going to be able to save someone by doing this for him?

"If it gets you in the spirit of the game, I'd be willing to concede this once." Jude held their clasped hands as though in the midst in agreement. "Does that sound fair? Whoever gets my bite won't even remember the night, only that it was sweet."

Slowly, Katelyn shook his hand, regret mingling briefly with intrigue like freshwater eddying into brackish. But no one would die—just a pinprick, like giving blood. Offer them a cookie afterward, and everything should end fine. Right? The devil had already made his deal with her. The devil already *had* her. She might as well accept his generosity when he offered it.

"Then which woman do I want?" he asked.

Katelyn returned her observational skills to the small crowd. It was getting late, and more people were coming in. She had to discern who had been there when he'd asked her to choose the first time, who had left and who had just entered. Easy enough. She wiped anyone new from her vision and focused on the women remaining, briefly disregarding her theory on blondes. However, after enough perusal, she'd narrowed the room down to six women, all of them blonde. The one at the bar was still in the running, but there was a young woman who kept drawing Katelyn's attention.

She wore a paisley scarf and an honor society pin, although Katelyn couldn't tell which from this distance. Her blonde was mostly natural. She enhanced it with color, but the roots showed a slightly less saturated golden. She was visibly nervous being in the bar as she drank her virgin cocktail, so this was probably her first time, and she clearly wasn't experienced with men, which begged the question why she'd decided to seek out experienced men in the first place. Based on the warmth with which she conversed with the man at the standing table, fantasies had likely brought her here, a preference that probably had her daydreaming her panties wet during college lectures.

She held herself away from the crowd, avoiding contact with those passing by, although she didn't flinch from the man with whom she was speaking, who could brush her shoulder or touch her hand and inspired the brightest smile from her more reserved demeanor, so no history of abuse but a well-defined personal bubble, an introvert taking a walk on the social side. The girl was nothing special, really—the quintessential college girl. With her choice in shoes and dearth of accessories beyond her scarf, Katelyn thought that even if she'd pledged, she'd never have made it into a sorority that wasn't academic-based.

However, there was a quality. The closest word Katelyn could come up with was 'vitality'.

Katelyn nodded at her. "Blue top, purple scarf, skinny jeans. UTM student. I've crossed paths with her a few times, but I don't recognize her from a specific class or event. Probably a sophomore at the oldest. Your choice of venue makes a little more sense now."

Jude shook his head. "It's not youth I seek. I chose Humberto because it's quieter and less crowded, and I wanted to be able to speak with you. In the future, we won't need words."

"Just meaningful, second-long glances?"

He smiled. "You're correct, however. You just saved this lovely young woman. I'm sure you're pleased."

"As punch."

"Now it's your turn. I don't have your knack, but would you like me to pick which one you'd want the most?"

"I'm not interested in anyone here," Katelyn said. "I never saw the point in going older."

"It was part of your deal to choose a man. If you don't want one to play with, choose one you would want drained. Vague revenge served cold. Who would you like to fool around with and see afraid?"

"That's a paradoxical combination if ever I heard one," she muttered.

"Go. Mingle. When you've found one you want, let him take you to the alley. There are several niches in the back deliberately ignored by the staff, dark corners ideal for a spur-of-the-moment rendezvous. And no, Katelyn, I won't let you run. I think once you get your taste—of the risks, the perks, of blood and other things—you'll take to it like a tiger to water." He gave her a less-than-subtle nudge. "Remember… You're here to enjoy yourself."

"I don't know how to—"

"*Go*. And if you try to leave—you won't be able to, but if you try—I'll kill them both, have myself a feast, and you'll have to jump into the deep end a little faster, because you'd feast right there with me. On the bright side, you would be left alone for a week or so, because I wouldn't need you for a while."

Katelyn clenched a hand into a fist, but she pushed herself out of the booth.

Jude covered her fist with his fingers. "I'm not saying these things to be cruel, only to be clear."

"Yeah, well, fuck you and your clarity. You turned me to be cruel. You say you didn't, but you did. I remember what you said, that you couldn't leave me alive but you wouldn't turn me into a vampire because that would be too much of a good thing. So you trapped me like this. Last time I checked, a trap wasn't cruelty-free."

Katelyn wrenched away from him and let the crowd draw her away, although she still sensed him in the distance, the way someone might feel a roaring fire even from the other side of a room. Without him, she mingled, rubbed her arms against others as she wove between men and women coming together, drifting apart, leaning closer, each trying to find that evasive connection, the chemical reaction that seemed to drive humanity, whether they admitted it or not.

Katelyn wasn't immune. She hadn't indulged as often as she thought she was supposed to, and that was something she'd never even talked to her friends about, along with the whole virgin thing. She'd mentioned it to one of her school friends back in high school, to much high-pitched disbelief and endless efforts to set her up with someone. But Katelyn couldn't think of a less interesting reason to get with someone than just sex. It made her feel good for a time, at least what sexual things she had engaged in, but emptiness returned so quickly afterward that it wasn't worth the hookup. She wanted more than chemical reaction. If that made her unrealistic, so be it. She'd rather be alone than used.

At least, that had been her philosophy before. She was horrified, mortified, by how much her desires had changed. Even apart from Jude, these little nudges and brushes wreaked havoc. The room was full of rushing blood, racing hearts, vessels moving to the surface under the influence of alcohol—blood filling and flushing, thickening and hardening flesh between legs, and although Katelyn couldn't pick out anyone's blood in particular, she inhaled it all. Unlike the smell of alcohol, she couldn't adjust. It constantly assaulted her senses and, in doing so, compromised her judgment. So close to so much blood, just a little bit of fabric or skin in the way, Katelyn thought if a complete stranger whipped her around and kissed her without any preamble, she'd let them, taste them, breathe in the cologne of their scent without resistance and lose herself within their mingling clouds in a heartbeat.

Not every man who crossed her path gave her more than a moment's attention. She wasn't everyone's type, just as they weren't all hers. Some of them were older than she'd look for, even in a place like this. Some of them were straightforward lechers that she couldn't convince herself to settle for, even to get it over with.

Most men who received her second glances were already occupied, their flags planted with the young lady of their choice. Once again, the sheer visual fact that very few of these women were like her tried to pull her into a morass of self-conscious self-loathing, but Katelyn fought to halt that line of thinking before it started. Regardless of what she looked like, when a man had the possibility of young sex dangled before him, it wouldn't matter if she was softer in the middle—or everywhere—than his average fantasy. Odds were he'd be so distracted by her boobs, he'd barely notice the rest. She wished she'd worn something more low-cut today. It would make this whole thing easier. Not that men weren't looking, but she'd be a more effective lure with a greater amount of cleavage. That was just hard, practical fact.

After a distinct lack of anyone finding her immediately appealing enough to swing her to their table, she took a seat at the bar.

The bartender was a woman in her fifties. Katelyn could see the benefits in employing an older woman in a place like this, at least if they wanted repeated business from the women. She wouldn't be inclined to be sympathetic to a belligerent man, and she wasn't likely to be hit on here as often than if she'd been younger. She was worn and attractive and wore the accessory of her age without needing to pretend otherwise. She keenly tracked the room, even as she acknowledged Katelyn and didn't make her feel ignored.

"What'll it be?" the bartender asked.

"Diet Coke."

"Anything else?"

"Just the Coke."

She poured Katelyn a glass without comment.

Katelyn turned around in her seat and leaned back against the bar as she drank, opening her shoulders to present her breasts, her legs crossed to draw additional attention to her thighs. When sitting at bars, she usually put out the vibe that she didn't want to be disturbed. It didn't work with the ones too drunk or too indifferent to care, but these men were older—still capable of getting drunk but not of getting it up as easily when they were. They'd recognize an invitation when they saw one. All she had to do was wait for someone to take her up on it.

It didn't take long. Katelyn had expected to finish her glass.

"From the man over there." The bartender grinned as she passed Katelyn another glass of Diet Coke. "He said he'd buy you another of whatever you're having."

"How generous," Katelyn replied. "Thanks."

She took the glass she was drinking and the one he'd bought and went over to meet him, though she hadn't even had a second look.

He would do.

* * * *

Katelyn wasn't exactly known for her flirtation skills, since she rarely had to make use of them with her friends around her. Yet there she was with Robert Carlisle, an account executive from the business district who was ostensibly at the bar for stimulating conversation with someone still in possession of her intellectual knowledge, the kinds of things that tended to drift and fade from a person's memory after leaving college.

He was a nice enough man, even if his excuse for coming to Humberto was flimsy at best. He was just on the tasteful side of scruffy that would be acceptable in a boardroom. He made her think of an absentminded librarian or professor on TV or in movies, not the ones she knew in real life. He wore a tweed jacket with leather elbows, a scarf that wouldn't be out of place on a French hipster and boots that looked like they'd been made from leather book binding. He drank brandy. If he had a house of his own or a large enough apartment, Katelyn suspected that he had a study and had read at least half of the books he kept in it. The poor man had a nostalgic attachment to his time at university, when he'd played on his school's lacrosse team.

Katelyn didn't mind indulging him for a little while, although he didn't do much for her other than flatter her by his choice.

Robert finished his brandy and passed sixty dollars across the bar, presumed tab and tip. "Want to get out of here? I live only a few minutes away. I could make us some coffee."

She set down her glass of what he probably assumed was her second rum and Coke of the evening. Then she drew closer, amazed at her own bravado as she tucked herself against him where he half-stood, half-sat on his bar stool. She embraced him with one arm, almost straddling his leg. After trailing her free hand down the buttons of his shirt, she passed them over the front of his trousers, caressing him boldly, thinking of the couple on the dance floor.

"There's a place out back."

Robert made a choking sound, stiffening in more ways than one. It wasn't like she'd done anything but the standards during their conversation—laugh, bite and lick her lips, look down coquettishly, sometimes stare at his mouth, all calculated to indicate her interest. It felt more and more natural the longer she did it, especially since his interest in her hadn't seemed nearly as calculated. He had the barest confidence that suggested he'd come to Humberto before but hadn't been lucky every time. Well, this time he'd hit a jackpot, and his disbelief was oddly endearing.

Blood swelled him under her fingertips. His fragrance hit her like a fine mist of wine. She parted her lips and leaned close to his parted mouth.

"Out back?" he repeated.

She kissed him, paying particular attention to his lower lip as he tried to maintain composure. She couldn't believe she was doing this. Public displays had never been her thing. Exhibitionism hadn't entered into her repertoire, because people tended to think that anything public was free to comment on, and she didn't want anyone staring or judging who the guy had chosen to make out with. However, as Robert continued to harden with each brazen stroke over the placket of his trousers, and as he slowly met her kisses with more heat, his stubble chafing her chin, she thought she could get used to it.

"Out back," she answered.

"Now?"

She brought her lips to his ear. "Unless you want me to get down on my knees right here."

"Fuck," he breathed. He grabbed the hand she stroked him with and held it tightly as he wove them through the throng and out of the bar. Once there, she took the lead, finding the side alley that led to the back. He laughed as she ran them into the darkness.

Guilt hit her without warning once they reached the back alley and he pushed her by her breasts into one of the shadowy nooks that Jude had mentioned. He kissed her again, kissed her breathless, his excitement mostly selfish, but she could hardly fault his eagerness—and that eagerness *was* for her, not just for sex. He moaned with delight as she brought his kneading hands under her shirt to touch her more directly. Her nipples hadn't softened since Jude, not with the scent of quickened blood keeping her on edge, and now she whimpered as he found them, tweaked them, stroked her into lightning bolts of arousal that made her scent swirl with his in the air around them.

"Condom," he said frantically before kissing her neck. "Back pocket."

She slipped her hand into one of his back pockets. Underneath the wallet, she found the little foil package. She palmed it but didn't remove it from his pocket. She cupped his ass, coaxing him against her abdomen, where he happily rubbed his erection.

"God, you're amazing," he groaned. "So fucking gorgeous."

Katelyn wrenched away, yanking her hand out of his pocket without the condom. She pushed against his hands until they were out from under her bra and shirt, then stumbled from him. "I'm sorry. I'm sorry. I can't do this."

"What?" Robert looked like he was still trying to figure out why the girl he'd been pawing wasn't still up against a wall. "Why? I thought you liked me. I thought you were liking this. Are you nervous? I'm not going to hurt you, I promise."

"No. It's not that. I just… I just can't. I need to go," Katelyn stammered, backing away and hoping that Jude wouldn't emerge from the shadows like a panther to pounce upon Robert. He wasn't the best man in the world, but he didn't deserve to be lured for his blood rather than his body. He didn't deserve her deceit. He was nice enough, and if it weren't for Jude, she wouldn't have seduced him in the first place.

Her settling shouldn't have been a near-death sentence. She couldn't do this to him…to herself.

"No, wait. Whatever I did, I can fix it." He followed her with awkward gait affected by blood flow, his arms outstretched to beg her, stop her, keep her from doing anything other than what they'd been doing. In his pursuit, he tripped on an uneven bit of concrete and stumbled against the brick corner of the niche. "Ow! Shit! Damn wall."

Katelyn paused in her escape. "Are you okay?"

"Yeah." Pain had interrupted the progress of his lust, at least for a moment. He brought his hand away from his face and stared at it. "Fuck, I'm bleeding."

It gleamed on his palm and cheek like garnets, even in the darkness, where she shouldn't have seen the color as well as she could. She stared intently at the place on his cheek where the blood welled and swelled until it was too heavy to sit suspended and dripped down into his stubble.

Katelyn took his hand. He stopped muttering in irritation as she ran her tongue slowly, deliberately, along his fingers. She gasped, licking his palm and fingers again, to catch what she'd missed.

"Is that— I don't think that's safe. I mean, you're not supposed to— You don't know—"

She grabbed him by his lapels and raised herself on tiptoe to catch the drip of blood along his cheek to the source, moaning as she closed her mouth over the wound and sucked.

"Oh my God," he muttered, as though he couldn't believe that he found something so dangerous so hot. But he stumbled back, bringing her with him until this time he hit the wall. She cradled his face, sucking and licking at him until the blood stopped coming. Then she dragged her mouth to his, where he met her with now-equal passion, groaning every time she caught his lip between her teeth.

He didn't resist when she turned them so that he pushed her against the wall again. She braced against it as she raised her hips to meet his. After one more swipe of her tongue over his blood—fresh, fresh blood, brimming with life—she dropped to her knees and worked furiously at the fastenings of his trousers.

"Fuck, fuck, *fuck*..." he breathed, slamming his hands against the brick. Even the most intellectual person could lose their articulation under the right circumstances. He didn't make another mention of a condom, and she didn't have the patience for one. She couldn't get pregnant from a blow job, and she was already sick with a blood-borne disease that he couldn't catch. She just wanted the blood, the flush, the hard fullness of his arousal that called to her as strongly as the scrape on his cheek.

She yanked down his boxers and immediately nuzzled his erection, breathing him in like a starving woman presented with a feast. And like a starving woman, she didn't waste any time taking him into her mouth.

He shouted, hitting the wall with one hand, as she swallowed him down as far as she could go, almost to his base.

She groaned, clutching at him for purchase but unable to find a handhold strong enough for her. She'd never given a blow job before, at least to a person. During a memorable hazing ritual, pledges had deep-throated cucumbers, and each of them had been critiqued and coached on how to improve. Her cheeks hadn't stopped flaming for days.

She flushed now, but for an entirely different reason and not just because of his blood, which pulsed so temptingly underneath the thin layer of his skin that it was all Katelyn could do not to bite down. But her cravings seemed to understand the difference between the blood she foundationally craved and what else he could offer her here. Pre-cum seeped from the tip, smearing over her tongue as she took him in again and again. She couldn't remember anything that her sisters had suggested as far as technique. She had only her instincts and her need to have more of him, more and more of what was trickling through his pre-cum.

"Holy shit," he gasped, curling his fingers into her hair and easing her back a bit. "A little hard, honey. You're going to suck me right off if you keep going at it like that."

"Sorry. I just..." Katelyn laved him from root to tip, wriggling her tongue along the prominent vein on the underside of his rigid cock. "I just want you deep. As deep as you can go."

"No need to apologize. I... Fuck... You keep doing that, and I..." He groaned as though they weren't still outside where anyone and everyone could hear. "I can't believe this is hap-happening."

She took him all the way down again, this time pushing beyond her impulse to gag and swallowing around him, her throat clamping down on the head and her tongue undulating against him. More. She had more of him, and it still wasn't enough...watered down, tepid, bland. She needed more than this cheap imitation. She pulled back from his cock with a gasp and a cough. Then she dove back down again, moving her head back and forth on the way down like a serpent to tuck him in as deep as he could go.

His fingers in her hair tightened, pulled at the roots, holding her still as his hips jerked of their own accord.

"God, I'm going to come. Don't stop. Don't stop. *God*. Yes, yes, God, *yes*."

His words meant nothing to her, as affirmation, validation, compliment or warning. All that mattered were the hot pulses of cum hitting the back of her throat. She pulled back just enough to catch a few thick, sticky strands over her tongue with a helpless, desperate moan. Like Jude's blood, Robert's semen seemed to coat her mouth, and when she tasted it, everything in her body buzzed, as though every part of her could taste him. She gasped, crying out around him as she acted on instinct and brought one of her hands down between her legs to press against her pulsing clit. A slow, rolling orgasm swept through billions of thirsty, ecstatic cells.

Katelyn was reluctant to let him out of her, but his cum eventually stopped welling into her mouth, and he sidled away as his erection began to soften.

"Whoa, there." He drew her off him, laughing and gazing down at her with light in his eyes. "That was fucking amazing, woman."

"I completely agree," Jude said, blacking out even the dim streetlight and grabbing Robert by his shoulder. He placed a hand on the side of Robert's head, then pushed it to the side. Before Robert had the opportunity to protest the sudden intrusion, Jude plunged his teeth all the way into his neck.

Katelyn just stared, mussed, shaken, the taste of blood and semen still coating the inside of her cheeks. Robert's eyes went wide, his mouth open in a silent scream, but Jude brought his hand around Robert's head to cover his mouth in case he made more than the stunned grunts gurgling from his throat.

Then Robert's eyes rolled back in his head, and his cock thickened once again before her as though he wasn't well over forty and just through with one climax. Her mouth watered at the implied promise of more cum, but that wasn't what drew her to him now. That kind of life was all well and good—her body shot its richness through her veins like adrenaline—but it wasn't what limned Jude's lips as he glanced up to meet her mesmerized gaze.

He slid his teeth out, slowly, so that she could see every bit of them exiting Robert's flesh. Robert groaned the same way he had with her mouth around him, but even when Jude had unsheathed himself, he remained slumped in Jude's strong arms, limp, his bobbing cock hanging out of his undone trousers. For all the effort Robert put into visible academic dignity, he didn't have much of it left now.

Katelyn didn't care. All she wanted was the red at Robert's neck—a more generous spring than the scrape on his cheek or even the tip of his cock—and the blood on Jude's lips.

"Have some," Jude said hoarsely. He held Robert's shirt out of the way of the seeping wound. "A token of my appreciation. You've done well tonight. Every moment I watched you, you didn't disappoint—even when you almost ran, because you stayed anyway. Taste him. Really taste him."

He didn't have to tell her twice, not this time. She swayed in and practically fell against the bite. She clamped her mouth around it the way she had taken his cock into her mouth. Sounds escaped her that she'd never heard before, the lunatic cries of desperation. *This.* This was everything she wanted but didn't have the equipment to take on her own, not without some heavy-duty rope and a good knife. As good as her orgasm from his cum had been, this was better. Robert's hands opened and closed, blindly grasping in his unconsciousness, but it was Jude who closed a hand through her already tousled hair and held her down against the wound.

And it was he who pulled her away.

"No," she whimpered, struggling against his grip. "There's more. There's so much more."

"Yes, there is, love, but I thought you didn't want to kill him."

"I– I– Fuck." Katelyn reeled back against the wall, holding her head as though it would explode. She pressed her mouth closed tight and only breathed when she had to, because every time she inhaled, the scent of Robert's blood filled her head. She wanted it. She wanted it as much as she wanted Jude's blood. More than her own life, she wanted someone else's. She needed it, and the more she resisted, the drier her mouth became, despite the blood and cum still coating it.

Jude drank a little more, a minute's worth that lasted hours for her. Then he took Robert in his arms and rested him against the wall. He even did up Robert's trousers. Robert had come again. His semen glistened on his shirt.

Jude gathered some on his fingers, then did the same over the bite mark. It closed with supernatural speed after Jude licked at the wound.

He offered the mixture to her. She couldn't hold her breath forever, and when she breathed it in right in front of her mouth, she had nothing left in her to resist. It wasn't enough, but it was something, his warm fingers probing over her tongue with the last bit of scraps from his feed. She shuddered through one more hard orgasm, whining around his fingers, her juices uncomfortable between her legs as she pressed her thighs tightly together.

"I am pleased," Jude said quietly. "Very pleased indeed."

* * * *

She sneaked into the sorority house well after curfew. Debbie came out of her room when she heard someone shuffling in the kitchen, but she just gave Katelyn a look that said she understood but that she wasn't going to understand twice.

Katelyn gulped against the obstruction in her throat, which had been there all the way from Humberto back to campus. Jude hadn't said a word in the taxi. He'd simply handed her an envelope when they'd reached Greek Row. She hadn't needed to open it to know what it contained—for services rendered.

He'd stroked her mouth with his thumb before directing the cabbie to leave. His fingers had still smelled of blood, the way rosemary and basil clung to skin.

Katelyn's legs weighed twice as much as she climbed the stairs to the third floor. This was college on a Saturday night, so lots of girls were still awake, either in their rooms or in the common areas. She grabbed her pajamas and headed to the communal bathroom without meeting anyone's eyes.

No one talked to her, so news of her weirdness from this morning, plus the rumors, had done their work. She didn't mind being ignored. If no one cared, no one would notice as she slipped through the cracks and quietly lost her mind.

She turned on the shower, stripped down, and stepped under the spray. Then she stuffed a washcloth in her mouth, let the images of the last two nights wash over her and screamed.

Chapter Seven

She was in the middle of Medieval Lit when she spotted the small wolf spider in the corner.

No. Not here. I can't do this here.

The drone of the professor's lecture dissolved into white noise as her world narrowed to elegant legs and a plump gravid abdomen. Not just one life. Dozens of lives, all locked in a body barely bigger than a quarter.

She clicked her fingernails on her desk. Her tongue stuck to the top of her dry mouth. She'd felt like shit this morning, her hair lank and lifeless, dark circles under her eyes. Her fingernails were in dire need of moisturizing, and a few clusters of pimples had sprouted under her ear and near her temples, plus one inflamed zit at the side of her nose. Foundation could only hide so much. No one had told her to put more makeup on, because everyone probably assumed that she looked terrible because she was either the murderer or bereaved. Even her Medieval Lit prof had given her a sympathetic glance as she'd entered the classroom.

But it wasn't just grief or even guilt. She felt physically sick, like she was coming down with something, and she looked as bad as she felt.

She thought of Robert's blood inside her from days before…and the sow blood. There were horror stories about people who thought they were vampires drinking human blood that was the wrong blood type. And there was a reason meat was cooked all the way through. Even stored in the fridge, who knew what had been in that pig blood?

Besides, blood type aside, Robert could have had something in his system he hadn't even known about that she'd absorbed and that might be making her sick right now.

God, I hope it's not gonorrhea.

Last time she checked, though, sexually transmitted diseases didn't make live spiders as appetizing as double cheeseburgers.

She tried to laugh it off, forcing herself to look away, face the professor and type up her notes. But the words were meaningless, might as well have been a foreign language. Her thoughts kept turning to the spider and whether she'd missed her chance.

Her chance. Her chance at what?

Imagine her in your mouth, spindly legs writhing over your tongue, and her and all her babies sliding down your throat and into your stomach. Imagine her juicy little body and those of her eggs dissolving, spreading, making you whole again. You're dying, Katelyn. You're dying every day. Your friends died in a car crash slash murder, and now you're dying even faster. You don't want to be like them, do you? A life for life. Many lives for much more life. It's a simple equation.

She almost wished those thoughts came from Jude, because then she could blame her state on him. But it was broad daylight outside, and he wasn't whispering in her head. This was all her.

All I need to do is wait for when he calls. Then I can get blood again – safe, clean blood, she argued with herself.

But think of all those lives. You need it.

I'm not eating a fucking spider*!*

The maggots had been disgusting enough, and that had been back when she hadn't known what was happening. The spider wasn't anywhere near her. There was no reason to lose control, no reason to go over there and do what her mind whispered at her to do, complete with tantalizing suggestive images. She didn't *need* it the way her cravings told her she did.

She could handle this. All she had to do was pretend nothing was wrong. All she had to do was pretend the spider wasn't there.

Then came the shriek.

"What's going on?" The professor stopped his lecture and climbed a few stairs toward the girl who had cried out.

"It's a giant-ass spider is what's going on." The girl clambered over seats and people's legs to get away from it. "It was coming right at me."

"It's not going to hurt you," the professor said. "Most spiders can't even bite through human skin. Please sit down and try not to disrupt my classroom again."

"It was going to crawl into my purse."

Katelyn fought against her impulse to stand. She lost. She ripped a piece of paper out of her notebook and picked up her empty coffee cup. "For God's sake, stop being such a girl. I'll get rid of it, Dr. Lavenshire."

"Kill it!" the girl shouted. "Stomp on it!"

"It's just an innocent spider doing its part," Katelyn said. "I'll take it outside, if that's okay, sir."

Dr. Lavenshire waved a hand in dismissal. "Yes, yes, that's fine."

Katelyn couldn't get to the spider fast enough, but she tried to be more circumspect about her urgency than the other girl. Once she found where the nearest boy was pointing, she knelt on the floor and put the piece of paper in its path, goaded it forward with the coffee cup and tried not to drool in front of everyone.

Once the spider was on the page, she covered it with the cup, then slid both the paper and the cup over to the edge of the step so she could get a hand underneath. The spider moved over the paper, its little weight shifting along her flat palm.

"Be right back," she muttered.

No one paid her any attention as she scurried up the steps. By the time she reached the door, she was in a full sprint. She shouldered open the doors to the outside and barreled through a group of students trying to enter. They apologized. She didn't.

Katelyn ran around the side of the building to the back, where the air conditioner rumbled like a broken washing machine. No teachers taking smoke breaks. No janitors taking the back way. Just her, some half-dead grass and a spider under a cup. She hid in the enclosure that housed the air conditioning anyway.

Once she'd set the paper down, she raised the lid. For a moment, she fully intended to let it go free and run like hell. But as soon as she saw the spider, slightly damp from the leftover coffee in the cup, which had also stained the notebook page brown, she grabbed it and stuffed it into her mouth, groaning as she did so.

Her teeth cracked the little legs and burst the abdomen, which exploded into her mouth. She couldn't swallow it fast enough.

As soon as everything left of the spider and its eggs were in her stomach, she leaned back against the building and stared up at the bright blue sky, her hands clenched into tight fists at her temples. She smothered a whimpering sob.

What the hell am I doing?

* * * *

The blood and cum from Saturday night on its own hadn't helped nearly as much as Tinsel had said it would.

Jude didn't call her for the rest of the week, and she sure as hell wasn't going to seek him out. He'd all but guaranteed that the next person he drank from would die, while he'd never put her out of her misery that way.

She'd taken to opening her window and leaving partially eaten lunches and dinners on her desk. She'd lay on her bed and watch the food until the nourishment she really needed showed up, not the dead crap that the cafeteria tried to feed her and that she used to like just fine. She choked down what she could. The rest she left for the flies.

It would start with one, but one wasn't enough. So she would wait. In they'd come to the siren call of spoiling food. She'd creep toward them. They'd buzz about in anxiety at her movement, but as much as her reflexes had improved, she could also keep herself inhumanly still. Then she'd swoop her hands over the lot of them and close them together in a hollow ball.

She'd interlock her fingers so they had no escape, bring her mouth between her thumbs, part them and suck the wriggling flies in to swallow them whole, like pills.

For the flies she missed, she waited until their maggots hatched. She got something out of them sooner or later.

Flies weren't enough. They were small, their ichor not quite bloody. She heard rats and mice in the walls, the minuscule scurrying of cockroaches, beetles, spiders. But those creatures were stealthy. Flies were easier to trap without making too much of a mess.

Her hyper-attuned senses kept her alert to all the blood pumping through the sorority house, sickeningly aware of every menstruating woman and every bloody tampon in the trash, some of which she couldn't help but suck on when she was in the stall, her face screwed up tight to keep from crying for the fifteen-hundredth time. It was disgusting and delicious, and she couldn't help it.

The first tampon she sucked on, she threw up immediately after, which just made her even hungrier. There was no use trying to stop it. She had no control over what she ate. All she could control was where. As long as her craving knew she would satisfy it, it gave her time to close the stall or lock a door.

In a pinch, she sliced her own skin, but just as Jude had told her, it just wasn't the same when it was hers.

And after every life she took, even something as insignificant as a fly or a little bit of endometrial tissue, her skin cleared up, tightened, smoothed, the most acne-free she'd been since before puberty. Her cheeks turned a healthy pink that made some of the sisters tentatively compliment her makeup. Her eyes were bright. Her hair had never looked so colorful, with threads of chestnut and gold emerging from the dirty red—such fragile vitality that crumbled away within hours without every tiny bit of life she consumed to sustain it.

That only fueled the more suspicious flames. What kind of girl thrived after the deaths of her friends?

Some of her sisters decided she was guilty and treated her that way. Others decided she was innocent and defended her. Katelyn didn't share an opinion either way. She wasn't entirely clear on her culpability, but guilt ate away at her where the lives eaten could never reach.

It was a few girls from the latter group who knocked on her door.

Katelyn kept the door mostly closed to hide the food on the desk. "What?"

"There's a cop here to see you. An Officer Dunn? He said he has news."

Katelyn stepped out, locked the door behind her, then followed the girls downstairs. She surreptitiously wiped her mouth in case she had anything caught on her lips, and she checked her teeth with the tip of her tongue. All perfectly innocuous reactions to meeting a somewhat handsome police detective at the door. No one would ever know what *kind* of food she was trying to hide.

Detective Dunn raised his head when Katelyn arrived at the door. "Ms. Dillon. I know I could have called, but I just wanted to let you know that, after investigating the murders of your friends, we've determined through a distinct lack of physical evidence that you were *not* involved. I apologize for any emotional turmoil we might have caused you after losing your friends, but—"

"But you were just doing your job," Katelyn said, more coldly than she intended. "Any idea yet who actually did it?"

Detective Dunn glanced behind her, where the group of curious sorority girls had grown. News of her being cleared of suspicion would travel the grapevine all the faster. "At this point, the trail has gone cold, but I assure you, we're still looking. If you ever want to ask about the progress of the investigation, or if you have something you need to talk about—something that other people might not understand—here's my number." He handed her a business card with both his and Detective Black's names and numbers. "You'd be surprised at what a good listener I or my partner can be."

Katelyn slipped the business card into her bra. "I'd like to go now."

"Of course. And Ms. Dillon, I'm sorry for your loss."

"Thank you." That, at least, was sincere.

* * * *

"Come to me."

How considerate that he'd waited for the end of her last Friday class to call. That week, she'd eaten a total of three spiders, seventy-six flies and fifty-seven maggots. It had been all she could do not to start laying mousetraps behind the sorority house and waiting for the sharp clap of something fresh.

She didn't attempt to resist the call, which meant she could use her rental car rather than steal another bike.

This time, when she entered the butcher shop, Cody nodded at her and indicated that she should go ahead into the back. Katelyn pushed through the metal swinging door into the meat freezer. The layer of frost muted the scent, but what helped control her appetite in Jude's absence was the knowledge that there could be blood at the end of her journey.

It waited on the counter, a quart bottle this time. Katelyn twisted off the top and chugged it as though it was a Friday night kegger.

"Long week?" Jude asked when she slammed the empty bottle down and gasped for breath.

"Don't even start."

"It should get easier."

"That's what Tinsel said last week. It has *not* gotten easier, Jude."

"And it won't get easier tonight, love. It's time for you to do what you were created to do. You'll receive your usual fee, of course."

Katelyn nudged the bottle. "Can I have another?"

He stayed on the other side of the island, his expression inscrutable and oddly indifferent, coldness that she wasn't accustomed to from him. "And remove your incentive?"

Tinsel entered the kitchen, wearing another sparkly halter top, this time gold instead of silver, which complemented her blonde pixie cut.

"Tinsel will be joining us tonight." Jude leaned down to kiss Tinsel hello.

"I want to see if your abilities deserve his praise," Tinsel said. "*I* don't need your help. I've never been as particular in my feeding as he is."

"Only in the ones you turn," Katelyn said. "Since they'll be living forever instead of just the next hour—and probably with you."

That earned Katelyn a tight smile. "More or less. I don't have a type, but they need to be worth keeping around."

"You have a type. You just don't know what it is yet."

"Do tell."

"I don't have enough information to tell you that. I don't suppose *you'll* let me have more blood before we go out."

Tinsel pressed her lips to Katelyn's cheek. Her breath was colder than Jude's. "Not my familiar, not my call."

"You're his sire."

"You beg nicely. I'd love to explore this side of you, but you're still not mine, and he hasn't loaned you out to me yet." Tinsel patted Katelyn's cheek, then continued past her.

Katelyn grabbed the neck of the quart bottle, but Jude slipped it from her hand before she could make it shatter again, this time deliberately.

"Now, now, let's save the feistiness for the dance floor, love. You'll get blood tonight. Fresh blood. Human blood. Better than the flies you've been subsisting on, although even that has done wonders for you."

His gaze traveled over her face and loose hair, down to the cleavage that she'd made a point to show off tonight, knowing that Jude would take her out. She couldn't wear a halter like Tinsel, but her top was still low and off the shoulders, the edge of her black bra visible and the thick straps breaking up her bare, pale skin. She'd chosen to go sexy, short-skirted, boots to her thighs, but with only Tinsel and Jude there, not to mention the taste of maggots still in her mouth along with sow blood, she didn't feel sexy.

"Time to go." Jude beckoned for Katelyn to follow. "Is Cara feeding tonight?"

"We'll see," Tinsel said shortly.

* * * *

Katelyn had never been in this club before, its atmosphere geared more toward young professional than college, because there was enough nightlife in Meridian that they could make these distinctions. It wasn't quite as neon as 360°, and like Humberto, the scent was less hoppy than she was used to in her usual clubs. The music was mostly the same, the clientele slightly gayer, but in general, this crowd was more familiar to her than Humberto's.

Once on the dance floor, Jude and Tinsel broke away from each other. Katelyn noticed that they didn't look in the other's direction after that, not even for a second this time.

Katelyn wasn't creating monsters—they'd been monsters long before she came on the scene—but she was certainly making monsters more effective.

Jude brought her with him to the dance floor, to a surprisingly slow song with a thumping beat like a heart thrumming through it. He surprised her by turning her away from him and holding her against him with his arms crossed above her chest. She tried not to read more into it than that he wanted to keep her close so that they could speak, but Katelyn couldn't control the way her body responded—as though she were safe, secure, loved.

That was the cruelest part of the joke.

Jude moved them to the rhythm of the music. At his size, their position could have been so awkward, but he rested his cheek on her hair, possessively bent over her, and they didn't bump and grind so much as sway—undulating like rocking water, body to body. Still, the very physical sensation of him, the flex of his muscles against and around her, distracted her more than she wanted it to.

She wondered if Jude could sense it as he lightly stroked the top of her breasts with his knuckles, almost like petting a cat. She hoped he couldn't. She didn't need him to know what he made her feel when he was like this, since he obviously didn't care, except for what it did for his ego.

He was a vampire. She was a familiar. Familiars served vampires. She understood perfectly well, even if the nuances had yet to be hammered out. He could hold her like this, but it was no different than a child hugging his teddy bear, entertainment and emotional practicality and nothing more, despite her familiar instincts wanting more by nature.

It was a terrible thing to do to a person, change them into a lesser being designed to be denied.

However, the longer they danced—her skin tingling and her body moving itself against his of its own volition—the longer she would be no threat to anyone. She didn't have to look around for potential prey, nor did she attempt to find other vampires in their midst. Jude had said his blood in her would protect her, and she trusted him that much. If another vampire's bite would turn her, all the more reason for another vampire not to seek out the taste of familiars who hadn't earned the right.

As the music quickened, he slid his hands down over her breasts, tweaking the peaks on his way, then settled them on her hips, his fingers light on her abdomen over her shirt. He raised his head from her hair and kissed her temple, down her cheek. Against her ass, his erection stirred, grew, as their hips moved faster, less sinuous and less subtle. His smile on her skin told her he enjoyed their game.

"It's time to find me a girl for the night," he murmured, his lips and voice stimulating her ear.

She forced her knees not to weaken. The huskiness in his deep voice wasn't for her but for the woman she'd bring to him.

"I think there's a flaw in your brilliant plan," Katelyn said.

"And what's that, love?"

"It was one thing for me to lure a guy out behind a bar, and in theory, I'd be able to find someone for Tinsel that way, too, although I don't have the first clue how to flirt with a woman. But that's the problem… Even if I could lure her in the first place, a woman interested in me is probably not going to be as interested in you."

"Then don't seduce her. I only wanted to know if you could, should the opportunity arise."

"What do you want me to do? Hogtie her and drag her out? Some of the new dance moves are pretty crazy, but I think someone's going to notice that."

He laughed, sliding his hands over the filmy material of her shirt as he stepped around her, his erection still against her. She couldn't avoid the tide-forming force of him, the light-blocking size of him, the strength everywhere she looked and touched. He was inescapable, and he was laughing at her for it.

"How about using your unique perceptiveness to befriend her?" Jude said.

"You really are evil, aren't you?"

It wasn't enough that he wanted her to seduce men to their deaths. He wanted her to befriend women to their deaths, too, which struck her as the greater betrayal. Men historically made a mess by following their dicks, but friendship, even of the acquaintance sort, required a certain level of trust, which she would almost immediately break.

There was a special circle of hell for people like that.

"Think of it as selling a product." Jude pulled a small stack of cards from his pocket and slipped them into her bra. "There are whispers on the street of an extremely exclusive club. No one knows where it is. Only a few can claim to have ever been. All you need to do is promise them VIP access. You'd be surprised how many people take the bait."

"How do you keep them from immediately sharing all the details online?"

"It's only a name with a reputation as something worth attending if you're lucky enough to get an invitation. They can only say that they were invited somewhere, not where they're going. Turning off and giving up their phones is a condition of their entrance. We haven't been caught yet, and in this perpetually archived world, that's no small feat. We know how to protect ourselves, Katelyn. And all you have to do is provide me with *one* attendee."

"So you're banking on people's excitement at exclusivity to capture them all and eat them like Happy Meals?"

"We've left a few alive to tell the tale, dazed but ecstatic. Just enough to ensure future feasts follow us willingly."

"Did I mention you're evil?"

"Did I mention that in a debate on food ethics, I'd win?"

She thought about trying to hit him again, but his smirk told her he wouldn't let her get that far.

"Please don't make me do this." In a place like this, even as close as he was, his mouth inches from hers, he shouldn't have heard her. But he caressed a lock of hair framing her face, his amusement dissipating. For a moment, she thought he would kiss her, but he lowered his eyes and withdrew.

"It's why you are what you are," he said. "If I must command you every time, I will, but it'll save time and effort on your part more than mine if you embraced your purpose."

"You wish you could be so lucky."

"Very well." He brought his lips to her ear. "Find me a girl I want, Katelyn, and convince her to come with us to the Slaughterhouse."

"That's the name of the club?"

"Mm-hmm."

"And people agree to come?"

"Danger thrills them. No more delays. Do your duty."

Katelyn shoved herself away from him, schooling her expression to hide her displeasure and fury. She was not only an accessory for a vampire, but he was also officially making her an accessory to murder. Because of him, she might never lose the tail of suspicion. No matter how surreptitious Jude and Tinsel thought they were, she didn't have the expertise to hide her tracks.

"You have your own skills. You know how to conceal yourself in plain sight, and you're in a much better position to do so than Tinsel and I are. You have such little faith in yourself, Familiar."

She pretended she hadn't heard him and continued to mingle in the crowd. She noticed Tinsel dancing in her periphery, but she didn't turn to look.

Instead, she pretended that neither vampire was there at all, that she was at the club alone. She almost imagined that she was there with her friends, but she quickly pushed that thought aside when it triggered tears.

She was here for business, not pleasure, and she needed to act the part from beginning to end. She could appear to enjoy herself, but a too-sudden switch in persona would trip a girl's red flag faster than a man's. Sure, women weren't as threatened by other women unless a man was involved, but women were generally more cautious about being separated from the fray and brought somewhere alone.

Really, trying to find a man would be much easier.

His laughter rippled in her head.

Katelyn closed her eyes, taking a position somewhere in the middle of the dance floor—close enough to the speakers to avoid conversation but far enough that it didn't deafen her. She moved to the music, accepting any partner who decided to join her for this song or the next. She accepted but didn't encourage them or take the dance to a more personal level—nothing like how close she'd been to Jude when he'd danced with her. None of them lasted longer than two songs before moving on. Groups of women tended to close out interlopers, but a few came her way in unconscious solidarity with the single chick. They, too, moved on. When she wasn't closing her eyes to allow the music to envelop her in a smooth wave of liquid sound, she passed her gaze over the crowd with a small smile on her face—enigmatic without putting anyone off.

Katelyn had to sell *every* moment, because someone out there might be paying attention the way she had been. Jude and Tinsel had been fortunate she'd been the only one who'd noticed them and that it had been so easy to neutralize her—and put her in play on their side.

As she scanned the crowd, she didn't quite know what she was looking for beyond his physical requirements. The only time a girl caught her eye was when she glimpsed Tinsel. Her heart would race at finding someone, then calm when she realized this wasn't a girl whose life she had to destroy.

"We're not leaving without someone."

"Patience. Unless you really don't care who I bring, in which case there was no point in turning me at all."

"You're a saucy minx, love."

Somewhere between eleven and midnight, Katelyn found her.

Her light blonde hair feathered close to her scalp. In the club lights, it would have been easy to miss, but her eyebrows were mostly drawn on. She wore false eyelashes. There were several rough patches of skin on her chest and arms that she'd covered with foundation.

There were also healed track marks on her hands, forearms and the crooks of her elbows. A recovering addict seemed unlikely, given the venue. The fatigue that the woman tried to hide with concealer told

Katelyn that her first guess was correct. Based on the relative smoothness of the track marks, plus the length of hair, the woman was either in remission or waiting to see whether the treatments would take. She had enough energy to dance with two other girls, although she didn't chime in as often to the conversation between them.

It wasn't the girl's weakness that caught her eye, but what glowed through her eyes, through the color in her drawn skin, the new roundness to her face.

Katelyn's heart sank into her stomach acid as she stopped dancing and made a beeline for the girl. She wanted to swerve away, let the girl have her victory, however temporary. The last thing she needed after everything was a violent death, but although Katelyn tried to look for someone else, anyone else, her attention always came back to the girl, and her direction didn't waver. He wouldn't let it.

"Invite them all. We have use for the others as well. But she's exquisite, my familiar. She's mine."

"I hate you so much right now."

"I know."

Her smile concealed her urge to scream. "Hi."

The three girls stopped dancing as well, more than a little miffed that they'd been interrupted by a stranger, especially a stranger who was younger and not quite at their level. Katelyn didn't take their involuntary biases too personally. She was used to it.

"I couldn't help but notice you while you were dancing." *Oh, wonderful.* That sounded like something Tinsel would say as a pickup line. She amended her approach. "Sorry if this seems so abrupt, but I'm a recruiter looking to spread the word—"

"We already have a church, thank you, and we're not looking to join another one," said one of the girls, a tall brunette with pretty lips and a half-shaved cut. "If you'll excuse us..."

Katelyn burst out laughing, which captured the girls' attention more than anything, as only sincerity could. "I'm not evangelizing, at least not in the religious sense. No, I have a small number of invitations for an exclusive party tonight at the Slaughterhouse. You might have heard of it."

"Oh my God, it's that place. You know, Bella, that place? That place that— God, I can't even remember how they described it," the shorter brunette said, with lots of animated gestures to make up for the fact she couldn't think of one solid fact about the club.

"That place that's invite-only?" Bella—the girl in recovery.

"Yeah, the one with the chains and the meat tray and the industrial gothic thing going?" the shorter brunette continued. "With the best bands no one's ever heard of, that sort of thing?"

"That's the one," Katelyn said, after silent confirmation from Jude, like a nod in her brain.

"No fucking way." The shorter brunette was clearly excited, which only sank Katelyn's heart deeper, this time entwined with her intestines among the shit.

"I have three invitations." Katelyn pulled them out of her bra and spread them like playing cards. "You would have to agree to be driven there and surrender your phones before you arrive. We don't cart you to the most underground club in town just for you to get lost in likes. Make memories, leave footprints. Sound fair?"

"What's the cover?" Bella asked.

Excellent question for the suspicious. "No cover, open bar. We have sponsors, not customers. The only cost is your discretion. Are you in?"

"Hell yeah, we're in," the shorter brunette said.

"This sounds like just another pity perk," Bella said quietly to her friend.

The taller brunette waved her concern away. "Embrace the perks, Bella. Being sick sucks. People throwing free things at you is one of the few things that doesn't suck about it. Come on. Let's have some *real* fun."

Don't take it, Katelyn begged inside, but she only broadened her smile when the two brunettes snagged the invitations and gave one of them to Bella, who eventually nodded in assent.

"You get a taste from all three, love – an excellent catch. Tinsel is ready with hers. Bring them with you."

"You're a despicable leech. She's a cancer survivor, for God's sake."

"You're the one who chose her for me."

"Son of a bitch."

"Familiar mine, you won't be singing such a nasty tune when you get what you want from them, too."

But I will after I've had it, she thought, to herself this time.

As though he were right there at her ear, the vibrations of his laughter made her shiver again.

"Very good," Katelyn said. "If you'll follow me, I'll get us on our way. Our bouncer will take your phones in the car."

"This sounds supremely sus," Bella said.

Listen to your gut. This isn't just sus. This is air-raid sirens. Don't come with me, Katelyn pleaded.

"If we post about it, *everyone* will know where it is, and *everyone* will be there," the shorter brunette replied. "Kind of defeats the point, doesn't it? What are you afraid of? That they're secretly a human-trafficking ring that'll snatch us up as soon as they get us free from our phones? It's just how this place works. I read about it somewhere. I swear there was an Instagram pic after someone left or something."

"Still sus."

"That's part of the fun," the taller brunette said. "Live a little. Live a lot."

Bella raised her chin, squaring her shoulders with a deep breath. "You're right. You're *right*. Live a lot."

Katelyn smiled—*so much fucking smiling*—and rested a hand on Bella's shoulder to guide the three girls off the dance floor and out of the club to the large dark-tinted SUV waiting for them. Jude rolled down the window, serious and professional, and held out a black box.

"Phones, please," he said.

All three girls relinquished them, the shorter brunette with one last tap on her screen before turning it off.

"Come on in."

Giggling with anticipation, the three girls opened the back door and climbed in with three other guests brought in by Tinsel, who sat on one of the guys' laps.

Jude indicated for Katelyn to sit in the front with him.

"Six souls," he murmured. "Wesley and Diane have another seven. A good haul for the night."

Katelyn buckled herself in and stared straight through the windshield, refusing to acknowledge his existence. He grinned and peeled away from the curb to the squeals of some of the passengers, willingly gathered for the slaughter.

* * * *

"This is it?" one of the guys asked. "Looks like the docking bay of a meat-packing plant."

"It's called the Slaughterhouse, numbfuck," another guy shot back. "What'd you think it was going to look like?"

"Not like a literal slaughterhouse."

"A little more horror-y than I thought it was going to be," the taller brunette said.

"I'm telling you guys, that's part of the fun," the shorter brunette replied. "Look, another car. See? We're not the only people here."

"Sus. As. Hell," Bella muttered, staring up at the back of the building.

Katelyn had only ever seen it in light, but they were right about it in the nighttime. There were rules about hot young things in a place like this—such as not being there at all unless they wanted to meet a creative, untimely end, especially at a club known as the Slaughterhouse. Whoever came up with that name was just a little too proud of themselves for telling their victims exactly what to expect.

She wanted to ask whether Jude thought it was dangerous to lead people right to the butcher shop, given that giving up phones wasn't the easiest thing for people her age to do, and it wouldn't surprise her if one or two people might squirrel theirs away in a pocket or their bra and act like they didn't have one on them. If that hadn't happened yet, it was bound to eventually.

If Katelyn had had a voice in the Family's decisions, she would have suggested that they stick to kidnapping rather than voluntary surrender. It was going to bite them in the ass eventually, because they couldn't completely control the circumstances. They could control a lot more if they tied someone up and frisked them.

But they weren't going to listen to her. They wanted their fun.

She pushed out of the vehicle and opened the doors for their guests.

"Follow me, ladies, gentlemen." She met Bella's eyes for a little longer than the rest, practically willing her to see the truth of what was right in front of her, but Bella was swept up in her friends' excitement and didn't notice.

Jude and Tinsel entered alone through the side door, and Cody met Katelyn with his haul before guiding all of them to the loading bay. The corrugated metal rattled as it raised to welcome them into the dark room.

Like entering a new haunted house, the humans clustered together, women clinging to men who weren't quite as strange to them as they'd been prior to the drive. One of the girls squeaked when the loading bay door lowered again.

"Welcome to my home." Jude's deep voice resonated through the metal room in an affected Transylvanian accent.

Synthesizer, strings and a throbbing heartbeat filled the room, with strobe lights flashing fast enough that everyone could see where they were going. Vision came in fits and starts that disoriented and jarred, but the Slaughterhouse's guests grinned wildly as they took in the venue.

Because that's exactly what it was...a slaughterhouse.

From the ceiling hung hooks and chains that swung with a vague sense of menace a few feet over everyone's heads. Dips in the floors led to drains. The room was lined with narrow pens and an elevated walkway for observing animals from above.

The room had been modified for use as a club venue and meticulously cleaned, but not enough to hide the distinct bouquet of bleach from a familiar's senses, and despite the bleach, Katelyn still smelled the old blood, human and animal, and deeper than that, decay and rot.

In the center of the room, the Family had put out a spread, with the aforementioned legendary meat tray as well as fruits, cheeses and desserts. Punch bowls and a margarita fountain provided much-needed alcohol. Katelyn almost wished she drank.

On the second-floor walkway, Katelyn caught strobed glimpses of other vampires dancing, almost architectural, like the gargoyles or angels on so many of the buildings in Meridian.

There were others on the first floor as well, as sparingly clad as the ones above. One shirtless man's leather pants clung tightly to his legs and left absolutely nothing to the imagination as he danced with a woman in a short leather skirt and a halter so thin, Katelyn could see the outline and texture of her nipples as her breasts bounced and jiggled from the dancing. Strategically placed to define a dance area in the large room with such a small number of guests, three other vampires danced alone, also dressed for sex and inviting the others to dance with them.

Between three cars of invited guests, it looked like there was just enough so that each vampire could have a victim, plus a few extra.

Katelyn was drawn to the intricately arranged meat tray. A few of the meats had been smoked more than cooked, and some of the fish was raw. She made herself a plate and ate as fast as she could on the other side of the buffet table from the makeshift dance floor. When she thought she could function with the heady scents still lingering in the air, she tossed the plate and walked the edges of the room to watch the vampires work.

With free drinks flowing amid lots of bare skin, the guests and vampires weren't even trying to dance in any way that didn't simulate sex anymore.

Tinsel was flanked by a man behind her and a girl in front. She writhed between them as she kissed him over her shoulder, then took the woman's mouth while the man showed his voyeuristic pleasure.

Bella had found herself in the company of the white-blond man who'd been grinding with the short-skirted vampire earlier, but she'd already been slated for Jude, so that was probably what the shorter brunette was doing there with them. The taller brunette was across the crowd with a similarly tall, skinny man. They looked like models being photographed in the dark as they made out against one of the metal columns.

Katelyn wished she didn't like watching so much. She heated from within, from the meat and from the carnal spectacle, imagining hands and bodies on her the way they were on the other humans and vampires in the room, all over her, multiples, many people, many limbs, all stroking her, and her clothes in a puddle on the floor…

Her skin prickled as though someone was watching her, too, but there was no reason why when there was such a scrumptious visual feast in the center of the room. Until a young man broke away from the group and headed straight for her, moving with the beat.

"What's a girl like you doing all by yourself over here?" The boy was slender, compact, his shirt clinging to a body that he obviously took enthusiastic care of. His face was defined in its angles, and his smile was too wide for his face, but genuine.

"I just work here," she replied.

"'All work and no play', as they say."

The boy took her by the hand and pulled her into the fray. He whirled her around, making her dizzy and catching her against him when she stumbled. He hummed in pleasure at the press of her breasts, stomach and thighs against him, and once he got his arms around her, he refused to let go. He nuzzled her neck, rubbing his erection against her as he slid his hands down to squeeze handfuls of her ass.

"God, you feel so good. Wish I could bury my tongue in you right now." He slapped her ass soundly, then slobbered and chewed over her neck.

Well, that escalated quickly. Not even the promise of semen was enough to make him appealing. He didn't seem to give a damn about whether she was enjoying herself, only in losing himself in a body without any regard as to whom that body belonged.

"Um, personal space, please," Katelyn said.

The boy spanked her again, squeezing her flanks after each slap. He dipped his mouth down her chest toward her prominent cleavage, bending his legs to reach.

"Hey." She pushed at him a little, thinking he might not have heard her or registered the fact that she wasn't dancing with him anymore.

"Fuck, so *soft,*" he groaned. He slipped a hand between her legs from behind, cupping her cunt through her panties.

"Get off." She pushed harder, but now he had a real grip, and he knew how to hold onto it.

"Oh, I will. Just relax. It'll be good for you, too. I know it's probably been a while, but no one else sees what I see, baby."

"You're drunk."

"Very. Want to try it?"

"Don't make me hurt you." She was pretty sure the massacre wasn't supposed to happen yet, but she was prepared to get the damn thing started, with the early stirrings of panic making her heart race and her pulse thud in her ears.

He raised his head from her breasts. This time, his wide, sincere smile seemed evil in the strobe lights and shadows. What bewildered her most was that he didn't seem sadistic. Her displeasure simply hadn't registered at all in his empty eyes. "Pain can be good. Want to move this to one of those niches? What are they, pens? Whatever. They're dark, and we can do whatever we want."

"No." This time, Katelyn was sure that the boy heard her, saw her form the words, knew what she meant, but there was no spark of comprehension that anyone could be saying no to him.

"What're you afraid of, baby? I'll be gentle if *you* be rough." He leered down at the way her cleavage pressed even more tightly together when he brought her against him.

Katelyn landed a solid punch to his face just in time for Jude to catch the boy from falling, which meant he'd already been coming to relieve her. But her heart pounded too hard against her ribcage, and her pussy felt as though the boy were still digging into it. His saliva cooled on her skin. She rubbed at it furiously with her clenched fists, ready in case he or anyone else decided to come at her again.

Most of the people on the dance floor stopped their foreplay, stunned from the break in rhythm of the evening, but not for long. Jude looked so much like a bouncer that none of them questioned when he murmured something in the boy's ear that made him lose his smirk even faster than her punch, then hauled him toward the pens. One of the vampires on the second-level walkway stared down hungrily into the pen where Jude threw the boy and latched him in.

The boy had opposable thumbs and could undo the latches, even while drunk. However, as soon as Jude turned his back on the boy, the woman from above dropped into the dark. Jude didn't even blink as he faced Katelyn across the room, his eyes seeming even darker against the flashes of light that gave them a baleful glow.

"I told you I'd protect you."

"You killed him."

"Only earlier than otherwise. Excellent right hook, by the way."

"Suck me, Jude."

"Now, now, be nice. If you don't want to stay for the feast, the only other option is to bring Cara hers. She'll feed if you draw blood. You might even find it a comfort that she won't let you have any of it."

Katelyn rubbed her breastbone and tried to look like she wasn't as shaken as she was. She needed to stay calm to not alarm the guests and to get her pumping blood under control, because the vampires were considering her now, off-limits though she was. She could whet an appetite as well as any human.

Maybe she didn't want to leave, if one of them could possibly slip.

All it would take was one bite for her to escape this nightmare, because then she'd be dead and the requirements of life wouldn't apply anymore. She wouldn't have to try to be normal at school. She wouldn't have to catch flies in secret. And when she punched someone's face in, maybe that would be literal, a nice crater the shape of her fist in their skull—or she could have taken the boy down herself, made him come in his shorts as she dug her teeth deeper into her neck.

She almost didn't notice her mouth watering or how she stroked over her neck and down almost to the peaks of her breasts at the thought. She abruptly stopped, mortified at the intensity of her own arousal and at the way Jude stared so deeply into her eyes that she knew he'd seen exactly what she wished she could have.

"Perhaps one day," he whispered. *"But not tonight. You've done your part. Stay or go, Katelyn. You'll get the scraps from our arterial sprays either way."*

"You say the most romantic things." But she didn't want to stay, because if she stayed, she'd have to see what happened to Bella, Jude's giant form engulfing her delicate frame, his cheek against her blonde hair, his teeth giving the girl what he refused to ever give her—everything Katelyn wanted...except her death.

That was what Bella had to pay, although Jude wouldn't even permit Katelyn the price.

"Taking Cara a woman will free Tinsel for more enjoyable pursuits, which is sure to endear her to you as well."

Sure, that's what she was going for.

Katelyn nodded, nevertheless. She wasn't ready to see in person the consequences of her actions. She'd barely seen what had happened to her friends. She thought something in her head would burst if she had to see it now, knowing that she was the one who'd caused it on purpose this time instead of by accident.

"Very well. Tinsel will meet you in the plant." No fire-code-approved emergency exit signs in here. If Jude hadn't pointed out the discreet door, even she might not have known it was there.

Katelyn wove through the dancers. By the time she reached the door, she almost stumbled through it, hands cold and shaking. She tried to recall what life had been like before she'd been sucked into this world. Had it been less than two weeks? She felt like she'd served for centuries.

Lord knew how Tinsel managed to get the girl away from her friends, but she came through the door with the shorter brunette in tow, already gagged and bound with duct tape. The girl was wide-eyed and bloodless behind the silver, and she struggled to scream and free herself.

Tinsel appeared less than concerned. "Do you remember where Cara is kept?"

Katelyn nodded. "But I don't know if I'll be able to unlock her door."

Tinsel nudged the bound girl toward Katelyn. "The measures keep her in, not us out, and you're more than capable—not as capable as us, but enough to get in and to take care of yourself in a crowd without Jude intervening on your behalf."

"She'll run if I let her go."

"Then don't let her go." With that, Tinsel turned on her heel back toward the Slaughterhouse. As soon as the vampire left, the short brunette immediately stopped trying to scream and instead pleaded through her tape gag. Katelyn couldn't make out what she was saying, but she could take a few good guesses.

Katelyn grabbed the girl's bound wrists and drew her down the hall. "I'm not going to sugarcoat it for you. This isn't going to end well. I'm sorry. I truly am. If I attempt to free you, they'll stop me. But I don't think you'll feel any pain."

Not much consolation, but now that the truth was out, Katelyn couldn't pretend she was taking the girl to some clandestine modeling audition or something like that. There was no point in choking on any more lies.

Once the girl realized Katelyn wouldn't help her, the tone of her muffled cries shifted to insulting, and she wrenched against Katelyn's lead, taking her by surprise and slipping from her grasp. The girl almost somersaulted backward in her fall, but she scrambled to her feet with surprising haste and careened across the packing plant floor. She made it halfway across before Katelyn grabbed her by her hair and flung her around to clang her forehead against a metal railing. For a moment, Katelyn feared she'd killed the girl, but though she fell to her knees and lost focus in her eyes, she remained conscious.

Katelyn took advantage of the girl's disorientation by taking fistfuls of the girl's hair near the roots and, apologizing every second, pulling her toward the stairs. She would have thought the stairs would pose a greater obstacle, but they didn't. She dragged the girl up each flight like a piece of luggage, with as much ease as over flat surfaces.

She shut out everything that reminded her this girl was human. She told herself she was bringing Cara nothing but a squealing pig to slaughter and continued up the second flight of stairs to the third floor.

The girl wriggled like a beached eel when Katelyn stopped in front of Cara's door to work the lever deadbolt down. Once she'd cracked all the locks, she whipped the girl into the room, then closed the door behind her.

"I'm not hungry," came Cara's voice from the pitch blackness.

Katelyn released the girl. There was nowhere else for the girl to go, so it didn't matter when she tried to crawl away. Katelyn tracked the girl's movements by her whines and sobs and the rustle of her clothes. "Yes, you are."

"No, I'm not."

"I'm not even a vampire, and I'm always hungry," Katelyn said. "You're not lying to me. You're lying to yourself. If you don't bleed her, they're going to make me do it for you, and you'll drink anyway."

Cold breath frosted her cheek. Katelyn hadn't heard a hint of Cara's approach.

"What if I just bleed you?"

"You wouldn't." Still, when Cara's lips brushed her skin, Katelyn shivered—and not entirely from the chill.

"Why wouldn't I, if I'm as hungry as you say?"

"Because I'm a familiar."

"You smell human to me." Cara's mouth followed the path of the boy's overzealous attention, but Katelyn stiffened for an entirely different reason. Cara hovered her lips above Katelyn's heart, which beat a little faster in response.

"You resent Tinsel for changing you," Katelyn said, maintaining her composure, only a slight break and breath in her speech. "The answer depends on whether you resent Jude, too."

Cara retreated. "Jude is her victim as well. He just doesn't know it. He passed that cruelty on to you, but I don't blame him. I'd only complete her work by feeding off you."

"Please," Katelyn whispered.

Cara's laughter could ice marrow. "I hope to God you never understand why I say no, that you never know what it's like to be like me. But it's okay, Familiar. I forgive you for your trespasses. You can't help that your soul is held in his own ignorant hands."

The lamp switched on. Cara calmly sat on the edge of the bed as though she'd been there the whole time.

"Leave," Cara said, "unless you want the bloodlust to hit you as well."

"You'll eat?"

"You might hear it through the door, God help me. Leave now. You risk your own death if you don't."

"I'm not afraid of you."

"Poor brainwashed pet. You're not strong enough to take me on. You should be locking me in. One human might not be enough, and you wouldn't be able to stop me."

Cara slid to the ground in a crouch, then leapt over the bed to where the girl was trying to wriggle underneath. In mid-air, her fangs slid out, gleaming in her open mouth. She grabbed the girl and yanked her out and up as though she were nothing more than a tiny ragdoll. Her eyes went blacker than Katelyn had seen in any other vampire, darkness expanding almost to the edge.

She reared up, then sank her teeth into the girl's neck like a serpent injecting venom. However, she didn't just let the blood gush into her mouth, mostly contained within the confines of her lips.

At the first taste, Cara lost control.

Growling, she ripped her fangs back and forth through muscle and sinew. Blood flew in arterial arcs from the severed carotid and jugular. It sprayed Cara's face and soaked through the top half of her white dress as she practically climbed on top of the still-standing girl to dig her teeth deeper. When the girl's legs buckled, Cara dug her claw-like nails into her to hold her in place as she continued to rip and tear and drink like a feral beast. Blood splattered and soaked the blanketed walls and the bed, shone on the girl's clothing and skin.

When the blood scent hit her, Katelyn swayed forward, but Cara unsheathed her fangs from the girl's neck and hissed, barely avoiding scratching Katelyn with her bloody claws.

Katelyn reeled back, hit the wall, then slid to the ground. She covered her mouth and nose with her sleeve and watched, unblinking, as Cara continued her feed. When nothing was left in the girl's neck, Cara moved on, ripping off any skin coated with blood, sucking at the clothes, spitting out everything once it had been drained.

Cara dropped the corpse and crouched over it, her teeth still bared, stained and dripping, and kept a wary eye on Katelyn as she dipped down to lick at the girl's blood pool. Licking wasn't enough after a time. Cara started slurping, even biting at the metal to get as much of the blood as possible. Her white dress was now almost completely red.

The worst part wasn't what Cara had become, with her deathly pallor and glass marble eyes looking somewhere to Katelyn's right.

It was that Katelyn's mouth was watering so hard that she'd soaked her sleeve with saliva.

Once most of the blood pool on the floor had been taken care of, Cara focused her wandering feral gaze on Katelyn. Katelyn whimpered, but before she could try to run, Cara jumped high into the air with a snarl.

The door burst open. Jude cuffed Cara across her head, adjusting her trajectory. She hit the bed rolling but whipped back onto all fours, hissing, spitting and howling like a cougar.

Jude bared his teeth back, braced to fight. "Get out of the room, Katelyn."

Survival instinct briefly overtook her cravings, and she ran out of the open door. Jude backed through with her, then slammed it shut and latched the lock in a short series of economical motions.

The floor trembled as Cara pounded on the door, screaming.

Now that her life had been saved, the cravings returned with a vengeance that equaled Cara's own. Katelyn pressed herself against the metal, gulping in what little scent managed to permeate the nearly airtight door or that had escaped when Jude had opened it.

Jude sucked at the thin smear of blood where he'd hit Cara. "I don't think you'll be able to burrow through, love."

Katelyn rested her cheek against the door. "You wanted me to see that."

"Between a small slaughter and a large one, I thought you'd do better starting small. You're a sensitive girl under your bloody desires. Adjustments must be made. Acclimations."

"Validations. Perspirations. You have only yourself to blame, you asshole."

"There's blood to be had in the Slaughterhouse. By now, the bodies should be gone. You won't have to concern yourself with where the blood comes from." Jude stroked her hair. "You were in no real danger from her. I promised to protect you."

"Yeah, sure you protected me, after putting a whisk in my brain and giving it a good swirl." She panted, trying to hold herself back from running her tongue over the door in the hopes that blood would seep through by the sheer force of her will, but when he pulled her away, she followed him like a leashed puppy.

Back in the Slaughterhouse, the strobes had stopped flashing, and the cage lights among the hooks illuminated the bloodbath left behind. No bodies, although she detected the faintest hint of smoke and charred meat from her position at the entrance.

That meant nothing to her. The only thing that mattered was the blood dripping slowly toward the drains, washing away, away from her, so much disappearing, wasted, before her very eyes. Everything became silver metal, golden light and scarlet, until the red was all that was left.

Chapter Eight

She came to wrapped in a blanket and smelling fantastic. When she looked down at herself, she realized why.

Underneath the blanket, her clothes had been soaked through with the blood she'd practically been swimming in to get as much as possible—no less an animal than Cara. She'd gorged herself until she couldn't move. Even though blood didn't burden her, at some point she must have truly had enough. She hadn't known there was such thing as 'enough'.

She smelled like she'd been on her period for five weeks straight, but she wasn't trying to eat through her clothes, so that was an upside.

"I promise it gets better."

Jude sat across from her in the large communal bathroom. It wasn't like the ones in her sorority house or freshman dorms—more like a locker room, with half stalls and metal bathtubs.

"I thought you said I wouldn't be like her," Katelyn said.

"I haven't lied to you yet. You weren't like her. You were compliant enough when I pulled you away from the feed. Cara needs to be chained to her bed for anyone to clean her room after she's finished—whatever's left, anyway. How do you feel?"

"Embarrassed. Ashamed. Crappy."

"Physically?"

Katelyn leaned back against the wall and closed her eyes. "Fucking amazing."

"Good. You won't be able to go home in those clothes."

"I won't be able to do anything in these clothes ever again. What day is it? Is it still Friday?" Katelyn tried to extricate herself from the blanket.

"Technically Saturday. You haven't lost much time. Don't rush, if you don't want to move. When you're ready, you can wash the blood off."

"I can't go home naked. And I don't know whether you noticed, but no one in your skinny-ass Family is exactly my size."

He smiled. "We'll make do with what we have."

"That doesn't sound good."

"We can start keeping clothes for you here."

Katelyn untucked the last part of the blanket. "I feel like a sanitary napkin," she groaned as she got to her feet. "You know, I used to imagine moving in with a guy would be more romantic than this."

"I wasn't aware you were moving in."

"You want me to bring over clothes. Next thing, I'll be bringing a toothbrush and toothpaste to get the smell out of my mouth before leaving. Then I'll need to overnight after another blood coma. Then I'll be kicked out of Delta Tau for missing too many events and becoming the live-in shut-in, and I'll need a place to stay until the end of the year. Then I'll fail classes because of my addiction. I'll be kicked out of school, and I'll be so goddamned ashamed at being an abject failure of a daughter that I'll throw away my phone and have to move in full-time anyway."

"We have the space. It would be more convenient."

"I'm not making this more convenient for you—not while I still have my mind." Katelyn stared down at her clothes and tried to figure out what could be salvaged. There wasn't an article of clothing that hadn't been soaked through, including her panties. She was pretty sure she'd never been that wet on her own.

"I know," Jude said—a tad indulgently, but the fact was, her will *was* his indulgence, so if she rebelled, it was only because he was okay with it, which took the punch out of rebellion.

She played with the sodden hem of her shirt. "Turn around."

Once again, he indulged her, albeit with a reluctant sigh. She reflected off the walls, unlike him, but the brushed metal made her little more than a flesh-and-blood-colored blob. She peeled off her shirt, skirt and boots, then her panties and bra. She was disappointed most about the bra.

Once she entered the shower, Jude kept his eyes averted until he'd sat down on a bench to the side so that he couldn't see over the half-stall walls of the shower.

"Do you all just shower together, or am I in the men's room? Or are *you* in the women's room?"

"We share. Since all of us either sired or were sired, it goes without saying that most of us have seen one or more of us naked before we even turn."

For a moment, she could practically feel his fingers in her mouth, the taste of him a fog in her mind. "Is that what siring is, just another kind of sex?"

"Usually someone is turned because the sire wants a companion. Often, that companion is sexual. It doesn't have to be binding. My relationship with Tinsel has been more familial than sexual following my transformation. Sometimes, that's all there is, despite the sexual element of our bite. Siring has been forged from friendships as well."

"Is friendship what Tinsel wanted from you? Or did she need a bodyguard against everyone who made fun of her for that name?"

"Ours was a fiery but brief romance. We do better as family. She likes small women and either big or pretty men."

"That narrows it down."

"More than you'd think."

"It's more than *you* want."

"My tastes are narrower, yes," Jude replied, "but not exclusive."

"Could have fooled me."

She turned off the showerhead when she was confident that she'd washed off all the blood and double-checked every nook and cranny to make sure.

As she wrapped herself in a towel, she said, "I can't stay. There's a thing tomorrow. I'm going to get privileges revoked if I don't participate more often."

"Does it last the night?" Jude asked.

"You realize I'm in a sorority, right? Yeah, I think we'll be up late."

"Can *you* make it that long?"

"If I find enough spiders in the corners, probably," she said grimly. "And this'll be at a fraternity. They don't clean much, at least what normal people call cleaning. So it's all but a guarantee."

Jude came up to her as she stepped out of the stall. She'd never been this close to naked with a man before. All she'd need to do was drop the towel and...

And he'd pick it up like a gentleman and hand it back to her. But there was nothing she wanted more than for him to gently remove the towel himself, then none too gently shove her against the wall, bury his teeth in her, bury his cock, it didn't matter which. She didn't even know what it was like having a cock inside her, but at that moment, nothing seemed more right, as though she'd been hollowed out just for him, a dull yearning ache low in her cunt.

He had to see it. He had to *smell* it.

But he just handed her a faded blue button-down shirt...and that was all.

"Seriously?" she said.

"As you pointed out, we don't have much in the way of clothes your size. I thought one of mine might cover enough to be decent on the way back to your home," Jude said.

"Your idea of decent and mine are two different things." He was a large man, and yes, it would probably fit her, but she didn't think he'd accounted for the two things about her that differed strongly from him—her boobs and butt. The back wasn't going to cover all of her ass, that was for sure.

"It's well into the middle of the night," Jude replied. "It'll have to do. We'll take better precautions next time.

You understand, I've never had a familiar before. I'm learning as much as you are."

"Don't even." She snatched the shirt from him and headed for one of the bathroom stalls.

When she came out again, he approached slowly, taking in the sight of her bare legs all the way up to the tops of her thighs, where the shirt managed to cover everything pertinent up front. But Katelyn had been right. It didn't cover quite enough in the back.

She tugged at it fruitlessly, but the shirt didn't stretch out except over her breasts, straining the buttons. She didn't have a bra on, so her breasts weren't as perky, other than the points of her nipples pushing against the fabric.

"You look..."

"Ridiculous."

"That wasn't the word I was going to use."

Tinsel strode into the bathroom with Cody, Diane and Wesley behind her, talking among themselves. When she saw Jude and Katelyn, she quieted, although the other three didn't seem to notice.

Jude, however, did. He took a step back and straightened. "Shall we go?"

* * * *

They developed a routine—a grisly, gruesome, serial-killer-type routine, but a routine nonetheless. She made up for the bloodiness by keeping some clothes at the butcher shop, and he made sure to hold her back from most of the mess, pouring her glasses from spouting necks before instructing her to help with the clean-up once she could pull herself together. She sometimes had to use the bathroom facilities, but more often than not, her stand-by clothes remained in one of his drawers.

He mostly called her one night a weekend and on the occasional weekday. When she didn't have anything that her sorority absolutely required her to attend during a weekend, however, he stole her through Sunday.

She brought him his blonde girls. Most of them were blonde, anyway. There was one redhead and that one Black girl that caught his eye who she'd retrieved for him before he could even point her out. But mostly they were blonde, petite, pretty, just like Angel. There was a little variation—in style, in curves, which he could take or leave. Always smaller and prettier and peppier, so that he could gather them in his arms and swallow them up with his body as he drained them with his teeth.

When she stayed for the party, she sometimes witnessed him fuck them first. She'd peer into the pen and see a leg, a shoulder blade, bulging biceps, glistening in the darkness. She'd hear them—her whimpers or cries, the low moan of his heavy breathing. Sometimes, he'd come out again with blood on his lips, snapping at her to deal with the body.

She dealt with the bodies now. The butcher shop wasn't just fitted with barbecue pits but an incinerator for meat waste—their own crematorium. No bodies, no crime. Just another random spike in Meridian's suspicious number of 'missings' that newscasters and morning talk show DJs occasionally mentioned.

With Cody and Wendla, one of Cody's women, she would stack the bodies on dollies and roll them to the incinerator. They'd heave the bodies into the incinerator three-deep and turn on the fire until all that was left was ash. Then she'd clean the dolly and go back into the Slaughterhouse to help spray down and bleach the rest of the floor. Each party was a Family party, and the whole Family contributed to the clean-up. The newest vampires got hose duty, and so did she.

Again and again, she went to the clubs with her master. She never called him that to his face, but it slipped into her mind more and more, to his delight. Again and again, she found him girls and brought along any friends who might happen to come with them. Again and again, she grabbed blood where she could get it, insects caught in her room, spiders found in corners, the occasional cockroach behind one of the two school cafeterias when she was particularly desperate and didn't want to go to the store for mousetraps.

Again and again, she dreamed of blood and teeth, dreamed of him so intensely that she knew he could see into her mind through the course of what imaginative scenarios her brain had concocted. And yet again and again, it was as though he laughed at her desire and discomfort. Never to her face, but it glittered in his eyes and played at the edge of his smile whenever she came running to him after his call.

It must have been nice to have a girl he could string along and never satisfy—not with his blood, which she still craved, and not with his body, which she craved more and more graphically. *Hopelessly devoted,* as the song said. Must have been really fucking nice to be the object of desire and not the subject, viewing her devotion from the outside, and not caring about her more than a friendly stray cat.

This was the life she could expect. There wasn't much use in finishing her Social Psych degree or going on to get her doctorate…not in the middle of suffering a serious case of irreversible, untreatable Renfield syndrome—aka bug-eating crazy.

She was getting better at hiding it, or maybe she was just getting used to whatever she did behind closed doors as she continued to isolate herself in the room she'd once shared with her friends.

She'd had to clear out the food and flies when Aly's, Angel's and Maria's parents had arrived to take their daughters' things home. Katelyn herself had cleared out well in advance. She hadn't wanted their parents to look at her and wonder why she was the one who had survived.

She'd hidden behind the cafeteria and filled her mouth with as many cockroaches as she could hold—just as bad as confronting the parents and more than what she deserved.

* * * *

She knew she'd hit the jackpot as soon as she entered Humberto and saw the girls congregating at the bar. They were all laughing together, an ugly, glassy noise, tucked away in their group as a massive joke. They'd hang out with older men to accept the flirting and free drinks, then mock their smile lines and gray hair when the men's backs were turned. As though golden hair and a golden tan were all that was worth its weight.

They weren't Jude's personality type, and they were a little more bronzed and pink-lipsticked than his usual fare, but when Katelyn looked at him over her shoulder, his eyes gleamed hungrily. There was more than one way a girl could satisfy him. A vampire's bite could be a last hurrah, but it could also be an execution, like when Tinsel had ripped her teeth through the girl who'd called her a dyke for hitting on her in the Slaughterhouse and into a man who'd insulted Jude for the color of his skin.

Funny how the nastiness really came out once people thought they were in a private, exclusive party.

Case in point—five girls, all aggressively blonde, two of them naturally so—too-tight cheap shirts, cheap leggings, push-up bras, cheap jewelry, expensive watches, expensive phones, overpriced purses, overpriced shoes. Everything about them just figured, from their makeup to the small Asian character tattoos on their arms.

Katelyn was familiar with the species. She saw them plenty in the Greek system. She'd never understood the appeal. Of blonde hair, sure. Of conformity, yes. But to the point of being indistinguishable from each other, cheapening themselves into mass-produced inventory…? She assumed they were different when alone instead of pandering to the expectations of a group. Still, this was as much who they were as what they became in private, and Katelyn could use that.

They ate the invitation up. With Jude behind her in his suit, the blondes overlooked Katelyn's lack of basic status symbol and accepted her as what she was…the help. This time, Jude played his cool right beside her, accepting their shallow compliments and wooing them as though they were high class. Because he was younger than the average Humberto man, they gravitated toward him. Katelyn also noticed how they checked his hands, but not for engagement or wedding rings. She suspected they were looking for championship rings or sports tattoos near his wrists—signs of the professional or retired athlete she'd suspected he was, someone with money to burn.

Once she'd paid their tab with Jude's money, Katelyn led the girls out to the car. After the first few fishing expeditions, she'd asked him what the vampires did about security cameras. He'd told her that cameras couldn't catch vampires on film and that most of the places they frequented didn't have cameras for anything except the cash register, in deference to higher-end clientele who didn't want to be recorded. According to him, Meridian in general was notoriously lax with their security.

The girls piled in, sitting on each other's laps when Tinsel added more people to the party from a nearby bar. Katelyn fought the urge to press her hands against her ears at the frequency and volume of the laughter, lubricated by champagne that someone had brought with them into the SUV.

Trying to get them to relinquish their phones was like pulling their professionally whitened teeth.

"If you don't give up your phones, you can't go in. Rules of the house," Katelyn said.

"I'm not giving up my phone," Girl Number One protested. "I'm not going to let some stranger take it away and, I don't know, sell it on the black market or something."

"Do you know how much I pay for this thing?" Girl Number Two asked.

"But what if I need it?" Girl Number Three said.

"You know, I take one selfie at your party, you'll have people pouring in. It's free exposure," Girl Number Four chimed in. "I have over a hundred thousand Insta followers."

"We don't *want* everyone pouring in," Katelyn said patiently. "Yes, I know how much your phones cost. We take good care of them. But if everyone knows where this place was, it won't be 'invitation-only' anymore. It would become a 'come-as-you-are'."

Bingo. God forbid just anybody could get into the Slaughterhouse. With Jude hovering behind her as a more intimidating presence, the girls relinquished their phones. Some nights were more difficult than others. If one person protested, that got the others going, just in case someone who wasn't them got preferential treatment.

She supposed spending so much time with the spider had lent her some contempt for the fly. Then again, she consumed both with equanimity.

As soon as the party was in full swing at the Slaughterhouse, with people and vampires doing their best to mate in the middle of the room and others actually doing so in the pens, Katelyn started to leave as she always did, to wait until Jude called her back in and presented the blood and money he owed her for bringing him blondes.

But Jude emerged from the flashing shadows and closed a hand around her wrist. "It's time for you to stay."

"I still can't control myself enough around fresh blood," Katelyn said.

He brought her hand to his lips and kissed it. "There are shackles upstairs."

"Do I want to ask?"

"Not all vampires can control themselves either in the early weeks. If they can hold a vampire, they'll be able to hold you—should you feel you need them. Just stay out of the way of the feast. The Family knows you, but you could get lost in the melee, and I wouldn't want something to happen to you that even you don't want."

"Is that all?"

"We use them for other things, too."

"Uh-huh."

He leaned in to whisper, "It's time for you to see what you do for me."

"I've gotten an eyeful a few times, thanks."

He pulled back, a little startled and confused. Then he understood. "Not that. That's...foreplay. I want you to see the main event, what a vampire truly does when there's no threat of being caught. Stay, Katelyn. I know you want to watch their blood rain. Your usual fee applies, of course, but now you will witness from where the wine flows. Go upstairs and lock yourself in if you think you won't be able to restrain yourself."

The command resonated through her like the pulse of the music and lights. She'd managed to avoid the reality of vampires' mass murders every time she contributed to the potluck, depending only on her overactive imagination to fill in the blanks. But there was still a world of difference between painfully realistic fantasy and outright reality.

Her leaden feet ladened her as she climbed the ladder to the second level, which wasn't just the walkway. There was a storage room to the side filled with wooden and metal crates. In the corner of the walkway next to the room were the promised shackles. There were two sets, one for each wrist and ankle, but Katelyn didn't see the point in locking herself in multiple times, so she clamped a shackle closed over one ankle. As soon as she did, she nearly kicked herself for not latching it to her wrist. Putting it on her ankle meant that she'd be able to reach the walkway edge and peer over the side. She wouldn't have been able to stretch herself far enough if she'd attached it to her wrist.

Now that she knew it would prevent her from seeing over the side and circumvent her master's order, she couldn't do it. His scold when she tried struck her mind like a light slap.

Her stomach twisting, she crawled slowly to the edge.

The vantage point gave her an excellent view down all the low-cut shirts and dresses that the girls wore, and now and again, she glimpsed proper bulges in some of the guys' pants. Likely *all* the guys' pants, but she couldn't see all of them.

She closed her eyes. The carnal mass reminded her for the fifteen-thousandth time how frustrated she was. Since Jude had first taken her to Humberto, there hadn't been anything approaching date-like in her life, and once Tinsel had stepped in, Jude's flirting had been little more than a polite tease, natural rather than intentional. She was a familiar, a working dog to be shown affection, given praise, then left behind in favor of more appropriate companionship.

If she sounded bitter, it was only because she was horny as hell, and she didn't like to be reminded of what she was missing, what she'd missed for so long, what she expected to miss for much longer. Considering she couldn't trust herself to pick up a guy when only Jude's moderating influence kept the more disgusting aspects of her cravings at bay, dating again seemed unlikely.

The strobe lights shut off and the cage lights flooded the lower level, obscuring hers in darkness.

Jude entered the light and spread his arms like a master of ceremonies. "Ladies and gentlemen, please do not try to run."

But his mouth broadened in a sharp grin as the crowd realized that their dance partners' smiles were just as toothsome. Many of them shouted or screamed, and everyone tried to run.

Some vampires immediately pounced upon the runners to drag their prey down or to the side of the room or into a pen for privacy. Some of the vampires had already stripped down so their outfits wouldn't be ruined by the spurts of blood that others didn't seem to mind hitting their clothes.

Cody had his fangs deep in the neck of a struggling yet moaning Asian girl who reached into the air as though groping for a handhold. Eventually, her arms went limp, and her moans climbed with pleasure.

Tinsel had bound a young man and woman together with duct tape and now bit from one to the other, mixing their blood in her mouth as the one untended gushed fountains. Every time she unsheathed her teeth from their flesh, they awakened from the pleasure of the bite to the pain of the wound. Then her influence would subsume them once again, and they writhed in confused but unrelenting arousal, Tinsel's power overwhelming their pain.

Diane and Wesley jumped from person to person until they'd each marked three, at which point they herded their prey into a terrified group clinging to the wounds on their necks in vain.

Wendla was surrounded by three men, the only seemingly willing humans in the bunch, as she sank into one, then the other, then the other, and as they sank into her mouth and cunt, their dicks achingly hard, apparent even from a distance.

Blood spurted, spattered, sprayed, painted the metal floors like Pollock possessed by Bacon. Bodies thudded to the ground, and other bodies writhed over them. It was as bloody as the scene in Cara's room, but the mess here was more deliberate, part of the art and joy of the hunt.

Katelyn practically drooled, but her cravings seemed to understand that she was shackled from any possibility of exorcising her hunger. Her vision remained terribly clear.

Jude penned Blonde Girls Number One through Five, then one by one bound their wrists in handcuffs before hanging them on lowered hooks, where they dangled like living meat. Their toes barely reached the ground, not enough to ease the weight on their wrists. They flailed and kicked at him, screamed holy hell, but no one helped them.

As they spat obscenities, Jude admired the five hanging girls. Then he took off his clothes.

Katelyn's mouth, conditioned to water in the presence of blood like a dog with a steak, went dry.

Suggestion in his smooth Sky Masterson ensemble didn't compare with exposure. He emerged like a dark god, his muscles bulging, coiled with fluid strength unhindered by his size. His cock gleamed in the light, its ridges and veins set off in exquisite detail, and jutted out without shame or restraint. He did nothing to cover himself once there was nothing left in the way, nothing to hide every Atlas inch of him, terrifyingly perfect from every angle.

He rendered one of the girls speechless at the sight, but as he approached, that erection straining straight for her, she joined in the chorus once again.

He ripped at her shirt and leggings with nails that had become claws, but it didn't seem sexual so much as violent prelude as he sank his teeth into her neck, shaking his head like a cat to rip through the flesh. He buried and bathed his whole face in the blood, catching it in his mouth when he pulled back a little before sinking back in once again.

The girl kicked and shouted, her fingers twisting against the hook, but her eyes rolled back and her face flushed until it could no longer spare the blood. He yanked out of her.

Then he lowered himself to his knees in front of the next girl, tearing through the fabric of her skinny jeans to close his mouth over her thigh. When he withdrew, the ivory of her femur was visible through masticated muscle.

With the next, he sliced through her abdomen.

Girl by girl, Jude indulged himself, unspeakably violent yet almost elegant. And their lives weren't extinguished or drained out in a matter of seconds. He'd destroyed major blood vessels, but the spray slowed to a spring, then a trickle. The low beat of their hearts slowed, stuttered, but hadn't yet stopped as he slipped into the darkness, leaving the bodies for whoever wanted to finish them off. He wouldn't give them that peace.

The metal ladder creaked, and the walkway shook with his ascent. She scurried from the edge, disorienting terror and anticipation crushing her ribs as she pressed her back against a crate.

He climbed onto the walkway, his black eyes as dark as they could become, his brown skin dripping with blood from head to toe.

"This is because of you."

Jude held his hand out to her. Red droplets hit the walkway in tiny circle splashes. *Human blood. Human blood for the taking. Human blood within her grasp. Her payment.*

Katelyn stepped forward. He met her halfway, bringing his fingertips to the seam of her lips. She accepted his bloody fingers into her mouth, communion as unholy and transcendent now as it had been then.

He pulled her closer by the curl of his fingers. She sucked hard as he eased them back, chased them when they popped out of her mouth, but he held them out of her reach and covered her mouth with his instead, sweeping an arm around her waist to draw her against him, his bare erection brazen against her abdomen. He groaned as she tasted the blood around and inside his mouth, and he pushed her back until she hit the crates again.

"I don't care," he murmured as she moved from his mouth to the thick layer of blood along his jaw and down his neck, tasting *him* under the blood—undeniably, unbearably *him*—firm yet gentle, cool yet warm underneath, perhaps from the veritable feast she'd helped him bring home. "I want you, and there's no reason in the world why I shouldn't have you."

He swiped at the crates behind her as though they were empty, although the heaviness with which they fell suggested otherwise. She stumbled back but caught up short on her shackle and fell.

"No. Don't be afraid. I won't hurt you."

He crawled over her, and she hesitated beneath his massive body.

"Come to me."

Katelyn wasn't even sure whether he meant to call her like that or if his desire pulled her in of its own accord. He dripped on her, blood its own siren song. He didn't need to call her twice.

She parted her lips for him, accepting his kiss like air, arching up against his body as he lowered himself with care on top of her, slotting his hips between her parting legs. *This*. This was what she'd wanted as much as the life force of all living—his kiss, his weight, the mounting lust that pounded through her with fragrant heartbeats she heard him inhale like perfume. He bathed her in the blood of the murdered as he tangled his fingers in her hair and pulled her head back to dominate her, control every aspect of the kiss, inundate her with his desire until she was gasping, clutching at his slippery skin.

He was magnificent, everything her hands had ever craved, hard, unyielding.

Moving down her neck, he licked the blood he'd smeared over her in the hollow of her throat, then down to the swell of her breasts over her shirt. Her arching body made her breasts shift heavily toward him.

He didn't hesitate. With his free hand and the tips of his sharp teeth, he tore her sodden shirt to shreds. She didn't give a fuck about that. She helped him pull the remains away, then pushed desperately on her skirt. He ripped that apart, too, growling like an animal as he crouched over her.

She reached behind her to clutch the edge of a toppled crate and work herself upright. The upper level was dark, and so was he, but for the crimson on his pantherine form and the moon-gleam of his fangs.

Now that he wasn't kissing her, touching her, she was suddenly aware of herself in a way she didn't want to be, every curve and lump and the way she looked in her bikini-cut underwear, which wasn't anything near what those girls he'd killed would look like in a G-string. She pulled her legs in, holding her knees. He tried to coax them down, covering her hands with his, but he didn't force her.

"What are you doing?" she asked shakily.

"I'm taking what I want. What I *have* wanted. And I'm giving you what you want, aren't I?"

But I'm not what you want. I know that better than you. And I only want you because you made me this way. And he'd just finished a wholesale slaughter with his Family, like some cheap horror-movie plot. Being total basic bitches didn't warrant being exsanguinated while still alive.

"Katelyn." He slid closer and pressed a kiss to her knee. "Open for me. Let me…"

He tucked himself close through her slowly parting, then reached behind her to undo the hook of her bra. She caught the front with one hand.

"Do you need this again?" He ran his fingers over his chest, drawing more blood on their tips to offer.

She'd denied herself alcohol for so long, but it occurred to her that she was already addicted to a liquid that impaired her judgment, and he was giving it to her to loosen her up in the exact same way.

But decay wasn't a typical withdrawal symptom, was it?

He painted her lips. She accepted the offering with her tongue, moaning at the fresh spread of it through her mouth. Jude guided her hand away from her bra. It fell onto his lap, and he discarded it.

Next, he curled his fingers down the front of her panties and tugged them down, crawling back until she was as naked as he was but once again without the dampening effect of blood and touch.

"Come to me. Lie down, Katelyn."

She slid forward until she was underneath the poised form that seemed to darken even more as he took in the sight of her with all the subtlety of a starving animal. Her hands trembled, her spine felt like a tree branch and she tried to close her legs against his scrutiny, but Jude ran his palm over her inner thigh, coloring her pale skin with the blood of his lambs.

"I won't hurt you," he whispered. "I would *never* hurt you."

He hovered his mouth over her navel, breathing onto her skin as he flared his nostrils to take in her scent. The tickle of his cool breath followed his mouth's path back up to her heavy breasts. He gathered them in his hands to run the smooth length of his fangs over the undersides, around her areolae, then finally latched onto a rigid peak.

She dug her nails into his shoulders, the squelch of blood under her fingernails only enhancing the pleasure he wrought from first one nipple, then the other. He was as gentle as he'd promised, nothing but the caress and light threat of his fangs—nothing that pierced through the skin. No matter how she arched against his mouth, he remained painstakingly, painfully careful.

He laughed into her as she tried to force his fangs to prick her, turn her. He shook his head again, tugging and sucking her nipple between his less-dangerous teeth, then setting it free, jiggling her breast from the snap.

"Now, now, I can't give you that," he murmured, tracing the abused, reddened nipple with his thumb.

"Won't."

"Won't," he agreed.

"But why—?"

He stopped her question by drawing her head up to his chest. She'd touched a man's chest before, but she'd never used her mouth to do so before. Her lips trembled before pressing against him, hardened muscle underneath velvet, slickened skin. She ran her tongue along the line of his muscle. The blood was coagulating in the cool room, on his cool flesh—the easier to gather with the tip of her tongue. She slid her hands up his abdomen to gather more for her questing mouth. Taking her by the wrists, he trailed them lower, to the V of his hips. He covered one hand with his and wrapped it around his cock.

She panted against his chest, fighting not to squeeze. This part of him wasn't cool. It was hot and pulsing as though he were alive, the flesh surprisingly heavy and harder than she'd ever conceived under the easy slide of his skin.

"Bring me into you."

Jude dipped down to take her mouth again, holding himself up with his elbows and the controlled flex of his thighs so as not to crush her. He took such care. He was in complete control, while her brain was slowly melting as she stroked his cock, explored it with fingers alone, tried to compare it to the one she'd taken into her mouth for him. She still tasted death on his lips and was helpless in its clutches. Her cunt felt hollow and deliciously swollen, juices dripping with each clench of arousal.

He rocked against her, rubbing his cock against her body, even with her hand around it, pushing through the circle of her fingers. As her breathing shallowed with diffuse fear, she ran the head over her clit, then through her folds until it probed at her entrance. With the next rock of his hips, he pushed through, straining open places that had never before relished the stretch.

The coronal tear meant so very little to her as he groaned into her mouth and continued to enter her. She yanked her hand away and wrapped her arm around him, lifting her hips to meet him until he'd thrust completely inside. She dug her nails deep into his back, tearing the skin, while he eased back slowly, then filled her all the way up again.

He jerked his hips inside her with a sharp intake of breath, then paused, opening his black eyes to peer down at her curiously as he worked in and out of her with more control. Then he braced himself on his elbow, holding tightly to her hair. He brought his other hand to his lips and bit into his thumb.

"Take me," he whispered into her. He squeezed the thick welling blood over her parted lips before plundering her suddenly eager mouth. Her cunt fluttered around the thickness of his erection as she bucked beneath him, moaning from the trickle of his vampire blood sliding down her throat again.

She felt complete, as though the time between her transformation and now had just been a prolonged interlude. This possession, this stinging pleasure, his care and her carelessness tried to be fucking, but no matter how hard he entered her now, how he maneuvered her mouth with his thumb inside and the rest of his hand with a dominant grip on her chin, her body lit up with unfiltered, uncontrolled lust at his undeniable affection.

She wrapped her legs around his hips and her arms around his back, digging in again and again with her fingernails whenever he inspired another unbearable wave that she couldn't take by her strength alone. She didn't hold back, because every time she did, he would groan and snap his hips to sheath his cock in her as far as it could go. As her aroused tension heightened and her cunt grasped at his erection as though to draw him in even deeper, he could do nothing to conceal her high moans from echoing through the room with the others, from human and vampire alike.

"Come to me. Come for me, Katelyn."

She stiffened, her scream scratching through her throat as she raised to meet him and he finally lowered himself over her, his thrusts becoming erratic and the jut of his hips bruising her thighs. Orgasm tightened her around him and radiated outward, pulsing with her racing heart.

The fragrance of her heated blood seeping through her skin, the congealing blood on his, the blood flowing down her throat and the scent of her juices and his pre-cum all joined together to bring her hunger and her orgasm higher as she drank and drank and took and took. Jude finally gave her everything he had, shoving into her then stilling, his sharp mouth open in a silent, predatory scream as he came inside her, his cock twitching with its own pulse.

He covered her, her breasts smashed against his chest, but he eased his cock out of her to shift to the side to keep from crushing her entirely on the metal floor. He didn't pant like she did, only quickened his breath out of habit, so he calmed down more quickly, massaging her scalp and stroking her lip with his cut thumb until the bite wound closed and she simply licked and sucked the flesh clean.

Clean. They were both naked, smeared like newborns. His cock was slick with his cum and her juices, and cool as he softened against her thigh. When she moved her legs, she could feel her own wetness, inside and out. Sweat joined with blood on her overheated skin, and she licked her lips for what remained of him. None of it was dignified in the least, much less clean.

"You have pleased me, love." He kissed her ear lightly, then nuzzled her neck to breathe deeply of her scent. As she gazed up at the chains, bolts and beams of the Slaughterhouse ceiling, he stroked her, kissed her. Hell, he was *cuddling*.

Absent the compulsion of desire, though, she understood that none of it meant anything to him. She was his slave, created to please him, and nothing more. The revelation settled into her vulnerable chest as though vermin had emptied her out and slept there, sapping what was left of her warmth while the metal and his lack of heat chilled her through.

He kissed down to her breasts, taking more time with them now that his pleasure was spent. He coaxed her nipples to harden again, using his lips, teeth, tongue, fingers, everything available in his arsenal as he watched her reactions from down her body. He drank arousal to the surface again with dexterity and skill, but he hadn't captured her mind again, so though she still pushed her breasts against his insistent mouth and hands, she bit her lip and squeezed her thighs together, trying to hold herself back.

Once he'd nibbled a helpless moan from her, Jude dipped his tongue into her navel, inspiring a surprising jolt of lust, before pressing his mouth against her mound just above her reawakened clit.

She clenched her thighs together more tightly.

"Mmm, I thought so. You *have* been keeping secrets from me, haven't you?"

"What secrets?"

"You've never done this before. I wish you'd have told me. I would have been more considerate of your introduction."

"Just because I didn't say anything doesn't make it a secret."

"I hope it didn't hurt too much." He stroked her folds down to her cunt and slipped two fingers in. Katelyn's hands made fists at her sides. "I didn't smell much blood, but a little goes a long way, my familiar. I can't tell you how difficult it is for me to simply…taste."

Jude ran his tongue over her clit, then through her furrow to the entrance. He curled it against the places that stung, soothing them before drawing out again.

He rested his forehead against her soft abdomen. Now he was panting. "If only you knew…"

He interrupted himself by closing his mouth over her sensitive, swollen clit. He tormented the little piece of flesh, lashing it with his tongue before digging the tip around its base as he sucked in wet but powerful bursts that had her hips bucking. Her fists opened, only for her to bring them to his smooth, blood-sticky head and hold him there. She alternated tightening her thighs on the side of his head and spreading them to ease his access.

As he applied himself to her clit, he continued to caress her with the two thick fingers inside her. In comparison to his erection, they were quite manageable. He smiled against her whenever he'd caress somewhere that made her wetter around his fingers or when he startled a gasp or a moan from her lips. She'd muffle herself, but that would mean relinquishing his head, and that might mean that he would pull away from her clit, and she just couldn't let that happen, not with the slow climb of arousal building back up inside her.

"I will make you forget your pain. I'll make you never able to forget this."

His mouth otherwise occupied, he poured his promise into her mind, meeting her eyes again from where he applied himself enthusiastically to her clit, lavishing every ounce of energy to conjuring only pleasure within her, not a discordant note of discomfort to be found. Her whole body tingled, prickled, heated once again, warming the metal beneath her. He tucked his free arm under her leg and caressed her right breast, tweaking the nipple to make her clit throb within the intensifying suction of his mouth.

She strained, squirmed, begged him in her thoughts if not her words, because forming coherent pleas eluded her. Rational thought fled in the wake of fire after fire inside her that continued still higher beyond her first orgasm as he quickened his mouth and his fingers inside her.

Finally, she couldn't take the tension anymore. Her orgasm burst through her, around his fingers, against his mouth. She writhed under his unrelenting ministrations, nearly crying when he simply wouldn't stop pulling at her pleasure strings, forcing the orgasm on and on and on until it buckled in submission and surrendered to the master who had given it to her.

* * * *

He carried her from the second level to the bathroom. Once under the spray, the hot water did most of the work, but he still ran his hands over her body to smooth the rest of the mess away.

She just stood there, unsure what he wanted her to do, even less sure what she wanted and what just came from her nearness to her master.

In the end, does it matter?

This was what she was now. She was his—mind, soul, now body. What did it matter what she really wanted, when he wanted her to want it?

She'd never been the kind of girl waiting for that special someone, for flowers, candlelight, R&B, sweet nothings. Katelyn thought they were lovely gestures, but she hadn't planned on everything being perfect her first time. At least, she'd thought she hadn't.

Really, what was she so glum about? Mind-blowing. Orgasmic…twice. Minimal discomfort, and that hadn't bothered her. Connected, with him inside her, with his fingers and his cock, with his kisses. The sex had been amazing, better than anything she could have imagined for the cherry-picking. *He* had been amazing, attentive, everything a hopeless romantic could want—except for the blood, the metal and the massacre.

Now the hollowness in her cunt had returned, less enjoyable than the ache of arousal. She knew she'd more or less returned to normal, but her insides weren't *used* to it. His tongue seemed to have healed any tearing from his initial entrance, yet she still somehow felt the loss of her virginity in a profoundly physical way.

She was just full of surprises she didn't care for. Things would be so much easier if she could be the girl she thought she was instead of the one she was—or the one she'd become.

Katelyn faced the spray, her eyes closed, as though she wanted it to drown her, but she pulled her head back and gasped for breath when she couldn't hold the air in anymore.

He wrapped his arms around her from behind, enfolding her in his effortless way. He did this with his blondes, too, but it was so much more effective with them. He tucked his arms under her breasts, one hand caressing the curve of her hip, but nothing of her was truly concealed when he held her this way. If anything, holding her seemed to expose her more, putting her breasts, belly and thighs on display, albeit just for him. To Katelyn's knowledge, no one even knew what they'd done. The sounds they'd made had blended in with the rest.

He rested his cheek against her temple. "What's wrong?"

"Nothing."

"You can't lie to me, love."

"Then you don't need me to answer."

Jude tucked himself more tightly around her. "Was it not quite what you imagined?"

"I hadn't much thought about it," she replied.

"I find that hard to believe, you not thinking about something that most people treat as a significant occasion."

"I'm not most people."

"Then what's wrong?"

Katelyn stood in the shower spray with him holding her but with her hands at her sides. She honestly didn't know.

Chapter Nine

Once he'd gotten a taste—once *she'd* gotten a taste—she couldn't stop. His body was as addictive as blood, and he often mixed such business with pleasure.

She didn't kiss him in front of Cody again or in front of the rest of the Family. He didn't show any signs of being ashamed, but when he would pull her into his arms and kiss the oxygen from her lungs, they were always alone or at least out of sight.

There were so many rooms in the building perfect for such a purpose—bland, largely unfurnished, too impersonal to belong to anyone, apartments waiting for tenants. Katelyn sometimes wondered whether the Family had plans for expansion, but the empty rooms they frequented were convenient, and Katelyn didn't ask questions anymore.

In his arms in the aftermath—sometimes bloody and sometimes just the normal stickiness associated with sex—he would ask what was wrong. But she'd rest her head against his massive chest as he cradled her to him, and she wouldn't answer.

Conversation in general had died. Who needed to talk when their routine needed no words? She didn't resist the call and knew how to find the girls he wanted, and she was always close by as the Slaughterhouse claimed its victims. She still sometimes brought Cara blood or bodies, but now Katelyn would leave before her bloodbath, which Cara seemed to appreciate. Katelyn had already seen in Cara what Tinsel and Jude had wanted her to see.

School took up most of her week, but it became an afterthought, the dreamy haze she endured until she could be with the man who made her feel alive.

Now that she had a regular influx of human and vampire blood to remind her what she really *needed*, flies and spiders just didn't cut it anymore—not that she could stop. Her cravings demanded payment with interest. Flies and spiders weren't enough, no matter how many she caught, no matter how long she kept her window open, although winter was creeping into Meridian, and she froze under quilts at night while hoping for cockroaches and other beetles to come in from the cold. Without roommates, nobody complained.

She shivered, wrapped in a quilt under the two she'd put over her sheets, but she couldn't cover all of herself. She needed to breathe. So her nose was cold and dripping, but she didn't have hands free to blow her nose.

She should have been sleeping, but insects weren't the only creatures seeking shelter.

There had been an article or two about the problem in the student newspaper, because where there were people, there was food. And where there was food, there were mice and rats, especially when there were open trashcans in open rooms at the corners of the open-air dormitories. Easily accessible trashcans in closed dorms and dumpsters behind the cafeterias and strategically placed around campus also offered a veritable buffet and theme park for wriggly-nosed rodents. They certainly helped keep the stray campus cats fat, but there weren't enough cats to combat the infestation.

Katelyn had been aware of the problem before Jude had changed her, but she hadn't really understood the reality. Here she was, in a seemingly clean, well-taken-care-of house with a stricter tidiness policy and less long-suffering maid service than the fraternities. But she had a much better sense now of how *nothing* was clean. She smelled so much more than she used to, not just blood and other bodily fluids. She smelled the filth of food decay, mold, dead skin dissipating to dust. And she still heard the relentless scurrying through the walls. If other people could hear what she heard, their skin would crawl.

This was her life, and some nights she couldn't sleep for the sound of creatures in the walls and the attic.

She wondered if there were bats up there.

Three o'clock came and went, and she was still awake, listening to the shuffle of little feet and developing ice crystals on her cheeks.

Finally, she threw back the quilts and unwound herself from the one wrapped around her. She grabbed her robe, then locked the door behind her.

The common rooms weren't deserted, but everyone was sufficiently distracted. They didn't notice her sneaking across the hall to the pull-down attic door. It only creaked a little as she opened it.

The other side of the door was pitch-black, with no windows, no lamplight spilling through the slats. Katelyn didn't think she'd ever been in the attic. In fact, if it weren't for a particular quality of the sound above her, she wouldn't have even known they had an attic.

Katelyn checked behind her. No one in the hall.

She climbed up the ladder in her socked feet. The musty scent of being closed in without much ventilation or shifting of air assaulted her senses—and the scent of animals. No mistaking that.

She pulled the ladder back in, closing the door.

Her socks upset the dust on the slats. Insulation lined the sides of the attic where the floor didn't reach. At her height, there was no need to duck in most of the areas, which was good, because she could barely see—although she was almost sure that before she'd been changed, she wouldn't have been able to see a thing, period.

She lowered herself to her hands and knees, letting her nose guide her to a corner of insulation where paper in the wall had been chewed through. Inside, baby rats felt their way blindly around their mother or suckled at her side.

The mother bit at Katelyn's fingers, tearing with merciless teeth, but that didn't stop Katelyn from wrapping her hand around the rat mother's head, squeezing, then twisting. After a series of snaps, the mother went limp.

The babies didn't know the difference. That was how she was able to grab them one by one, squirming and squealing, before snapping their necks and swallowing them whole like a snake.

The mother was too big for that. Katelyn bit down on the neck and ripped the head off. Still-warm blood squirted like errant ink on her face. She clamped her mouth around the fountain and tipped her head back to drain the rat dry, ignoring the gamey, wooden, rotten smells that came from it, the tickle of fleas fleeing their former host. After tossing the rat corpse aside, she brushed the fleas away. Their lives were nothing in comparison, the worth of them less than a second.

There were more creatures in the dark. Katelyn crouched, listening, smelling. Her eyes were nearly useless in this dark empty space, so she stopped trying to use them. She stayed as still as she could, her robe edges joining her socks in gathering dust. She wrinkled her nose but held back the sneeze.

Scurrying to the side.

She sprang and landed with her hand on the wriggling, biting mouse. She snapped its back, then used her own teeth to tear open its belly and drink what she could out of its small body.

When it no longer had any use, she tossed that body away as well.

Only in the absence of prey did she horrify herself.

Other scurries were too far away to draw her, and she'd lost track of the door. She swept her hand over the slats, searching for a seam, whimpering like prey herself as the darkness closed in.

These days, Katelyn knew what lurked in the darkness. Sometimes, those monsters were still human, just…sick.

But monsters nonetheless.

"Nothing wrong with being a monster, love."

"Get out of my head. You did this to me. If you absolutely have to stay, help me find my fucking way out."

"There is nothing in this world that will touch you. You have my protection."

"You're not here with me to protect me. And I don't want to be here at all." One of her nails broke, leaving behind a jagged tip as she scrabbled at the wood.

"I take care of what's mine, Katelyn."

"Then get me out of here!"

"What if I gave you what you really wanted? Would you believe me then?"

"Yes! Just get me out of here." Another snap of fingernail, one after the other. Some of the blood on her hands was her own.

"That's not what you really want."

The room filled with the shuffling, scratching sound of tiny feet climbing into the attic, through the insulation, up the walls. The shadows glittered with beady eyes. Other than little footsteps, there was no other sound, no protest, no fear. The creatures piled on top of each other, reaching heights above where she crouched on the slats.

"For your loyalty, I will give you millions of lives, as many you want. They won't run. They won't fight. You'll have all night. And you won't have to contend with the tedious ritual of capturing flies. They'll find their way to you as well."

She fell back, clasping her arms around her knees, and stared at the veritable feast just waiting for her to consume them. Saliva hung in thick strings from the corners of her mouth. There was nothing sane or sexy about this need, this bone-shaking desire, when she was surrounded by lives—so many lives, enough for weeks.

"Why are you doing this to me?"

"Because you're my good and faithful servant. This and more, Katelyn. I offer you this and more."

"Turn me. If this is my life, I don't want to live."

"You know I can't do that."

Katelyn bowed her head, hiding her face against her thighs and trying not to smell the fur, trying not to hear the thousands of quick-beating hearts. Saliva continued to drip down her chin, and she smelled of rodent death. Her broken nails snagged skin wherever she put them.

It wasn't that he couldn't do it. He could do it in a second—and he wanted to. He panted over her skin and groaned in frustration when he couldn't fuck her with his teeth. It wasn't that he couldn't. He just wouldn't.

The only answer she could come up with for why was that he already had everything he needed. He didn't want a companion. He wanted a slave—a pet to lavish gruesome gifts upon, but certainly no equal. He wanted her, but he threw the word 'love' around without meaning it, especially when she knew intimately where his eyes strayed and what his heart truly desired. And it wasn't her.

"Why don't you believe in me, Katelyn?"

She did. That was the whole problem, wasn't it? She didn't have a choice, but he wouldn't admit to his own choice with her. There was no equity in this arrangement, no true relationship. She was his—his freak, his monster, his murderer. He thought all the treats in the world would make up for that. To him, he was doing her every favor—and part of her agreed. So how could she deny him?

"They are all yours. As many as you can swallow. Take them. Accept my gift."

The horde swarmed closer, moving as a unit to crowd around her. Even if she wanted to leave, she was either sitting on the door or there were rodents in the way. She trembled so hard that her back threatened to seize, and her skin prickled maddeningly from her scalp to her toes. She thought of all the disease in the room with her. It seemed unlikely, but there could even be a strain of rabies somewhere in the crowd. Would it even faze her if there was?

"No disease. No pain. You have nothing at all to fear. Yield to me, love. Take what has been offered. Gorge yourself with my blessing."

The first cold, wet nose touched her foot. She grabbed at the mouse, snapped its back, then tore at it with her jagged nails until it popped and hot blood filled her mouth. She bit down into the matted fur to draw out more. When it was drained, she threw it aside and grabbed the next…and the next…and the next…and the next.

And the next.

* * * *

The frenzy ceased only when the rest of the rats and mice dispersed, leaving as unwarily as they'd arrived. Whatever mesmerism had kept them there also shielded them from the horror that had decimated their numbers.

She had no way of knowing for sure without light, but she felt as though the sun had risen. To her, no time had passed, and as always, her stomach seemed to stay relatively empty, no matter how much blood or living meat she consumed—as though she hadn't singlehandedly made a dent in the entire UTM rodent population. She knew what she heard every night—dozens of rodents living in the sorority house. Not hundreds. Not thousands. But that's what had come to her.

As soon as she'd started, her rational, observant mind had fled, but now she inhabited the monster's body once again, dripping blood rather than saliva onto the wooden slats. She didn't know the damage she'd done. She only knew that she was wet and dirty and smelled—and that she sat in a pool of blood that couldn't possibly be staying just on the floor. Even if light couldn't get through the slats, blood could. It would only be a matter of time before it soaked through the plaster.

Katelyn shifted where she sat, groaning. Her jaw ached. After a while, she'd stopped breaking their backs and had just bitten into their slack bodies.

Her whole body shook. Cold sweat beaded from her forehead and under her arms. She couldn't see much, but she could see enough.

She managed to get onto her hands and knees, feeling through the blood again to find a seam, swallowing back her screams because the last thing she wanted was someone to see her like this. Nothing was more important than hiding what she'd done or making sure that when it was discovered, it didn't tie back to her. She wouldn't be able to find her lost fingernails in this mess if she couldn't even find the attic door, so she prayed that when this massacre was discovered, the obviously nonhuman victims would discourage more thorough forensics.

A lot of hoping, wishing and praying. But last she checked, she had no other choice.

She scrabbled at the handle when she finally found it, then pushed the door down. Blood spilled over the sides, but she focused on climbing down as fast as she could and shoving the door back up to minimize the mess left behind.

"Oh my God."

Katelyn whirled around.

Five of her sorority sisters... Two of them wore sweats and held flashlights that had since been turned off. The other three looked like they'd just woken up.

Katelyn ran over the options. Not one worked in her favor. A few didn't work in the girls' favor, either, but she drew the line at that. Jude could kill humans and offer her their blood, but she was never going to wield the knife. Murder, while the best outcome for her in terms of minimizing witnesses, was off the table.

Which meant that Katelyn was royally screwed.

"Katelyn? Is that you?"

"What happened? Have you been up there this whole time? What did you do to—?"

"I thought I heard a noise." Katelyn's words came out garbled and wet with what was still left in her mouth, not just blood but meat and fur between her teeth.

"And you decided to become a Japanese horror demon? Nina woke me at five. No one came in or out. What the hell were you doing? Is all that yours?"

"Is all what mine?" Katelyn asked.

"All that blood? I'd say you must have had a bad period, but the blood's...in your...around your...mouth."

As Katelyn stepped forward, each of the girls stepped back.

"I need to go."

Horrible, filthy, disgusting, disgusted thoughts rushed through Katelyn's head, and everything that came out of her mouth made her sound drunk. She'd never been more awake, more alive. Under all the blood and dust, she'd probably never looked better.

That wasn't much consolation, though. The girls backed away from her as though she were a rabid fox with a foaming mouth – as well they should have. Their fear made them fragrant, and because her belly was a bottomless pit when it came to blood…

"What the hell happened to you?" one of the girls squeaked.

She wasn't going to make it to the showers without a problem, was she? Katelyn considered climbing out of one of the windows – perhaps in her own room, if she could manage to keep her fingers from slipping over the key under her sodden shirt.

"I heard a noise. I went up to check on it. I must have gotten lost," Katelyn said.

"Lost in a fucking attic?"

"When the door closes, it's hard to find again. I wasn't thinking straight. I must have freaked out, blacked out. I don't remember a thing. I just… My mouth hurts, I hurt all over and I just want to get cleaned up." The shaking was real. The slurred speech was real. The staggering was real. Her fear was real. There was no need for acting when she did such a convincing job being almost honest.

Her socked feet tracked blood on the thin carpet.

"Look at her mouth. She doesn't have a busted lip." But the girl stumbled back when Katelyn turned toward her.

"I think I bit my tongue," Katelyn said. That wasn't a lie either. "Please, I need to take a shower. I'll clean all this up later."

"Oh my God, it's dripping from the ceiling!"

They weren't going to buy the confluence of a tongue-bleed, nosebleed and heavy menstrual flow for much longer.

Katelyn made a break for the showers. Self-preservation—or at least preservation for the integrity of their clothing—forced them to let her through, although one of the girls with a flashlight swung it at her head. It grazed her ear and tossed her hair, which left splatter on the wall.

Girls coming out of their rooms either for innocuous reasons or to see what all the fuss was about reeled back as she passed them, a blood-soaked Valkyrie in pajamas and robe.

"Someone call the police!"

Panic rose inside her like hands choking her windpipe from the inside.

Katelyn yanked open the communal bathroom door. "Everybody out, *now*!"

When her words weren't enough to convince, one look at her made the rest run screaming. Once most of them were out and only one or two were cowering in the bathroom stalls, Katelyn locked the bathroom door. She left a bloodstain everywhere she touched.

When she turned around, she faced one of the giant mirrors lining the wall over the sinks.

The whole bottom half of her face, down her neck to under the neckline of her shirt, as well as her shirt and robe were coated in rich, dark red—some relatively fresh and some old underneath to richen the color and add texture. Flecks of flesh dotted her cheeks, neck and the terrycloth of her robe as well as the top half of her shirt. The bottom half of her pants and the robe up to her knees were soaked through as well, probably from kneeling while she ate and drank. The entire inside of her mouth had been coated the same red, even her teeth, which had visible pieces of flesh stuck between.

The girls had been right. She looked like something out of a horror movie, one of those too-real vampire-type movies.

And the irony, of course, was that she was just a vampire wannabe.

She stripped off her bloody clothes and left them in a pile on the tile. There was no point trying to hide them.

Another series of horror-movie screams told her at least one girl had opened the attic door, perhaps even climbed up. If they hadn't called campus security or the police by now, it wouldn't take them long.

She barely registered that she was out-and-out ugly crying as she shoved her way into one of the shower stalls and turned the water all the way to hot. She danced out of the spray when it burned her skin, but she kept it almost too hot as she stepped back in and raked at her face, chest and hair. Her broken fingernails striped her skin with thin new cuts, new blood.

As soon as the water at her feet ran clear again, she stumbled out of the stall, barely able to see through the blur, and fumbled around for someone's discarded towel before searching through abandoned toiletry bags for a nail clipper and floss. She clipped her nails first, down to the quick. She didn't need a freaking manicure. She just needed her nails not to cut her anymore.

She flossed the flesh out of her teeth. Then she found someone else's toothbrush and brushed her teeth forever, rinsed ten thousand times. Afterward, the toothbrush found a new home in the trashcan. The girl probably wouldn't want it anymore.

Someone banged on the door. A man, by the full sound of the fist.

It shouldn't have taken them so long. Perhaps they'd thought the first call was a prank.

Miss Debbie would have a key. Sure enough, the main lock and the deadbolt unlocked. Katelyn twisted them locked once again and held them in that position. The person on the other side continued trying to unlock the door, but Katelyn wouldn't let them. She was strong right now—terrified, confused, lost, and more than a little rattled, but strong.

"Ms. Dillon, open up." He sounded familiar, but the door distorted his voice.

"I didn't do anything!" A bald-faced lie, but in the grand scheme of things, she didn't think what she'd done was a crime. People exterminated mice and rats all the time, using traps and chemicals and poisons, and she hadn't eaten them out of sadistic cruelty.

"Ms. Dillon, we saw the attic. Did you?"

Fuck, fuck, fuck. Detective Dunn. If he was here, it was because he'd caught wind of her name and thought it best to investigate in person rather than leaving it to campus security or some beat cop.

"Your friends tell me you were shut in that attic for hours. Did you shut yourself in there?" Detective Dunn asked.

"I couldn't find my way out."

"I don't mean to be rude, Ms. Dillon, but it looked like you sprayed blood, guts and rodent corpses through a hose."

Oh God, he's being polite. That wasn't someone trying to capture a murder suspect. That was a hostage negotiator.

"I'm not going to hurt anyone in here. I just didn't want anyone to come in," Katelyn said. "I didn't realize how bad I looked. I needed to clean myself."

"You want to tell me why you went into an attic in the middle of the night?"

"I thought I heard something. In retrospect, that was a stupid reason to go into an empty attic without a flashlight or a phone. But I couldn't sleep, and I wasn't thinking straight." It was all such a poor attempt to salvage the situation, but as long as Detective Dunn sounded reasonable instead of out of patience, she was willing to talk. "I guess horror movies never taught me a thing. I've never been a big fan, anyway."

A low chuckle through the door. Not forced. That was good.

"So you heard something in the attic, went up and…"

"Only when I pulled the ladder in after me did I realize there wasn't any light. I panicked, and I couldn't find the door again. I heard mice, rats. At least I assume there were rats, because some of them seemed bigger. I thought they were attacking me."

"So you decided to reenact a massacre on a rodent scale?"

She rested her forehead against the door. "I don't remember."

"That seems to be happening a lot, Ms. Dillon."

"You cleared me."

"I did. And the evidence still bears that out. But you're not telling me everything about that night or last night, are you?"

"I don't know what you want me to say." Katelyn slid her hand down the door, freeing the deadbolt. "I can't remember."

"I believe you, Ms. Dillon."

"No, you don't."

"I believe you're having trouble. Maybe it's related to the car accident. Maybe it's related to what happened after the car accident. Maybe it's your mind playing tricks on you. Either way, I give you my word that we only want to help."

She knew that tone of voice, too. Not hostage negotiation. He was placating her—warm, reassuring, gentle, not a touch of the aggression that he'd shown with his knock.

There weren't just police on the other side of the door. There were people waiting to take her away. She could practically smell the clinical sterility that clung to their skin—anti-bacterial soap, unscented moisturizer, talcum powder, latex.

Many cities had their psych wards in hospitals, and there were private clinics, too, but Meridian had one of the only public psychiatric hospitals in the country, renowned because it was new. Meridian, after all, had only been a big city for less than three decades. Everything was new, even the places that looked old. A venerable building, filled with the newest psychiatric ideas and the most modern technology and treatments, it was a state experiment—one had that proved largely successful so far, although it would take at least another ten years before that could be definitively determined.

Such information was one of the benefits of being a UTM psych major. She'd planned to sign up for an internship for her graduate program.

Never had she imagined she'd walk through those doors as a patient.

"You think I'm crazy," she said.

"I think you're traumatized. Did you see yourself in the mirror before you showered?"

"Yes."

"Then you know what your sisters saw when you came down. And you can imagine what I saw when I went into that attic. It's pretty gruesome, Ms. Dillon. 'Crazy' is an oversimplification. You and I both know that you've been profoundly affected by what happened to your friends. Your sisters and house mother have noticed you've withdrawn, and some nights you disappear altogether. What do you do when you leave?"

"I go out. That's not a crime. I go for a walk. I go dancing. I go out to eat. That's all."

"Are you sure?"

Katelyn paused a little too long.

"Look in the mirror now, Ms. Dillon. What do you see?"

She turned her head just enough to catch herself in the mirror, barely covered by the towel, her hair weighed down by water, her face pale except for the full flush of her cheeks and lips from feeding. But that could do nothing for the reddened whites of her eyes or the puffiness underneath them from crying. Gazing beyond the supernatural health and beauty, Katelyn saw only a scared little girl—the kind who would be a victim of the monster she'd seen in the mirror less than an hour earlier.

"I didn't do anything wrong," she said. "The blood's gone. Only mine is left."

"The blood isn't gone," Detective Dunn said gently. "It's all over the attic. You cleaned it off, but it isn't gone. I think we can help you, but only if you let us."

"You're going to take me away."

"With any luck, it will be temporary. I think you're in pain. I think you're going through something terrible. You seem like an intelligent young woman. I think you know you need help, and that's what you've been so afraid of. But you don't need to be afraid anymore. Your parents have been contacted, and the university agrees that this is the best course for you as well. It will be easier if we don't have to break down this door."

There were frosted windows along the outer wall, but she was on the third floor. Even if her recent influx of blood could mend broken bones, it wouldn't be able to do so before whoever they had outside could get to her. The only way out was through the door. There was no other recourse.

That wasn't entirely true. But even after last night and the knowledge of what was going to happen, she couldn't convince herself to let the blood pooling under her body be her own. Part of her even thought that would be the right thing to do. She just couldn't do it.

"I'm not dressed," Katelyn said.

"We've retrieved some things from your room."

Katelyn pounded her forehead against the door. The image of her bedroom popped up with perfect clarity. The scarf she used to bind herself to the bed on the nights when the cravings went beyond rodents and insects. The open window. The three quilts. The plate of rotting food. The cutting paraphernalia on the dresser—razors, antibiotic ointment, cloth-based bandages—for when she used her own blood to take the edge off. She could barely point out the places she'd cut, just slightly smoother and more silvery than her own skin. That would be fun for the professionals to figure out.

"Yes, we saw some interesting things. We can talk about that later. No one here wants to hurt you."

"I haven't hurt anybody."

"Let's keep it that way. If you open the door, we can give you some clothing, and you can get dressed and come with us. I think that will end the best for everyone involved."

She kept hitting her head against the door.

"Ms. Dillon, I give you my word, you're not in any trouble. You've done nothing illegal. You've alarmed your sisters and your house mother, and they're concerned for your well-being. So am I. You know there's something wrong, or you wouldn't have locked yourself in. We can help. I *want* to help."

Without looking up, she undid the main lock and stepped back.

Detective Dunn turned the knob and slowly pushed open the door. He met her eyes first before taking in the state of her. Then he beckoned to someone behind him. He handed her a pile of clothes—university sweatpants and a sorority T-shirt, utilitarian undergarments, things a house mother would feel more comfortable handing to a male police detective, but also clothes that wouldn't eventually be confiscated. Even her bra was one without an underwire.

"I'm going to close the door again. Do I have your word that you won't lock it?" he asked.

Katelyn nodded.

He took in her appearance in again—nothing that made her feel dirtier than she already felt. He didn't have to work too hard to observe incongruities that Katelyn already knew were there, but he didn't comment, just closed the door and gave her the time to change. She came out after she'd put on her slippers.

Detective Dunn took her by her upper arm and led her downstairs to his police car, even doing the head-push thing that forced her in without hurting herself.

"Am I under arrest?" she asked.

"I told you, no. I just volunteered to escort you. The people behind us are the ones who will officially take you into custody." Detective Dunn closed her car door, then slid into the driver's seat.

"Where's your partner?" she asked.

"On another case."

"I'm not going to sign myself in voluntarily."

"We can do a psychiatric hold if we believe that you are a risk to yourself or others. You did a real number on those rats in the attic, Ms. Dillon, and I think you remember more than you admit. In the great State of Texas, we *can* have your parents commit you to the facility if, after seventy-two hours, we continue to believe you are a risk to yourself or others and that you're cognitively impaired."

"I'm not going to make that easy for them."

"You came with me easily enough," he said.

"I saw the wisdom in avoiding a more violent encounter. There's a difference."

At a red light, Detective Dunn turned around to meet her eyes. "May I call you Katelyn? I think we're beyond the formalities."

"I prefer the formalities, Detective."

"All right. I'm almost certain what's going on here, Ms. Dillon. You'll be in that facility for the rest of your natural life."

"Is that why I'm here? So you could lock me up for *something*, even if the prison is a little cushier and more medicated?"

"I think you're sick, but the illness is a little more metaphysical. Wouldn't you agree?"

Katelyn stared him down and didn't blink. Was he saying what she thought he was saying?

"On the surface, there are people who'd envy you. I've never seen clearer skin on a college student who wasn't on some kind of clinical product—except for the scratches, of course. My ex would kill for your hair. But you...*you* don't look good. From what I hear, that's very common for your condition. And there's a cure that you may not have considered."

"I don't know what you're talking about, but I'm pretty sure it's not department regulation," Katelyn said.

"I'm given some latitude when it comes to certain cases."

"That sounds like a shining example of police policy in this country."

"That latitude isn't counter to the spirit of the law, Ms. Dillon. It just accommodates things in this city that might not fall within the law's jurisdiction."

She hadn't expected that he'd almost say the quiet part out loud. What did he hope to accomplish by making his position clearer?

"The light's green," she said, stalling.

Detective Dunn returned his attention to the street in front of them and continued driving.

"Don't you know how dangerous it is, you saying that?" She glanced at his dashcam but hoped he caught her double meaning.

"A certain tipping of the hand is necessary now and then, especially since the message isn't for you alone."

Holy shit. He really did understand. If he hadn't figured it out the day he'd rescued her from the car wreck—and now she was questioning that much—this smart cookie had figured out what she was by now and who might be listening.

"You're going to be held at the Mattea Psychiatric Hospital these next seventy-two hours for observation and evaluation. Given the circumstances, the scrutiny will be intense, and given that Mattea has its own small wing for people like you, it goes without saying that your proclivities will be very difficult to hide. Mattea is the only hospital in the world with a specialty in zoophagia. In Meridian, it's practically an epidemic, right up there with clinical lycanthropy—not even speaking of the non-clinical sort."

Katelyn buried her face in her hands, hunching over her thighs. "Why the fuck are you telling me this?"

"I'm not an enforcer," he said. "I know that sounds counterintuitive, but this badge means I'm discouraged from the kind of vigilante justice that runs rampant and largely unchecked on the streets of Meridian. As long as they don't negatively impact the legal citizens of the city, there's never been a reason to get on their case. Do you understand?"

"I'm still a legal citizen."

"Yes. So maybe you should have a talk with your extralegal companion about their extralegal activities. I would hate to have to kick this up a less sympathetic chain. I want to help you, Ms. Dillon. There are three ways to clear up your condition. One of them... I'll take that recourse if I have to, because your friend isn't under my jurisdiction, but you are. Do you understand?"

"You lost me."

"Make use of phone privileges as soon as you can when you arrive."

He knew very well she didn't need a phone call. She didn't even know the number for the butcher shop. Who needed a phone number when he had a direct line to her head? She couldn't feel him there, but that didn't mean Jude wasn't crouched in her consciousness, keeping his ear open for everything the detective was saying. And if he wasn't there now, he'd sift through her memories later.

"You know I'm not crazy, but you're taking me to a mental hospital anyway?" Katelyn said.

"I didn't say you weren't mentally ill. It's just not anything this hospital can fix. In the end, all they can do is contain. It's a damn shame the doctors don't have any idea what they're dealing with. The ignorance is really quite shocking."

"Except when it isn't," she muttered. The Rosenhan experiment went a long way to explaining how doctors could be blinded by their own specialty. "If you don't think they can do anything for me, why send me there?"

"You exposed yourself. There's nothing we can do but address the issue at hand. If I hadn't taken the case, another officer would have done the same thing—or worse. You tore into hundreds of rodents. As a method of extermination, it's unorthodox at best, but certainly alarming. There's no way to spin what happened, whether you remember you did it or not. You're quick on your feet. Think about the position this put you in."

"I couldn't help—"

"I know the blame isn't entirely yours. You would do well to remind your friend of that."

"If you keep talking about my friend, someone's going to think I'm schizophrenic. Not my diagnosis."

"I'll write down that you came with me willingly," Detective Dunn said. "You don't have to sign yourself in, but it would help your case even more, and you'd have a better chance of signing yourself back out again.

I'll do what I can for you. I just hope your friend isn't in the habit of leaving strays like the others do."

Chapter Ten

She sat on her bed. They'd let her keep her bra and slippers, so her feet were warm and her breasts harnessed, which saved her some embarrassment, although she wouldn't say she looked her best. After the public humiliation, it was hard to care.

Even without the videos and pictures doubtlessly taken of the bloody mess of her or the attic, there'd been police cars with flashing lights and the ever-reliable rubberneckers to witness her being put in a police car like a criminal. She was pretty sure Delta Tau wasn't going to let her back in. *An honorable discharge to the loony bin.* She was also pretty sure that if she went back to UTM, they'd have a hell of a time assigning her a new roommate.

If she could go back. *If* they let her come back. *If* she could stand to go back. At this point, she might as well be Lizzie Borden. There'd be skipping-rope rhymes about her for years to come.

Because Jude had ensured that she would get caught.

She couldn't see any other way around it. What else had he expected to happen once he'd promised her a world of life and helped her eat through half of it? Her sorority house wasn't the butcher shop, where a majority of the inhabitants were bloodsuckers and a familiar could get away with a bloody mouth. She literally couldn't believe he hadn't thought through the consequences.

He had to have known he was making her the monster for everyone to see.

She could draw only two possible conclusions. The first was that it had been his intention to integrate her fully into the Family by depriving her of the last vestiges of humanity she'd barely been clinging to.

The second was that he was full of crap, that he'd deliberately led her on with words of love and devotion and lulled her into a false sense of relevancy. Perhaps taking care of a familiar had been more of a burden than he'd been looking for.

"I just hope your friend isn't in the habit of leaving strays like the others do."

Like the others. A whole section of the hospital devoted to zoophagia meant that there were other familiars here. And if there were other familiars, that meant that other vampires had abandoned them, like surrendering a pet at the pound.

Katelyn couldn't trust her own evaluation of Jude. He was her master. She was his bitch. Even now, she couldn't quite believe he could do this to her on purpose.

But he was so silent in her head. Conspicuously silent.

Her temporary roommate entered the room with finger in a book. "What're you in for?"

"You first." Katelyn's hair hung in curtains on both sides of her face. She barely looked up before casting her eyes back to the heinous ivory linoleum—soft on the feet, an affront to interior decorators everywhere. One would think a more modern building would have better taste.

"Tammy. Bipolar. Went off my meds. Manic episode. Danced on the edge of a roof. Parents made me come here for a few days to equalize. That's the word they used. I think they meant 'find my equilibrium', but whatever." Tammy settled back on her bed and crossed her legs. "Your turn."

"Katelyn. I committed large-scale slaughter on a bunch of rats in the attic of my sorority house. Ate their babies. Drank their blood. Kind of freaked people out."

Tammy's book fell from her finger, losing her place. "Are you serious? Dude. I mean…"

"You're safe. I'm watched."

"Well, as long as it was just rats…"

"They found my flytraps, too," Katelyn said, still staring at the floor.

"Are you *serious* serious?"

"Dead serious."

"You're seriously crazy, girl."

"Yeah, I'm getting that."

Tammy smoothed her hands over the woven hardback. "Is it, like, a taste thing? You like how they taste?"

"I like their blood," Katelyn replied, her tone flat, emotionless. Why beat around the bush? It wasn't a secret anymore. "I can't control it, but I need it."

"Wow. Like one of those weird vampy people who hangs out in clubs and thinks they're real? You sure I'm safe? Delusions and all?"

"Like I said, they're watching. And I have a code. Haven't broken it...so far."

"Suddenly my life doesn't seem that screwed up. I'll see if one of the nurses has a cross for me to wear tonight."

"I'm not a vampire."

"Then what are you?"

"Nothing. Nothing at all."

* * * *

A few months before, Katelyn had been having ice cream sundae shakes at two o'clock in the morning with Aly, Angel, Maria and some other Delta Taus. She'd always found it useful to have a five-year plan in lieu of New Year's resolutions—goals to work toward, even if things had to change midyear as focuses shifted and predictions needed revision. Her plans weren't hard and fast rules for her life, just an arrow pointed in a general direction—or else late-night ice cream wouldn't figure into the equation.

Humiliated, disgraced and abandoned in a psychiatric hospital for a severe paraphiliac disorder hadn't been part of that plan. Sure, plenty of people with mental illness went into psychology because they could relate and wanted to help other people like them, but somehow she didn't think the right people would sign off on her any more than they would someone with a felony criminal record.

She slept like the dead until lunch, aided by the fact that Tammy seemed intimidated, if not quite afraid.

The doors stayed open and the lights stayed on, but given that she hadn't slept at all the previous night, she took what she could.

After lunch, one of the nurses suggested in a way that wasn't simply suggestion that Katelyn stay awake until early bedtime, when the lights would go out and some of the doors locked. Two nurses would be on watch all night. She and Tammy were danger-to-themselves material, but Katelyn was still on watch for potential danger-to-others, which was why they'd want to give Tammy an unlocked exit in case it was needed.

Katelyn figured most of this out on her own. No one explained to her why things were the way they were. They just told her where to go and gave her antipsychotics that had no effect on her cravings whatsoever.

Full evaluation was set for the next afternoon. If she couldn't figure out how to get out physically, she'd have to figure out a way to convince a doctor of mental illness that she wasn't crazy when the best a person could ever really prove was that she wasn't crazy right *now*, not that she was going to stay that way.

Her parents were freaked out. The university was freaked out. Hell, she was freaked out. She needed to find a way to not freak the psychiatrist out as well. If she was assigned to the familiar wing, she was history. She needed to figure out how to get out of here without being locked away for a good long while…or forever. As long as her vampire lived, in fact.

She wondered when the hospital would realize their familiar wing housed secondhand immortals. Would they still be considered crazy then? Or would they simply be passed along to people better suited to deal with their unique, untreatable paraphilia? The kind of people permitted to exact vigilante justice on vampires, for instance.

Katelyn picked at her dinner, ignoring everyone around her more out of shame than antagonism. She was crazy as a bedbug, no doubt about it, and she heard whispers that made her think Tammy had spread the word on just how much, but she felt like a fraud and an insult. She couldn't in good conscience share a self-deprecating laugh or talk rehabilitation or medication or knock normal with the other people in this wing. If they thought she believed she was too good for them, fine—even though it was the other way around.

Bedtime came ungodly early. Who the hell under sixty-five went to bed at nine o'clock? But the nurse's advice to wait bore fruit. She fell asleep almost immediately, despite Tammy's bedside lamp.

* * * *

She had no idea what woke her up. She'd been asleep and now she was awake.

Katelyn sat up. The room was eerily silent, not even the hum of the heater. She could only hear Tammy's breathing. Moonlight poured into the room through the windows, barred with the ugly-pretty gothic wrought iron that vined over the building.

"You are not alone."

Katelyn nearly lost her balance, lightheaded with complete and utter relief that almost had her in tears.

"Open the window. Just a crack is enough."

"I'm not sure if I can." The windows were capable of opening, but that didn't mean they'd been intended for opening. There were emergency exits for evacuation,

but in case of fire where someone was trapped in a room, it looked like it didn't matter if the chestnuts burned. They weren't leaving through the windows without the use of a metal saw or particularly good bolt cutter. Besides, the sliding window looked painted to the sill.

"Try."

Katelyn clicked the latches and grunted as she shoved up with all her might. She fell back when the first gust of cold air rushed against her skin like an eager army forcing passage. Her shirt was short-sleeved. She rubbed sudden goosebumps on her arms.

They spilled in with the purer moonlight, emerging as though stepping out from the air.

Tinsel looked around. "Well, you certainly got yourself in a pickle. I'm surprised they don't have you in a straitjacket."

"They don't really use those anymore, unless it's an extreme case. They're more for magicians these days."

"Fascinating. I didn't know they still used this color green. Pistachio would knock *me* off my rocker. Are they *trying* to make people stay, some state-reimbursed-per-person grift?"

Katelyn ignored Tinsel's commentary. She was pretty sure the green was supposed to be soothing, although it had dried a bit livelier than the ward designers had probably anticipated.

She concentrated instead on Jude, standing dark and large in the light-colored room. It seemed like an obvious thing, how big he was, after all this time discovering his body, but he was that level of big that was hard to wrap one's mind around.

"Did you think I would leave you?" he asked, filling the room like a soft storm.

"If it had been your fault, I would have told him he should," Tinsel said, still inspecting the room and finally setting her sights on the girl in the other bed. "But it was *his* reckless error in far too public an arena. I put him in the same category as those annoying women who dress up their dogs, paint their nails and talk about how little Teacup needs to meet with the pet psychologist about repressed memories."

"I was foolish," Jude said. "Overindulgent. You have that effect on me, love."

"The next time you lose your things, Jude, I'm not helping you find them again."

"Hey," Katelyn whispered as Tinsel stroked Tammy's hair away from her neck. "Not here. Not her."

"It's not up to you who I drink, familiar." Tinsel blew her cold breath over Tammy's face. Tammy's forehead furrowed, and she shifted under her blanket, pushing it down in spite of the open window that blew right on her. Tinsel trailed her silver-painted nails down Tammy's neck, over the jut of her collarbone, past the neckline of her shirt to the tightened tip of her nipple. "If we want to take the whole floor, we will."

"Don't these people have enough problems?"

"It's a better death than any they've tried to deal themselves." Tinsel traced the dark, pearly lines on Tammy's forearm.

"It's not the same thing at all. Doesn't mean she's suicidal—or suicidal right now, at least. Doesn't mean she wants to die. Doesn't even mean she's miserable right this second. For God's sake, leave her alone."

Jude shared a look with Tinsel, who rolled her eyes.

"Fine. We have plenty to eat at home anyway. But just a taste. She won't even feel it."

Katelyn knew Tinsel had given a mile by agreeing not to kill, so at Tammy's quiet cry, Katelyn turned away. Jude caught her hand and brought her in, enfolded her in his embrace. Katelyn buried her face against his chest, but she balled her fists under the jut of his ribs.

"I know you're upset with me."

"Upset?" Katelyn said into his shirt. "*Upset?* Do you have any idea what you did to me? Do you even *care*? Or was that your aim all along, to get me out and ostracized and branded the crazy girl in the attic of Delta Tau? They'll probably talk about me in front of the fireplace on Winter Night for years to come. It'll turn into a ghost story or variant of Bloody Mary or something."

"There are worse things than becoming a legend."

"There are better things than becoming a monster."

"You're not a monster, Katelyn. I am."

The smooth press of his fangs against her lips made her knees give way. He held her to him with his powerful arms as though she weighed nothing and leisurely explored her mouth, nudging her with those teeth, the sheer carnal sensuality of him sweeping through her in imperious waves. She didn't appreciate the manipulation, but she couldn't deny it even if she wanted to.

"Oh, for the love of Pete, let's go."

Katelyn melted out of Jude's arms. Tinsel was wiping her mouth. Tammy still lay in chilly repose, a line of blood making its way down to the white bedsheets.

"They're going to think I did it," Katelyn said.

"They already think you're crazy," Tinsel replied. "You should be grateful I let her live, and I only did that to keep you from causing a fuss. Are we leaving, Jude, taking the whole floor—or were you planning a Bedlam screw?"

"We can get through any lock," Jude explained to Katelyn. He didn't release one of her hands, clenched though it still was. "And we can take whomever we want. Do your tastes run toward anyone here?"

"Can we just leave? I don't want to stay." What she didn't say was that she feared the longer they stayed, the greater the chance they wouldn't take her with them.

"I told you I would protect you, Katelyn. Why do you still doubt me?"

"I'm in a fucking *asylum,*" Katelyn whisper-shouted. "You disappeared from my mind. I couldn't find you. For all I knew, this was all part of the fucking plan."

"I sleep like the dead. When I awoke again, you were already in here."

"Then you can't protect me all the time, can you?"

"She's got you there, Butch," Tinsel said.

"There are other familiars here," Katelyn continued, as though Tinsel hadn't interrupted, "in another part of the hospital. Did you know that? That damn detective told me. So did the admitting nurse. So you wouldn't be the only vampire to break that promise. Once I was exposed, the easiest thing to do was let me go. As long as I'm under scrutiny, being near you only draws suspicion."

"Girl's got a point," Tinsel said.

Of *course* Katelyn had just landed the perfect argument for *not* taking her out of here.

"You don't ever have to go back to that school. You don't ever have to come back here." Jude didn't need inflection or emphasis to make his word final. "I'll take care of you."

"That's not what I want," Katelyn said.

Tinsel snorted.

"It's not. I mean, it is, but it isn't. The part of me that wants him to take care of me...that's not me. That's what he *did* to me."

"I understand," Jude said. "Shall we go?"

"Please, before I vomit," Tinsel replied.

"I'll make it up to you, Katelyn," he said before they left the room for the main floor. "I promise. For everything."

If he'd had an inkling what was going on in her mind, he would know he couldn't.

"We're not leaving through the window?" Katelyn asked.

"We can. You can't," Tinsel said. "We have to do this the hard way. Thank God it's late. Minimal security. Just some light mesmerism, and they'll all marvel at how the doors just unlocked and opened for you. All you have to do is not touch anything. They won't be able to see us on the cameras, and we won't leave fingerprints. It'll be like magic. *That'll* be a good campfire legend. Watch and learn, blood sack."

Tinsel took point and worked her will on nurse after nurse and guard after guard. Jude slipped through cracks under the doors and opened them from the other side. If the door required a button pushed, he'd enter the security booth and unlock the doors that way.

Watching them slip through cracks was like watching sleight-of-hand illusion that she couldn't decipher. It wasn't quite mist, wasn't quite that they became paper thin, wasn't quite that they disappeared. The closer she looked, the more her eyes hurt, so she stopped trying to understand something that was physically impossible.

Tinsel swept her arm out in a dramatic gesture as the front door opened for them, the now-deeply dreaming security guards drooling on the controls. "Freedom."

Katelyn was pretty sure Tinsel had intended her to catch that irony.

"Shall we go home?" Jude asked.

Katelyn turned to face the behemoth of a hospital, not quite institutional in its architecture but an imposing, crouching place, nonetheless. Now that she knew the spirit of the city, she had to wonder what ghosts and demons haunted the ward, this precipitate to such an insane place, normal though the city seemed on its veneer. There was something rotten in the State of Texas, and it wasn't just the State Legislature in the capital. Its dark heart was right here in Meridian.

Katelyn shivered but let herself be led to the dark SUV. She climbed into the back, blissfully alone.

She stared out of the heavily tinted window, the city little more than ghostly shapes and lights. The cool window did nothing to help her pounding head.

When they arrived at the Slaughterhouse, Katelyn didn't wait for Jude to open the door, although he'd started around the van to do so. She headed in after Tinsel, who hadn't felt the need to care whether she was coming. Jude's footsteps behind her were softer than one might expect from his size.

Inside, the strobe was in full swing, early guests drinking mini cocktails and waiting for more people as they watched the vampires dance together.

Katelyn felt decidedly out of place in her sweats, loose hair and slippered feet. The presence of the bleeders reawoke her appetite in a heartbeat. She'd eaten half the rats on the UTM campus, and already she wanted more.

It never ended, this hunger. No matter what she did, she would never have a moment's peace or any semblance of normal.

Jude slid his hands over her shoulders and down her arms. "One of the others is finding me some lovely chalices tonight. Do you want to get ready?"

Katelyn turned around as though through molasses. Jude took a step back when she met his eyes.

"Take me away," she said.

Jude tilted his head. "I don't have to feed tonight, if you'd prefer to spend its entirety with me."

"No, you don't get it. You have no idea what you've done. It doesn't even matter to you that I can never go back, that you stole my entire future. This…this *thing* that you've made me… All I'm good for is serving you—or is it servicing you? Hard to tell these days. All I know is that you don't have to share anymore. You get your servant full-time. And I get to stand in the shadows watching you yearn for other women before coming to me just because I'm the only one left alive."

Jude interrupted her with a kiss before the rest could spill out like bile instead of blood down her chin. He slid his fangs against her lips and dug his powerful fingers into the meat of her arms.

"No," he whispered. "You don't understand."

He tried to draw her closer, trap her with the allure of his hard body against hers, but she put her hands on his chest and forced herself back, because heaven knew she couldn't move him.

"Take me away. You said you could. Take my will. I don't want it anymore."

Jude's hand paused heavy on her cheek. A rush of emotions passed over his face, not all of which she could discern or name.

"Is that what you really want? To disappear. To leave— " He shook his head as though to clear it. "I just got you out of one kind of prison. Now you want to go back into another one?"

"It's all a prison," Katelyn said. "Maybe the one you send me to will be better than the others."

"I believed..." Jude stroked her lower lip with his thumb. "Is that *really* what you want?"

She nodded. "I don't want to be here anymore."

"I'm sorry it has come to this." Closing his eyes, he covered her face with his hand and passed it down, wiping her from her own mind like erasing notes from a chalkboard.

Chapter Eleven

Katelyn drifted in a cool red haze. There was no need, no hunger, no craving, no loss of control. Blood scent surrounded her, but she could barely smell it anymore, except to know that it was good. She didn't *need* it. It was simply there.

Within the haze, she was conscious but unaware, with no entertainment but also no desire to be entertained. She simply was—no stress, no accusations, no anger, no devotion, no love. Absolutely nothing. Not experiencing bliss was bliss in itself.

Yet she did have a sense, in that red heaven, that things were happening on the outside, that her body moved and her mouth spoke, but she wasn't the one doing it. She sensed time passing, but she didn't know how much or how fast, nor did it matter.

She could live forever in the absence.

* * * *

But just like that, she was ripped from the haze and into a dark room. A series of clanks made her jolt.

Bright cage lights flickered on above and beside her.

She was hanging from one of the ceiling hooks, her wrists cuffed in sturdy brown leather, the chain over the hook. She was completely naked, and she wasn't alone. Two clothed young women hung on either side of her, their legs dangling in the air over wide, gleaming metal bowls, while she could stand on tiptoes. Their ankles were duct-taped. Both of them struggled on their hooks and tried to scream through duct-tape gags. Blindfolds dented their perfectly tended, dye-job-blonde hair.

"You chose them for me, Katelyn. And, as usual, you chose well." Jude emerged into the light wearing black trousers and a crisp white shirt partially unbuttoned, with shirt sleeves rolled up.

"Not much has changed since you left," he continued, slowly stepping closer, pitch-black shadows in his wake. "You still do for me what you did. You're as keenly observant as ever, but with none of the ethical concerns that plagued you before."

She kicked her legs out. "Then why did you pull me out? Put me back! I want to go back!"

"No."

She'd forgotten what the warmth of his voice could do to her skin when it went that low.

"You did everything you were supposed to do, no more. Your body responded to mine, but you didn't. There was no spark of life, intelligence—a puppet going through its paces. That's not why I changed you."

"No, you changed me to punish me, remember?" When her kicking feet connected with his legs, he flinched in reflex, but he also smiled.

"I changed you to harness your magnificent perception. I didn't *turn* you to punish you."

"Same diff."

"It really isn't." He caught her legs and pushed them down. With him less than a hand's length away now, she couldn't do much to kick him, and she was pretty sure kneeing him in the balls wouldn't be too effective, although she tucked that idea away in case she needed to use it.

"I didn't create a familiar to humiliate you, Katelyn. I deprived you of something else, but what you *are* isn't intended to be torture."

"Then why am I hanging from a hook?"

"Not that kind of torture," he amended.

"Then what kind? The affectionate kind that puts me in a psych ward?"

"The kind that shows you the truth that even an observant woman like you doesn't seem to be able to see."

Jude lifted his trouser leg to pull a polished stainless-steel knife from the sheath attached to his calf.

"I have many natural weapons, but it's sometimes useful to have other tools at one's disposal. I am a butcher. I never know when I'm going to need a good cut."

He brought the triangular point of the knife to his lower lip, then licked it. He winced and hissed as a thin red line formed over his tongue.

"You drank what blood you needed and no more," he said, though slightly muddled from the cut. "None of mine in weeks."

"Has it been weeks?"

"Seven, to be exact. You don't need my blood beyond the first drop, of course, but I've missed offering it to you, missed your yearning for it."

"You made me."

"Did I?" He raised her chin and brought his mouth just short of hers, his lips parted. The swirl of his blood scent entered into her, as far from the hazy heaven as it could be.

She whimpered as her stomach and her cunt clenched in tandem. The chains leading to the hook rattled as she strained toward him. He stayed just out of reach until he couldn't resist her efforts any longer and gave in to her mewing cries with a rumbling groan of his own. He filled her yielding mouth with his bleeding tongue. Then she could do nothing but succumb as he ravished her mouth and poured thin streams of sire blood down her throat.

He withdrew from her slowly, making her work to keep him close until she couldn't strain her neck any farther. His eyes were hooded in satisfaction, and he licked his lips, leaving a smear of his own blood that called beyond her reach. She bit her lower lip in frustration. Just an inch away, so close but completely unattainable.

"My blood isn't something you need," Jude said huskily. "Do you think other familiars crave it so? They'll drink it, but it's *life* that they need, to prolong their own. My blood does nothing except cement the bond between vampire and familiar. It's your desire that drives that continued bond, love. The cravings for insects, rats, raw meat, human blood... That's the familiar in you. But your craving for me? That's something else."

"You've never had a familiar before. What makes you the sudden expert?" Katelyn asked.

"I have no reason to lie."

"You have every reason to lie."

He wiped the knife thoroughly on his pristine white shirt, marking the fabric with dark crimson. "While you were under, I inquired after other vampires with familiars. They all respond differently, depending on both the vampire and familiar. Those that crave the blood of their sire have one thing in common with each other."

"What is that?"

Jude traced down her sternum between her breasts with the now-clean knife point, watching her flesh quiver at the metal's coolness and from her uncertainty.

"They crave the master as well."

Katelyn adjusted her toes on the cold floor. Then she giggled.

Of all the reactions, that clearly wasn't one that Jude had been expecting.

"Do you realize how you sound?" she asked. "If you think I'm going to fall for any of this… You're so full of shit, which is also conveniently yourself."

As soon as he leaned close enough, she was kissing him again, licking the blood from his lips and taking in what was left from the healing cut on his tongue, but he angled his body so that her cold, bare flesh stayed untouched. Her breasts and cunt ached for some kind of contact—or at least freedom from whatever hold he had over her. Her skin marbled with the chill, heightened by the contrast of heat at her core.

"If you won't believe me about yourself—if you cannot accept your own role in this twisted arrangement we've created for ourselves—perhaps I can convince you that you place much higher than the women you believe I prefer over you." Jude brought the knife between them again, creating a barrier between their mouths before stepping away.

His trousers were so well-tailored that they couldn't hope to conceal the growth of his erection. She remembered exactly what it felt like in her hands, under her lips, the head in her mouth, the shaft sliding through the entrance to her cunt.

She swallowed against the salivation stimulated both by his blood and body.

The knife glinted as he moved it against the beams of unforgiving cage lights above. He never reflected in it, but Katelyn caught glimpses of herself, what she looked like trussed up naked like a sacrifice to his ego.

"You have no idea what your blood does to me. Mine would boil if it could when your scent seeps through your skin and into the air around you. Being near it takes all my control not to sink my teeth in and taste you. It is my right to claim you, to kill you, to turn you if it is my desire. But the second I take you with my teeth, love, is the second you start to turn. That blessed fragrance of your life would change. I would rather suffer the abstinence, take you in every other way we can devise, than spill a drop of your blood from my bite. Perhaps we can find a way around that tonight, another test to my self-control. But first…"

Jude backed away to the side, to the blonde on Katelyn's right. The girl squirmed as he slid the knife under her shirt. It slit open with little resistance, like the thin, cheap fabric it was.

At first, the racing of her heartbeat came from fear, but when Jude's fangs slid down over his eyeteeth, he nudged them against the girl's neck in an open-mouthed gesture of surprisingly sharp tenderness. The girl stopped struggling, the taut flesh of her abdomen twitching as her breath caught. The touch of Jude's fangs rendered her immediately compliant, pleasure fooling her into thinking that she wanted what those teeth could do to her.

Katelyn knew from personal experience.

"Cara's refusing bodies again," Jude murmured against the girl's skin, nudging her here and there with his bared teeth to keep her calm. He strewed the remnants of her shirt on the floor, then started on her leggings. "Tinsel's at her wit's end. Their affair when Cara was human is the only thing that keeps Tinsel from putting her out of her misery. She doesn't always show it, but she's a secret romantic and an even more secret optimist. I tell her to kill Cara or set her free on the city to get killed by some hunter looking for a sloppy feral. But she clings to hope that Cara will realize there's no turning back. Even if she denies the bodies, though, she still must be paid in death."

He sank his teeth deep into the girl. The sound of pierced flesh was delicious torment to Katelyn's ears.

As he drank, the bob of his Adam's apple slow and languid rather than his usual hungry insistence, he sliced the knife into the girl's thighs. Her legs twitched, her hips moving from side to side before canting toward Jude again, but any cry of pain dissolved into one of pleasure. The girl's face was flushed, her neck bared for Jude's ease. Though most of her face was hidden, there was no mistaking her body language.

Katelyn closed her eyes and whimpered again when the first hard droplets of blood hit the metal bowl beneath the girl's hanging body. The trickle became rivulets as Jude dug the knife deeper, never quite hitting the major vessels, so that the blood loss would stay heavy but avoid spurting. He wasn't entirely successful, but as the front of his trousers dampened all the way to the knees, he didn't seem to mind. The bright lights brought out each blood gleam as the girl's legs were slowly subsumed in scarlet.

The moans of lust dissolved into fear and pain when Jude retreated to view his handiwork. The girl tossed her head, her hair sticking to sweat on her shoulders. She flopped like a snagged fish, flinging blood, most of which the wide bowl caught.

"You weren't here to tell me what drew you to them for me, but I can tell you it's not their hair or figure, not the way you seem to think it is, although I've yet to be disappointed. When you don't seek to punish, you bring me girls with blood richened by depth not nearly as common as I wish it were – those who *live* their lives and don't just survive, those who have taken the reins in the course of their destiny. I interrupt that course, predator that I am, but it still affects the bouquet and the palate alike. Try it."

He crouched to dip his fingers in the bowl. The tips of his fingers disappeared beneath an already significant amount of blood. The girl was crying, but she wasn't struggling as violently anymore, nor was her face flushed.

"It may seem as though I show them special favor, and in a way, I do. It may also seem as though I callously discard them, and in a way, that is true as well."

Jude painted Katelyn's lips with the girl's blood until she trembled. He filled her mouth when she couldn't hold back any longer. As she sucked his fingers, he licked the blade, and this time he didn't slice himself in the process.

"I respect them, Katelyn. I really do. They have boundless resources to maintain that vitality, but I, like you, do not. Mine must always be replenished, and the heated bloom of life inside me is so very brief. When I am with you after them, when my body flushes with their fresh blood, it is as though I am alive with you, for what is arousal but a reminder of life?"

He slid a hand down his stained shirt to the strain of his erection against his trousers. He rumbled in pleasure, almost like a growl, at the way she couldn't tear her gaze from the sight of himself touching, cupping, squeezing, stroking.

"I've robbed countless lives of their potential since my rebirth. They become a part of me for as long as I live, even if their usefulness lasts such a short time. I have to be callous to take their lives, but that doesn't mean I do it to be cruel or because I don't understand what I end. And their deaths are not more significant to me, Katelyn, than your life, just because I've chosen to bleed them and not you."

By this time, the other girl had gotten the gist of what Jude was talking about and struggled extra hard when Jude moved toward her. He cut through her skirt and shirt as well, this time sinking his teeth into her over and over as he unclothed her to minimize the fear. When she was left in nothing more than her bra and panties—and a multitude of bite marks—Jude knelt and bit into her thigh as he sliced into her abdomen, then her calves. Blood poured over his skull.

When he finally withdrew, the girl's cries weak and the first girl now quiet, he looked like a serial killer. And by some definitions, he was.

He slowly coated his whole hand with the girl's blood and brought it to Katelyn.

She licked him like a cat. Her pale skin dotted and smeared red as he brought himself closer to her, her swaying body hitting his with the canting of her hips.

When she was finished with his hand, he caught her mouth in a quick kiss before letting her direct his head according to her seeking mouth—wet, licking kisses across his jaw, slow swipes over his shorn scalp, then down to the musky hollow of his neck.

She bit…hard. Her dull teeth pressed into the skin and almost didn't break the surface. Then the flesh gave. Thick vampire blood burst into her mouth like chocolate syrup. Jude's knees buckled, and he shouted, but though she thought he would strike her, force her out of him, punish her for real this time, he instead cradled her head in his bloody hand and pressed her mouth closer, stroked down her thigh to encourage her legs around his waist.

"Yes," he whispered.

She'd never heard quite that tone in his voice, although she'd heard it in her own plenty.

Desperation.

"Yes, just like that. Take, my love. Take all you want."

He couldn't keep his free hand off her, running it over her thigh, up her belly to her full breast, where he stroked and pinched the nipple until it was hard for a reason other than the cold. He rubbed his wet trousers against her folds. The width of his shaft parted her folds and teased her clit, the fabric too much of a barrier.

She gasped and panted as she lifted her head from his neck. "Please. Please bite me. Turn me. *Please.*"

He fumbled with his trousers, but not for long. It didn't take more than a few strokes of blood over the shaft and a quick positioning before he was inside her. He pushed up with agonizing deliberation, as though to savor the slide of every inch.

"I can't," he groaned. He sheathed himself completely within her, clutching at her ass as he tried to keep his composure.

"You *won't*. You just won't."

She screwed her eyes tight shut, holding in her pleasure like holding her breath as he moved inside her. He kept trying to justify this to her, but love and lust and hunger? Those things didn't come from a vacuum. She didn't want to love this. She didn't want to love him. She didn't want him to know how much she loved both. That would be more than submission. That would be the white flag of complete and utter defeat.

"I won't," he agreed. "Not yet. I won't lose this, love."

"What—?"

"This." He released her hair and brought the flat of the knife to her shoulder. Then he drew the edge along the firm flesh.

Katelyn hissed between her teeth, letting the air out in a rush. She'd done this to herself, but it surprised her how different someone else cutting her could be.

Jude lifted her shoulder to catch the beads of blood with the warm velvet of his tongue. He clenched his knife-free hand, digging bruises into her ass with his fingers.

"God, yes. Do you have any idea how much…?"

He dug the tip of his tongue into the wound, framing his fangs against her skin to suck her blood as well as he could without biting.

If she'd had her hands, she would have hit him, in spite of the way her clit and cunt twitched with every suck, the same way they did when he closed his mouth over a nipple. It wasn't fair. It wasn't fair that biting was the technicality, that he could have his cake and eat it too while refusing to give her what she needed, refusing to give her the choice.

He brought the knife to the top of her breast and drew a line of blood all the way down to the areola. The chains clattered and clanked again as she wrenched against the pain, but she didn't unwind her legs from around his hips, and her own wetness dripped down her thigh as he continued to fuck her in shallow thrusts. It could have been the victims' blood, but she didn't think so, not with heady waves of arousal following each cut as the scent of her blood mingled with the *drip-drip-drip* from the other two girls.

He mirrored the marks on the other breast and on her shoulder, not so careful or slow anymore. When he was finished, the knife clattered on the floor as he hooked his arms under hers to grasp her shoulders and pound into her as he drank from each cut, dragging his lips, tongue and teeth over her.

Katelyn used the cuffs on her wrists to pull herself up and drop back down to meet him. His thrusts rippled through her, and her breasts bounced against his mouth. Where the magic in his touch didn't reach, the stinging seemed to grow with every passing second. She couldn't touch him, couldn't taste him, could only let him take her as she cried out to the chain-ridden ceiling.

She felt as though she were chained not to the ceiling but to a car driving down the freeway and dragging her behind it. She was nothing but raw flesh and smearing blood. Her mouth tasted of it. Her body and his smelled of it. Where he bruised her, it came to the surface all the more fragrant.

Between her breasts, he murmured, "I wish I could make you understand that I love your life." He lifted his head to meet her eyes—his that engulfing black, the kind that seemed to pierce her with the depth of dark emotion. He slowed his thrusts, drawing out the pleasure, drawing out the desire. "I won't take that away from you. I won't deal you death or undeath, not with so much of you vital in life. Your hunger, your lust, your anger, your love… Would your passion cool under the frost of death, as it did for Cara?"

That was the most sense he'd made to her all night.

"Did your passions cool?" she asked. "The others? I watch them every night at the Slaughterhouse. No one's passions have cooled just because they're room temperature. Please, harder. Don't stop. Faster, *please…*"

But he didn't speed the steady motion of his cock entering her to the base before pulling back again, almost slipping out completely. As out of control as Katelyn was and despite the need in the sounds he made and the forcefulness of his mouth on her, he maintained strict control.

"New passions arise." Jude smudged the new wells of blood on her breasts over her nipples like old-fashioned rouge. "Old passions die. Novelty fades. It has not yet faded for us. Perhaps once it does, it will be time for a change."

"Then I don't…don't…want you… Fuck, yes. Just like that."

Lying was off the table, and he knew it as he quickened his pace and found an angle that sparked new pleasures, little bursts of red light behind her eyelids.

"I kill the ones who are expendable to me," Jude continued, between flicks of his tongue over her painted nipple and whole-mouthed kisses on her breast. "Dead or undead. You, my love, are not expendable. I won't kill you, Katelyn. Not yet. The sooner you accept your life, the sooner we can…enjoy…*this*…just like this. Always like this. More like this. Nothing in our way. God, Katelyn, I've missed this so much."

He tangled his fist in her hair and pulled, just the way he knew she liked it, and he brought her mouth to the place on his neck where she'd broken through. She didn't hesitate. The wound had mostly healed, but now that she knew she could do it, she latched onto his neck as he closed his mouth – but not his teeth – over her cut shoulder to drink from her blood as she did from his.

Their bodies became two parts of one machine, like a discarded piece of the industrial equipment left behind in the warehouse. He pumped in and out of her, tireless, unrelenting, and she met his thrusts with the rise and fall of her hips. Their bodies struck each other, thighs hitting thighs, groin grinding against clit, abdomen striking belly. He held her so close, her breasts against his massive chest, her nipples dragging with delicious sensation across the planes. They were both bloodstained, but it was such a common state for them that she barely noticed or cared about the mess anymore.

Jude wrenched his mouth away from her wound and plunged his teeth into his own arm. The twist of his neck meant his flesh ripped under her mouth and spurted more blood into her mouth like cum. Katelyn shook, her arms weakening and her wrists hurting, even with Jude's help. Tears built and fell from the corners of her eyes as her cunt tightened like a fist around his cock, over and over again, orgasm spilling through her like blood through veins. God, yes… She'd missed this, too.

He slid his hands up her arms and clasped her wrists, lifting her off the hook just enough so that he didn't have to pull his erection out of her as he did so. She sank down around him again, and he brought her bound hands around his neck to hold on as he turned them around. His sheer strength continued to impress her, thrill her. The way she held him, the way he held her, she experienced his body as a series of hard, flexing muscles. When she'd been purely human, she'd never thought this could be something she'd love, but this, at least, was something she was sure wasn't just because she was a familiar.

He sheathed his fangs to kiss her, raw and desperate as his pace quickened. Finally, he simply enveloped her tightly in his arms, keeping them both still but for the jerking of his hips and the twitch of his cock inside her.

"You see." He pressed his forehead against hers. "I can control it and still taste you the way I've wanted to since the night I turned you."

Katelyn nuzzled his neck where she'd bitten him, smearing his blood over and around her lips. "Not exactly the way."

"Close enough."

"Not for me."

"I can only bite you once. I can drink from your human blood with my teeth inside you *once*. If you want a repeated culinary experience as a human, you only need to regularly frequent your favorite restaurant, but unless we keep a human as a donor, we can only have the particular taste of human *once*. I want your blood, Katelyn, more than just tonight. The girls you give me are vital, but you *are* life, and I won't give that away as easily as you seem willing to. Because you have my blood, if I bite you even once, you will never be human again after that. There's simply no need to rush."

Katelyn tucked her chin over his shoulder. "You don't understand."

"Perhaps not your experience as a familiar, and I apologize for putting you in the position that I did. It was never my intention, despite your suspicions. I only wanted to show you all I could give, that you didn't have to fight the cravings so hard, because I could provide. But I have my own experience as a vampire that you cannot yet imagine."

He lifted her off his cock, but he seemed reluctant to let her go entirely. "Becoming a vampire is its own adjustment. Accepting what you are now will prepare you better for what you become in the future. Do you want me to put you back in your mind, Katelyn, or do you think you can live a bit longer, for me, for you?"

"My life that you say you appreciate so much is gone. I can't do anything *but* the work of a familiar."

He lowered her to the floor. "It's not the end of your life. It's just the beginning of another."

"Not the one I would have chosen."

"We don't always choose how our lives change."

"You are so full of bullshit. You *have* the power to change it."

He kissed her forehead with a smile. "Go on to the showers. I'll meet you there after I give Cara her blood." He slapped her right buttock to direct her out.

"Need to spend more time with your blondes?"

Jude tucked himself into his trousers, then shed his ruined shirt. "I've already told you, it's not… Hello, there."

Katelyn turned toward the door, where Cara stood like a shadowy demon in a white dress, staring at them with eyes more deeply black than even Jude's at his darkest bloodlust.

Tinsel held Cara's hand but spoke softly as though to not startle her. "The party will start soon. She wanted a chance to walk through the Slaughterhouse while drinking her blood like a civilized person. Maybe—just maybe—I might be able to convince her to stay for the massacre."

Those eerie black eyes fixed upon Katelyn. "You're back."

Tinsel tightened her grip on Cara's hand.

"I didn't know you knew I was gone," Katelyn said cautiously.

"You were able to bring me blood because yours didn't appeal while you were gone. It lacked a certain… But now…" Cara's gaze crawled along her chest like clawed fingers. "I could just eat you up."

Jude put himself ever so subtly between Cara and Katelyn. "Maybe you should go, Katelyn."

"Oh no, why don't you stay?" Cara said before Katelyn could take two steps.

"There will be plenty more humans, plenty more bleeding hearts, without feeding from a familiar," Tinsel said. "See? Jude bled you some fresh blood." She tried to lead Cara to the hanging victims, but Cara was too tense to move. Her mouth looked full as her fangs grew.

"But there's fresher blood right here," Cara whispered.

"This was obviously a mistake," Jude said, still keeping a keen eye on Cara.

"She has to start sometime," Tinsel replied.

"Why now? Why today?" Katelyn asked Cara instead of Tinsel.

"I couldn't stand those four walls one more second. I wanted to visit the rest of the prison for a change. I should have known your soul would return on the night I stepped out. But then, you *want* to become a vampire, don't you?" Cara stepped toward her, trying to slip from Tinsel's grasp. She bared her teeth like an angry wolf. "You want to become like me. You believe yourself so horribly put upon by bloodlust that you want even more blood on your hands."

Her legs kept moving, like those of a wind-up doll not yet worn down. Tinsel's slender arms flexed, trying to keep Cara back.

"But I can't really blame you. It's the way you're made," Cara said. "Just like wanting to rip your throat out is the way *I* was made." She wrenched against Tinsel's grip with a hiss.

"Get your familiar out of here." Tinsel whipped Cara toward the steel bowls of blood. At the same time, Jude swept Katelyn around him and herded her to the open door.

"There's something wr—" Katelyn began, but Jude interrupted.

"Go. I'll keep her here while you ready yourself for the evening. We retrieved most of your clothes and belongings. You'll find everything you need in my bedroom. I'll meet you later." He swiftly kissed her, then closed the door on the darkness behind her.

Katelyn shivered, gooseflesh under the whole-body smears of blood. She idly sucked on her fingers on her way to the showers, glad that most of the Family was out gathering more guests for the Slaughterhouse rather than seeing her naked.

Strange, though, how she wouldn't be mortified by them seeing her, simply uncomfortable. Had time in heaven affected her so much, that blood-dripping nudity among vampires barely fazed her? Not as much as Cara would if she were walking these less-than-hallowed halls.

Katelyn walked a little faster, but she couldn't shake the obsidian-glass glint of Cara's gaze upon her healing breasts.

She showered first, then towel-walked to Jude's bedroom for clothes. She still didn't encounter anyone on the way, and although she was less naked than before, she appreciated the solitude so she could continue contemplating how she felt about Jude bringing her back.

Oddly enough, it was what Cara had said about life that reverberated through the memory of Jude's mouth all over her, the echo of his declarations, the phantom sensation of his body against hers even now. It left behind an odd tingling sensation, like an aftertaste.

As she shed the towel and placed it on the bed, she couldn't help but reach between her legs to swipe her fingers through her folds, pressing up against an almost heavy ache. She remembered other nights on this bed—and obviously, there were some she didn't. She thought she'd be creeped out by that, but instead, she heated over her cheeks and deep in her abdomen.

Welcome back, she told herself as she retrieved clothes from the drawers he'd allocated to her. There was even a small armoire that hadn't been there before, with some of their nicer things hung up inside.

After the distress that had led to her leaving and the distress that had followed her when she'd returned, she was surprisingly calm, if not quite at peace.

Since she wasn't recruiting tonight, she didn't have to go full club attire, so she stayed basic—a little black dress and killer heels, albeit wide enough to maintain her balance on the second-level walkway, not to mention on blood-soaked metal floors. Nice enough she wouldn't be questioned by the guests, yet not so wild as to attract attention. She'd just come back from heaven and been bled and fucked between two exsanguinated women. She didn't think she had it in her to be sociable.

Before returning to the Slaughterhouse, she stopped by the kitchen for a sandwich. There was a whole blood-free shelf in the fridge with her name on it. Food didn't have the same appeal it used to, but she still needed to eat.

On the way back to the Slaughterhouse, she thought the smell was just her at first. Both the human and vampire blood in her system had sped up her healing, but the cuts on her breasts, exposed by the low neckline of her babydoll dress, weren't completely gone. In addition, the butcher side of the business ensured the Family kept the building obsessively clean for health inspection purposes, but blood scent sometimes lingered in little draft-blown pockets.

However, the closer she came to the Slaughterhouse, the stronger the scent.

Maybe she'd taken longer in the shower than she'd thought. But it *felt* too early for the massacre, and there was something different how it smelled.

The second she opened the door, dread akin to her early horror in the Slaughterhouse sluiced through her.

The cage lights and hooks swung and clattered together. The strobe caught everything in glimpses and snatches. Only one cage light shone, swinging with the rest and adding to the effect, catching on colors that the strobe dulled.

So much red had splattered in giant inkblots on the floor, staining clothes of all colors into one, dyeing hair, rouging skin, flowing in enticing rivers down the several drains.

But the blood that misted the air wasn't just human, nor were the bodies.

Tinsel's Family lay strewn, headless, among the rest. The heads themselves were attached by the neck to the hooks, blunt tips right through the throat. Some of the heads had already listed upside-down from gravity, but there were a few shocked, right-side-up faces.

Only one body was still attached to its head, and she kicked violently while trying to extricate herself from the hook. Air and sounds escaped her mouth, but Tinsel couldn't speak or scream at the woman standing amid the carnage, her formerly white dress dripping at her bare feet.

Once Katelyn had processed the scene—from sight to sound to smell to even the organic and inorganic metallic taste in the air—her only thought wasn't helping Tinsel down from the hook or keeping Cara from noticing she had arrived.

In the whole room, she couldn't find Jude—and losing him wasn't easy.

Katelyn darted in, closing the door to block the extra light before Cara noticed, although she was quite occupied. Far from the crouched animal Katelyn remembered from the last feed she'd witnessed, Cara was standing, her arms locked around a man and her teeth buried in his neck as he groaned loudly. Katelyn hoped that and the man's rushing blood covered the click of the closing door.

The wider heel kept her shoes from striking the metal too harshly, but she couldn't stay completely quiet. She ran as carefully as possible along the wall to the pens, then darted in and out of each. There were bodies. There were even blonde women. But no Jude.

"I am here. Stay where you are."

Katelyn leaned against the wall, her hand on her pounding heart. She closed her eyes in relief.

When she opened her eyes, Cara was right in front of her.

Katelyn screamed as Cara snatched her by her hair and dragged her out of the pen into the beam from the single cage light. Tinsel had had no luck with the hook. It was a matter not of strength but of delicacy, and Tinsel had neither the presence of mind nor the balance for delicacy. Her feet were well off the floor.

Cara tilted her head as she stared down at Katelyn. "I should do the humane thing and just put a creature like you out of its misery."

She whirled around with a snarl to yank Tinsel down from the hook. Her body tore free, hitting the ground with a thud. Blood oozed from the neck, and more dripped like molasses from the hooked head.

Cara turned back to Katelyn. "Delusional and hopelessly, jealously romantic till the end. But for the fond memories she gave me, I would have killed her sooner. Too bad she ruined everything by killing me."

"What the hell happened while I was out?"

The whole bottom half of Cara's face covered in blood made her smile seem extra sharp. "Jude never said anything?"

"I just woke up."

"He might not have known, anyway. Once he realized your blood didn't call to me when you weren't present, he had you bring me blood and bodies every night, whatever was on the menu at the time. I've seen quite a bit of you these last two months. Tinsel didn't like it, of course, but it was the easiest way to force me to feed. I'm not heartless. I could tell you weren't in there. I couldn't fight you like I could Tinsel and her children. Well, I could, but what good would it have done? Your death would have been for nothing."

Cara crouched next to Katelyn and stroked down the side of her face. "Violence I have dealt in spades, killing my second nature. But a death that truly meant nothing… If there was one person in the world I didn't want to kill, I certainly wanted to keep her alive, didn't I? I felt almost normal with you, Katelyn. If Jude was at your side, I could tolerate him as well, because he created you—but *only* when he was by your side. I asked him about you, why you were gone, what happened to lead up to it, so I know you understand. You understand how helpless the hunger is. And maybe now you understand that it doesn't end with the turning."

"Not fun having to do everything your vampire tells you to do, either," Katelyn said, "or that a lot of what you want from him is because of your fucking familiar changes, not free will—not to mention getting caught with rat in your mouth."

"He told me about that." Cara's bloody smile was almost tender. "I blushed."

"I'm back now. Why aren't you draining me dry?" Katelyn asked, more disturbed by Cara's sweetness than Tinsel's decapitated body lying not three feet away.

Cara sat back on her heels and held a hand to her stomach. "I haven't been well and truly full in years. It's so wonderful to be full." She slid to the side and lay next to Katelyn, gazing up from the floor at where Katelyn sat upright. "Besides, you smell different now that you've returned. Still delicious, but…mine."

Katelyn scrambled away. "What did you *do*?" The words echoed in the dead room.

Cara lifted herself back up as though floating. "He said you were smart. I think you can figure it out. I didn't even know whether it would work, and if it did, I thought Jude would know. But he never came after me. When I sensed your presence the second you returned, I knew it had worked."

Katelyn brought a hand to her mouth, as though she'd be able to remember Cara's blood on her lips from while she was 'away'. "Why would you do that? Familiars only serve vampires. I can't help you become *less* of one."

"It was a whim." Cara placed one foot in front of the other, deliberately pursuing Katelyn, no matter which direction she tried to escape. "You were as trapped as I was in a body with desires you never asked for. I thought you might… I thought you'd be a better companion to me than Tinsel, who was always trying to make me more vampire. And I could be a better companion than Jude, because I understood, too. I thought we could become more than what was made of us."

"What exactly are you proposing? A vampire and familiar duo who can't stand what we are and can't control ourselves because neither of us will drink the blood we need? That's what the hunters are looking for."

"Maybe that's what we need. I can't put myself out of my misery, so let them try. I'll only protest until the stake's in my heart—force of habit, living even after you're dead." She giggled, swaying slightly before crouching and leaping after Katelyn. A hunter might have been a more equitable adversary, but a familiar—her familiar—was not. Cara snatched Katelyn against her from behind.

"You're blood-drunk," Katelyn said.

Cara slid her hand around Katelyn's throat, squeezing only to taunt. She must have fed well, indeed. Color raged in her cheeks and lips, and her hand nearly seared.

"Do you know I never got drunk until Tinsel convinced me to? And what she did to me with her power..."

Cara stroked a line from just under Katelyn's breasts to her navel. Then, after a moment's hesitation, she slid her hand down. Katelyn grasped Cara's wrists, but she couldn't budge vampire strength. It certainly didn't help that Cara hit her with lust far more intentional than any attraction Jude had inspired with his touch.

Cara pulled Katelyn's neck back until she had to rest her head on Cara's shoulder. "What she did to me was wicked, perverse, what some might call abomination."

"Like what you're doing to me now?" Katelyn said breathlessly.

"I was innocent. You were once innocent. Now you're a familiar. Do you know what that means, being a familiar to evil? You want me to bite you, don't you, Katelyn? Sink my fingers into your cunt and my teeth into that pretty, tender neck. You're *trembling* for it."

Katelyn felt like the first time Jude had touched her, but she was all the more aware of the strings Cara pulled to get her there. As Cara ran her mouth along the exposed parts of Katelyn's neck, she breathed Katelyn's heated scent in, a growl edging her inhales. It wasn't long before Cara shook as well, still tracing Katelyn's slit and folds over dampened fabric.

"Tell me to turn you. We'll die together in a river of blood. Or tell me to keep you for myself. I don't see your other vampire anywhere to be found. He knows you're in distress as surely as I do, but he isn't here, is he? I would have killed him with the rest, but the man has an unusual knack for concealment, considering his ridiculous size."

"That's because no one ever looks up."

Jude slid from the ceiling with his legs around a length of chain and one hand loosely keeping him on. In the other, he held a fire ax.

He landed about twenty feet away from Cara, the body of his sire broken and seeping in front of him. His jaw tightened, but he seemingly forced himself not to look at Tinsel.

"Well, aren't you resourceful?" Cara licked up Katelyn's jaw, but her eyes were on Jude. "You going to kill me, the co-sire of your familiar?"

"I didn't offer her to you," he said. "I trusted you, and you *took* her. And now you're doing to her exactly what Tinsel did to you, as though paying it forward pays off the injustice."

"I'm giving her the choice I was never given."

"You didn't give her the choice to become your familiar."

"Neither did you," Cara shot back.

"I'm within the boundaries of my own ethics. You've long since crossed yours. You've slaughtered vampire and human alike in bloodlust and self-hatred. You're not to be trusted."

"If I turn her, whose blood do you think will win out in her transformation?"

Katelyn bit her lip at the wet slide of Cara's fangs as they brushed her skin.

"She's so sensitive, isn't she? So responsive. She's had more of your blood, so she smells more of you. But if my teeth turn her, will her vampire blood declare loyalty to me, her full sire? If so, how long do you think it will take for the madness to reach her? She's already showed signs. You rescued her from a fucking psych ward."

"She's not mad," Jude said.

"That's up for debate, but *I* certainly am. You think I would have done anything like this before I was turned, if I weren't insane with hunger I never asked for?" Cara asked with a growl. "I barely remember half of these people in my mouth. I'm lucid now, but the madness never leaves completely—and neither does hers."

"It's your resistance that maddens you."

"It's what I *am* that maddens me, as it does her. You gifted her three thousand rats, and you didn't think she'd resist?"

"She didn't, until she stopped drinking from them."

"Tell him," Cara whispered in her ear just as she slipped her fingers under Katelyn's panties.

Katelyn arched and made a helpless sound of startled pleasure, then tightened her grip on Cara's wrists. "Tell him what?"

"Tell him how when the blood flows, the madness is satisfied, but when it ends, the true you returns. Tell him how accepting it makes monsters of us all. At least we know what we are, Katelyn. We don't pretend to be a good, sensitive man who makes promises he can't keep."

"If you so much as break her skin, I'll cut your head off, and I'll make sure it takes two or three strikes so that you know what's happening to you the whole time. No madness in death." Grasping the ax in both hands, Jude bared his own fangs as Cara hissed at him.

"Is it madness?" Katelyn stared up at the shifting chains above, trying not to let her body run off without her. Cara's thumb circled and stroked her clit, and she was moving two fingers inside Katelyn's cunt, slow, deliberate, seeking, until they found the place where Katelyn thought she might shatter apart if Cara kept rubbing it. With added power behind what she was doing, every little thing made Katelyn feel on the brink of orgasm.

"What was that, honey drip?" Cara ran the smooth side of her fangs over Katelyn's neck again.

"I... Oh fuck... Is it madness to be what you are, even if it was how you were made? Or is it greater madness to try to act as though nothing changed? As though just because it shouldn't have happened, it didn't. There's a word for that kind of delusion... denial."

"Shut up." This time Cara squeezed Katelyn's neck to hurt. "Resistance is resistance. I don't have to be like them."

"What if you do? What if not being like them only makes you worse? Look what you've done."

"This place is where *they've* done it thousands of times over." Cara pressed her fingers more forcefully against and into Katelyn.

"All at once?"

"Almost every night. You helped them gather their sacrifices. Don't play dumb with me. It doesn't suit you," Cara said.

"No, they don't do *this* every night. *This* is if they all went into a hopping night club and slaughtered every last person there. *This* is why you were locked up. You singlehandedly killed all these people, and I don't think it's because you secretly want the hunters to find and kill you."

"Then why?" Cara asked, lips against the corner of Katelyn's mouth.

"Because this is what you really want—to feel righteous in your denial and exhilarated in your surrender. Otherwise, you wouldn't be having such a good time."

Her 'time' grew higher and louder as Cara relentlessly rubbed her clit and G-spot. Cara's vampire blood inside Katelyn pounded with heightened intensity that she could no longer talk through. Cara forced the orgasm through her, hissing into her skin the more Katelyn writhed in her arms.

"A good time? What makes you think I'm having a good time?" Cara laughed as Katelyn's legs stopped being able to hold her and all that kept her up was Cara's preternatural strength.

"L-look a-a-around," Katelyn struggled to say, but a scream tore through her throat as her climax continued to climb with each successive one.

Finally, Cara jerked out of Katelyn's cunt. She showed Katelyn how wet she was, the juices stretching in strings between Cara's fingers. She smeared Katelyn's mouth with them, then sucked them into her own, moaning low in her chest.

"Look around," Katelyn repeated, still shaking with arousal that hadn't dissipated just because her orgasms had reached their end. "There's as much blood going to waste as there was blood that you drank, from human *and* vampire. You don't need vampire blood, and if you couldn't resist human blood as much as you say, you wouldn't have left any behind to spoil. I've seen Jude spray a vein because he liked the aesthetic, but I've also seen him leave little more than a few drops behind."

Cara slowly opened the hand around Katelyn's throat, but the tension in her joints was unmistakable. If she hadn't already been pale, her knuckles probably would have gone white.

Katelyn pulled the hem of her dress back down, her hands shaking against the skirt. "You made a mess. You've always made a mess. The first time I saw you with a human rather than a bottle of blood, you lost it—not because it was blood, but because you gave in to the predator more than the rest of them. This is something you did on purpose, even if you don't know why."

Katelyn dared to face Cara, whose face twisted with fury.

"And I get it," Katelyn said quietly. "I hate that I love it, too. I hate that I love it all. I don't want to. But it only gets worse when you fight, because eventually you can't hide it in its rawest, purest form. And that's what you've become, Cara—a vampire completely in love with being a vampire. That's what you are."

Chapter Twelve

Cara screamed in neither fear nor pleasure. Katelyn would have covered her ears, but Cara swiped claws over Katelyn's face and across the front of her dress, tearing fabric, tearing skin.

"I thought you understood!" Cara yelled so hard that she bent almost double as Katelyn stumbled back and fell over Tinsel's remains. "Fucking familiar traitor! Bow to me, *bow* to me for forgiveness I won't give, because you're still mine, and I think it's time for us both to go. In blood or in flames, it's all the same."

A blade sank directly into Cara's shoulder. The bone made a wooden crack and crunch as it splintered. Cara's left arm hit the floor like a dry eel.

"Let her go," Jude said. As Cara's hawk-like screeching grew louder, the rumble of his voice grew softer, but no less potent.

"She's *mine,*" Cara snarled. This time she evaded the ax, ducking faster than Katelyn's eyes could see. "She's mine as much as yours."

"You stole what wasn't yours."

"You were neglectful. You have been from the beginning. Keep bowing, woman. Don't wipe your blood away. I'm going to need that in a minute. And I don't intend to use the loophole he did. You *will* die tonight. The only question is whether you'll wake up again."

Katelyn's body knew its mistress and stayed on all fours. All she could do was turn her head to watch Jude and Cara circling each other, Cara stepping over her arm as though she hadn't lost it at all.

Jude raised the ax again. "I don't want to have to do this."

Cara's saliva glistened on her bloodstained chin.

This time Jude anticipated Cara's feint. The second blow struck her other shoulder, severing the right arm as well. Cara screamed again, tossing her head like a wolf or a lion to shake the blood from the tips of her hair. Pain raked over the chalkboard of her screams, but Katelyn still couldn't tell whether the pain was physical or emotional.

Cara's pretty doll face had shifted into one far more demonic than Katelyn was comfortable with, as though the muscles writhed like small serpents under her skin. Without her arms, she appeared more lamia than human, just short of gorgon.

And Katelyn understood that Jude's calm exterior concealed something similar—something not just wild but unrepentantly wicked.

"Protect me!" Cara scrambled back with a sinuous weaving of her altered body. Her black eyes revealed the first hints of fear.

Katelyn stumbled to her feet to put herself between Jude and Cara, which forced Jude to abruptly yank his ax away, his eyes widening. Familiar healing wouldn't do much for an ax blade across her abdomen. But she cried out when Cara struck her again, this time across the back with the claws that had formed on her toes. Jude twisted sawdust from the ax handle.

"I could bleed her right here, kill her with her body between us, and you wouldn't be able to stop me, because you can't kill her yourself. You're weak, Jude. Tinsel made you weak. You could cut my legs out from under me, if you could stand to harm your precious girl, but I'd still be stronger than you. My resistance has made me stronger."

"That's quite the one-eighty," Katelyn said, "hating the vampire then declaring yourself the most vampire in the room."

"Shut your lying mouth." Another swipe of her claws.

Katelyn pressed her lips together and squeezed her eyes shut, but there was nothing to lessen the sting or make it mean something else—nothing but the pain that Cara wanted it to be.

"She's right, Cara."

As Cara ripped through her back again, Katelyn whimpered, her mouth still clamped closed because neither Cara nor Jude had released her from the command.

"Leave her out of this." Jude finally sounded like the violence against Katelyn was getting to him. "She's done nothing but tell you the truth."

"Too late."

"You're not going to live through the night," he said. "I hope you realize that."

"Big words, Big Guy. Of the two of us, you're the one with the greatest weakness. You'll stay away as long as you think she might have a chance. Come to me, Katelyn. Back up and show me that pretty neck again. You smell positively sinful."

"Please," Katelyn mentally begged—to whom, she wasn't sure.

"Run." He barked the order in a tone she'd never heard from him before. He'd commanded her in the past, but never with such force and intention. *"Run,* Katelyn. Run as far as you can."

"Oh, do stay."

Katelyn tangled over her own legs, one still operating under Jude's order and the other responding to Cara's.

"Escape," Jude said, but Cara immediately countermanded with "Stay with me."

"Goddamn it!"

Cara laughed. "Do retrieve my arms, darling. I'll be needing those after I feed."

Tears streamed down her face as Katelyn picked up the arms that Jude had cut off. She held them as though they consisted of all the dead rats and mice that she'd ever eaten.

"Fight her, Katelyn." Jude started circling again, continuing to clutch the ax, but even Katelyn could tell it was just for show. He wouldn't swing it if it could possibly hit her, and in that sense, Cara was right about his weakness, because Cara had no such reservations.

"I'm trying."

"You thought being her first would make her yours, but I'm the one who wants her more," Cara said. "I'm willing to give her what she wanted from the beginning—death, one way or the other. She'd rather be dead than yours for the rest of her life, wouldn't you, Katelyn?"

"If *you'd* rather be dead, Cara, I can oblige you," Jude said.

Cara bared her teeth once more. "I'll die, but not by your hand. I'll taste your blood before your ax tastes my flesh and bone again. I'll take all your power, and I'll take all my familiar once and for all. If I'm lucky, you'll still be alive enough to see it."

The entire room echoed with a deafening boom. Jude ducked, falling to the ground, and Katelyn brought Cara's arms to her ears as Cara's body hit the floor with dead weight, although she twitched, her face still writhing like serpents.

Blood seeped from a gunshot wound under her cheek.

Detective Dunn, then Detective Black, stepped from the strobed darkness near the entrance from the warehouse into the cage light beam. Their guns were up and aimed, body language tense and hyperaware.

As soon as Jude and Katelyn had pulled their hands away from their ears, Detective Dunn said, "This is just an ordinary gun. If I were you, I'd cut off her head before she heals around the bullet."

Jude was too startled by the presence of two uninvited humans in the Slaughterhouse, but Katelyn let go of Cara's arms, grabbed the ax from where Jude had dropped it and swung it down on Cara's neck. She'd never used an ax before, so she treated it like one of those carnival hammers that measured strength. It seemed to work about the same, but she didn't have Jude's aim. She struck too close to the collarbone rather than the neck. She had to press down on Cara's chest with her foot to yank the ax back up.

Cara's blackened eyes stared up at her. Her mouth worked wordlessly.

Katelyn screamed, her mouth as far open as it could go in contrast to when Cara had forced her to stay silent. She struck Cara right in the face with a sound like splitting logs mixed with stabbing a pumpkin with a butcher knife.

"Somewhere between the two," Jude said, still stunned, although he shouldn't have been so surprised by Katelyn's violence. She'd killed all those rodents he'd sent her, and she'd grown terribly accustomed to the sound of breaking bones.

"That one was on purpose." Katelyn took a breath now that Cara's face had been obliterated. She'd take much longer to heal from both the bullet and ax wounds like that, which gave Katelyn the time she needed.

It took four swings before she severed Cara's neck completely, difficult especially when she reached bone. When the ax hit metal and sent shock waves through the handle and up Katelyn's arms, she gladly let the weapon fall.

Then she turned to face the two detectives, forcing her legs to carry her and her shoulders not to slump. "Thanks."

"Looks like we didn't do most of the work." Detective Dunn lowered but didn't holster his weapon, not with Jude getting to his feet.

"You shut off her brain enough that she couldn't control me anymore," Katelyn said. "Made a huge difference."

"I hope you don't take this the wrong way, but what the hell are you doing here?" Jude asked.

"We've been keeping track of Ms. Dillon for several weeks now. Once we got wind of where the notorious Slaughterhouse was located, we watched the comings and lack of goings. When we couldn't stake out, we set cameras up all around. They don't record vampires, of course, but they recorded the humans coming in. We had a good enough sense of what was going on. You made waves with the murder of three university students, you and your Family."

"It's not *my* Family." Jude nodded toward Tinsel.

"Nevertheless, once Ms. Dillon mysteriously broke out of Mattea, we were tasked with finding her. In finding her, we found the Slaughterhouse, but once we were here, we had to determine if you were worth our time to bring down—whether you were more dangerous than any other Family in town, more dangerous than any individual vampires hunting alone."

The man had guts, armed with nothing but a gun. Jude had been limited in his fight against Cara because she'd used Katelyn against him. He had no such limitations with the detectives.

"And what was your verdict?" Jude asked evenly.

"Stay right there!" Detective Black shouted, leveling her gun at two moving figures in the strobing darkness. "Don't move!"

Jude raised a hand to the two vampires. They held up their own in reluctant surrender.

"We were going to leave you to your devices," Detective Dunn said, taking a more placatory tone, although he'd lifted his gun again at Detective Black's shout. "We hated to see the deaths of three young women discounted, as we always do, but you weren't doing enough to get *us* involved, as much as I didn't want to leave you behind, Ms. Dillon. We could tell you were different after Mattea, and it wasn't a better difference than the last time we met."

"Well, I'm back," Katelyn said.

"We can see that. And it looks like you've lost a few shackles there at your feet. Would you like to come with us now? We've reintegrated ex-familiars in the past."

Jude's gigantic form stiffened, as though he'd been turned into a bronze statue. Detective Dunn's gaze remained on Katelyn. It took her more than a few moments to realize why he wasn't side-eyeing Jude.

He thought Katelyn was Cara's familiar. She didn't know how much the detectives had overheard, but it hadn't been enough to know that Katelyn was Jude's familiar first.

"How'd you even know to come in here?" Katelyn asked, to buy herself more time to figure out how to play the situation.

"Detective Black isn't a witch or psychic or anything, but she has more than just women's intuition," Detective Dunn said. "She figured out something was going wrong inside. It looks like we arrived just in time."

"And we appreciate your help," Jude said. "We simply want to know what you intend to do now that you're here. Your reputations precede you, Detectives. We don't doubt you've informed your superiors of your situation, and you would be missed. That leaves us in a bit of a bind."

"We appreciate the situation," Detective Dunn replied. "We're just here to help Ms. Dillon in any way we can. Now that her mistress has passed, will you let her come with us?"

Katelyn thought fast, practically hearing the cogs and wheels turning in her brain.

"Let me go," she thought at Jude without looking. If Detective Dunn saw her share a glance with Jude, he'd make the connection, the way she had between Jude and Tinsel.

"But you're still mine. You still need – "

She didn't think it so much in words, just a general feeling of *trust me.*

"We could still have plenty of use for her," Jude said slowly, "but whatever makes you comfortable, Detectives."

"We'll leave you to you and yours, sir, if you give us safe passage. Ms. Dillon, please come with us."

Jude nodded, glancing at the other two vampires. Cody and the other vampire nodded as well, complying with the one who had obviously taken the mantle as head of the Family. Katelyn wondered how Cody had managed to escape the fray, since he was usually right in the middle of it. Maybe he'd been fortunate enough to be assigned to the storefront for late-night blood orders.

"Do you need to get anything?" Detective Black asked.

Katelyn shook her head. "Everything can be replaced."

"Come here, then." Detective Dunn beckoned to her as he lowered his gun.

When Katelyn passed by Jude, she sensed his mind in hers like a brush of fingers, but that was all. Detective Dunn put a hand on her shoulder and guided her back to Detective Black.

"We're leaving now," Detective Dunn said. "I hope we never have to see you again."

"Our hope as well, Detectives," Jude replied. "We were fortunate to have you close by. Have a good evening."

Detective Dunn and Detective Black led Katelyn out of the Slaughterhouse, flanking her with their guns ready. They didn't quite run, but Katelyn had to in order to keep up.

Detective Black opened the back of the unmarked car and helped her in. No cuffs, no Miranda warnings, and they didn't turn on their bubble lights or speed off, just immediately locked the doors.

Detective Dunn turned around in his seat after he'd caught his breath and reholstered his gun. "Feeling better, Ms. Dillon?"

She nodded.

"I'm sorry all this had to happen to you. I'm afraid we don't have much to help… enough for a motel room and takeout for a week. Or we could just let you call your parents."

She quickly shook her head. "I don't think that's a good idea."

"They're worried sick about you since you left Mattea."

"I know. I just… I can't face everyone yet."

"Of course. We can also give you contact information for temp agencies sympathetic to our division," Detective Black said as Detective Dunn pulled away from the butcher shop. "And we'll give you our cards again, of course. If you need anything…"

"How many of your cards have you given out?" Katelyn asked.

"More than you'd think," Detective Dunn said.

"More than we'd like," Detective Black added grimly.

"Once you've seen the other side of the curtain, the underworld never quite lets you go," Detective Dunn said. "If you can talk about it with someone who has a foot in both worlds, sometimes it helps. Whatever happens, whatever's going on, if you need to call us, we keep our phones on twenty-four seven."

"Either way, keep us as apprised of your situation as you want us to be," Detective Black said. "We'll need you to call us after a week to let us know if you've found yourself a job or you're struggling to find decent living situation. After that, we're not your parents. We'll assume you're okay if you don't call us again. We'd just like to be able to close one of our cases. It's always nice when we can do that."

"I think I can manage a phone call," Katelyn replied.

"Do you have any idea what you're going to do?" Detective Dunn asked.

"Not a clue."

* * * *

They set her up in a relatively cheap motel. They apologized that it wasn't someplace better, but Katelyn dismissed their concerns. Being an ex-sister didn't mean a little seediness would kill her. Far from it.

She accepted Detective Black's offer to buy her a shirt to wear instead of her shredded dress. The good detective managed to choose the right size, albeit deliberately oversized, and after a shower, Katelyn felt surprisingly like herself.

After giving her phone numbers, a bundle of bills and a paper with a typed-up list of resources for someone in her kind of peculiar circumstances, the detectives left, and Katelyn checked the corners for spiders. After swallowing just two, her cravings quieted. It was a good thing the detectives had left when they did, because the places that Cara had scratched her were already healed to a point that they would have questioned it.

Chapter Thirteen

"Go back to the beginning."

* * * *

Katelyn wove through dancing bodies on her way to the bar.

Ben wiped down the wood in front of her. "I heard what happened to your friends. I didn't think I'd ever see you ever again. Your usual?"

Katelyn nodded. "I thought it was time to come back. Kind of a grief thing."

He slid the Diet Coke across. "Want me to Shirley Temple that for you?"

"Let's live a little." Red dye wasn't quite what she was after, but grenadine made the drink less dull to her altered sense of taste.

"Well, I'm glad you're okay," Ben said.

"Thanks."

Katelyn kicked her heels against the bar stool, watched people dance and zoned out to the music and the hypnotic, chaotic sway of the dancers. She'd thought it would be more painful to come here, but after her time in heaven, mindless as it had been, her friends felt far away, not ghosts among the living. She'd received her punishment and penance, and wherever her friends were, she hoped they didn't have to suffer anymore.

"Hey, isn't that the guy?" Ben asked.

Katelyn snapped back into herself. "Hmmm?"

"The guy. The guy in the picture that the police showed us. The guy you said was stalking your friends and caused your accident." Ben had his hand on something under the bar, which Katelyn dearly hoped was a phone or a baseball bat instead of a shotgun in a crowded room.

Katelyn followed Ben's concerned gaze to the man who'd joined the rest of the dancers, a giant who towered at least half a head above the tallest men around him. He wore a green T-shirt that clung to his muscles and looked soft, even from a distance, jeans that hugged his ass without going skinny on his bulkier figure. She didn't know where he shopped, but he had a hell of an eye for what worked on him.

"Yeah, that's him," Katelyn said without alarm. "Turns out that was all a big misunderstanding."

"It was?"

"Oh, yeah," she replied. "He was there, but he's no criminal mastermind." She slipped Ben twenty-five dollars, more than enough of a tip.

"Whoa. Thanks. Katelyn?"

"Yeah?"

"You sure everything's okay? I can call the police."

"Everything's golden. We're actually acquainted now. He's not the one the police are looking for." She slid from the bar stool and drank half of the rest of her drink. "Have a good night, Ben."

"You, too. Be careful."

Katelyn entered the arena of dancing bodies, moving hers until she became a part of them not ten feet from where Jude was. She didn't look in his direction, but she knew the moment his body rather than anyone else's came up against her.

He encircled her from behind, one arm over her breasts, the other under, his cheek against her hair. Her wrap dress was a few shades darker than his shirt. They hadn't even planned it.

Her chest showed no signs of the knife cuts or Cara's claws. His bare arm rested against flawless skin. She'd kept up her diet as surreptitiously as possible, but it turned out that most people at a cheap motel weren't paying attention.

Neither of them said anything as they danced, but neither did they restrain their desire, not when all the people around them didn't care to contain theirs, either. Before long, his erection pressed against her lower back, and her panties were definitely wet between her thighs without a single touch.

She looked back up at him with a broad smile that he couldn't help but return. "Where have you been all my life, Big Guy?"

"My place is only a few blocks from here," he said.

"Then what are we waiting for?"

"I'll leave first and bring the SUV around."

"I get to be kidnapped this time?" She reached behind her and stroked up the shaft just to hear him groan in her ear.

"Whatever you want, woman." He broke away from her and was quickly swallowed by the crowd.

She waited, enduring a few pawings during the interim, then followed him out.

She opened the back door to the van instead of the passenger's side. "Do you know how many men touched my boobs after you left? You giving me all that attention made me precious—or maybe blondes really do have more fun."

"Not that I'm complaining, but why the change? I told you blondes aren't what I look for."

"And I told you that was a bunch of crap," Katelyn replied as they drove away from the club.

Jude laughed. "You found the qualities I like in a bunch of blondes, love, but I can also find them in brunettes and redheads just fine. *You're* the one with the fixation. Do *you* like it?"

Katelyn removed the rubber band holding her low ponytail in place. She pulled her hair over her shoulder to stare at its sweet, bright, new honey gold. She'd felt a little bad for using the detectives' donations on a dye job, but she hadn't needed to eat much, and after their week-later phone call, they were officially out of her life.

As far as she knew, they didn't suspect a thing.

"I do."

"I could tell. It makes me like it, too. You aren't afraid to be noticed when you're blonde," Jude said. "One more question before we arrive."

"Yes?"

"Are you wearing a bra under that?"

She didn't often go braless, but the wrap dress held her in surprisingly well, and that had certainly contributed to the less-than-subtle fondling on the dance floor.

Katelyn ran her fingers over where the nipples pressed hard and tight against the thin fabric. If she looked close enough, she could discern the texture of the areolae. "What do you think?"

"Fuck me," he breathed.

He didn't reflect in the rearview mirror, but she could see the way he looked into it. He didn't swear often. She considered it a compliment.

Katelyn pulled the sides of the wrap neckline apart, stretching the material until it tucked under her breasts, then flicked her nipples to make herself jump. Her breasts swung a little with every shift. "Watch the road."

"You are a wicked, wicked girl."

Jude seemingly couldn't get to the Slaughterhouse fast enough. He ran around the van to yank open the door and picked her up as though she weighed nothing. She wrapped her legs around his waist, giggling as he kissed her, which also hid her breasts from anyone else's gaze, although he'd promised that all the detectives' video surveillance had been taken care of.

"Do you want me to take you in the middle of the Slaughterhouse or in one of the pens like one of my victims?" he asked between kisses along her neck. He kneaded her ass and thighs as she rocked her hips against the head of his erection. "Or our room? I've taken ownership of the largest and stored most of Tinsel's things away. I think you'll like the new bed."

"Take me in the pen. Take me in the dark." She slid a hand up the smooth skin of his scalp, holding him close to her neck. "The party still going?"

He carried her to the side door. "We've made an alliance of Families to maintain the Slaughterhouse. It has a reputation as much in our world as yours. We didn't have to search long. We'll build up our part of the Family soon enough. Cody and Silas have their eyes on a few potentials."

"And me?" Katelyn asked.

Jude stopped fumbling with the doorknob and pressed her against the door instead so that he could look her in the eyes. His were big and black—bloodlust compounded by time away, but not as all-consumed as Cara. He was in control. She'd never doubted.

"Not yet." He stroked her cheek with his huge hand. "I know you want me to, and I've promised that I would. But…"

"But you want a little life first." She couldn't conceal her disappointment, but it didn't hit her with quite the gaveled fatalism as before.

"Yes." He kissed her again, lingering on her lips. "There's all the time in the world for death, love."

She reached down for the doorknob this time. He covered her hand with his to turn it the rest of the way, then closed the door with his foot, plunging them into darkness that the strobe barely touched near the slaughter pens. The first was taken. He stumbled into the second, so eager to fall to his knees that they tumbled onto the hard floor. Jude took most of the brunt of the fall on his elbows, but he laughed into her breasts with her as he pushed the sleeves down her arms with adolescent urgency.

"It's only been a few weeks," Katelyn said.

"My enthusiasm isn't solely for the end of your absence." Jude discarded her dress and hummed with an edge of a growl as he removed her panties. "I could have forced your return, but you called to me willingly, and I cannot—"

He cut himself off between her legs, licking between her folds and cresting at her clit. Katelyn dug her nails into his scalp. Not deep enough to break through, though the skin seemed so thin and delicate there. The evening already smelled of spilled blood, but in faded drafts, and she wasn't quite ready for fresh…not yet.

She didn't bother holding back her cries. It exhilarated her to be part of the orgy during the party rather than after, somehow more forbidden than when Jude came at her covered in blood. Maybe because it felt more normal, like something she'd missed from before her transformation. He was a little old to be a boyfriend—not even accounting for how many years he'd been undead—but he was skilled and more than a little frisky, so there were no complaints on her end.

Jude reveled in her thighs on either side of his head. He squeezed them, even slapped them lightly, stroked just behind her knees. He crawled forward until she was bent almost double. He seemed to enjoy forcing her legs up, her heels high in the air, her back arching as he coaxed shudders of pleasure through her. She felt fevered against his cool lips…close. She canted her hips up to meet his mouth, urging him on.

Then he surprised her by grabbing her legs and rolling them around so that she straddled his head. Her weight on his face and the press of her cunt against his mouth didn't stop him for a second. He doubled down, rather, groaning as she helplessly ground against his tongue. She nearly screamed from the slide of his fangs against her folds as he sucked hard and fast against her clit. That was enough to put her over, smearing her juices over his chin.

She lifted herself up as soon as she could convince her legs to move. He didn't need to breathe.

Katelyn jumped at the sound of tearing fabric.

"Really?" She peered between her legs at his now bare chest. "You had to do the male version of bodice-ripping? You just *had* to alpha-male Hulk-meets-the-Wolfman it?"

"I was inspired," Jude said with a bright grin. "Do you like it?"

"You have no idea."

She crawled back and licked at his face, tasting some of the life that he loved from her. He cupped her breasts, measured her hips, worshipped her ass. He couldn't seem to get enough of her. His kiss became more artless, their tongues twining but neither quite surrendering, and his fangs were always there to send shivers down her spine.

Jude wove his fingers through her hair and pulled them both upright. He swiped his tongue over her lips, her chin, then caught one breast in his eager mouth. She nearly teared up at the combination of his mouth and his teeth there, remembering the first time he'd tormented her with the very tip of his fang, almost biting her, almost taking her right there and then. She recognized his reluctance now for what it was.

"I want you riding me," he said, after holding the rigid nipple between his teeth. He released her nipple but not her hair and lay on the metal floor, guiding her farther back until she straddled his hips. He hadn't torn open his trousers, but his cock was certainly trying. "Just like you rode my mouth. I want to watch you take what you want from me. Let me see it. Let me see *you*."

She stroked down his chest, feeling more than seeing, enchanted by the slopes and planes, alive yet cool. When she reached the edge of his trousers, she jerked on the buttons and zipper to open them, pushed at his trousers the way he'd pushed at the sleeves of her dress, eager to have them removed—just enough for full access.

"Oh, there's a good girl," he moaned as she positioned his thick, heavy cock, then slid down, adjusting herself to his size. She wouldn't have thought two weeks would make such a difference, but he surprised her, nevertheless.

She didn't take long to start working herself over the shaft, though, the head stretching her entrance every time she raised herself up. It wasn't easy with her parted legs over his broad hips. She nodded, unable to speak, when he grabbed her by the ass to help lift her rather than expecting her to do it all on her own. She grabbed his arms so that she could feel the shift of stone-hard muscles under that velvet skin.

His black eyes glinted. He could see everything from his vantage point—the place where his cock entered her and slid between her clinging folds, the way her breasts bounced, the tossing of her hair as she struggled not to let her sensitivity bring her back to climax too quickly. It helped that he kept his teeth to himself, but the scent of newer blood had grown stronger on the drafts. It was only a matter of time before her cravings returned, hunger deeper than he could reach with his cock. After all, she hadn't had anything more substantial than vermin since she'd left.

"God, you're gorgeous," he breathed. "I'd love to see you bathed in blood—sitting in a tub, your breasts partially concealed, that blonde hair stained back to its natural red. Would you like that, Katelyn?"

She pressed her knuckles to her lips as her mouth watered.

"Another night." He pushed his hips up to meet her now, his cock punishing, his thrusts rippling over her flesh.

Suddenly, he lunged up to grab her by the neck and pull her down, using his strength alone now to fuck her. His arm encircled her waist. The other guided her head down to his neck.

"Bite me," he whispered.

"Bite me first," Katelyn said, but she smiled against him.

"Impudent girl. Oh, *fuck,* yes… I never thought I'd… *Yes.*"

She tightened her pussy around him at the taste of his blood bursting on her tongue, like returning home, and she dug her teeth deeper inside him. The heat of her lust made her breasts stick to his skin, but she moved her lower half like a serpent, undulating to meet his thrusts as she drank him in the deepest kiss she could give as a human.

It didn't take long before he clutched at her hips and brought her down all the way over him, as far in as he could go. He nipped at her shoulder to make her flutter around him, and she bit him still deeper through her second, more lingering, sweeter orgasm. The pulse of blood between her legs was almost as good as the pulsing hot blood in her mouth. His cooler vampire blood was more decadent, though, lengthening her climax well beyond his own. He clutched her to him through her shaking until she pulled back because, of the two of them, she still needed to breathe.

He didn't even bother cleaning her mouth the way she had him, nor did he retrieve her dress. He rocked them up until he could get his knees under him and stand, his cock still buried inside her. Then he kicked off his shoes and trousers, almost fell as he toed off his socks.

Both of them gloriously naked, he walked them out of the pen and back onto the Slaughterhouse dance floor, where the massacre had officially begun, although neither Jude nor Katelyn paid much attention. He accepted a wineglass of blood and gave it to Katelyn. She gulped it down, and he lavished her throat with the caress of his lips and tongue, as though tasting the blood through her skin. When she was done, he knocked her hand away, leaving the glass to break. He'd been softening, but he hardened once again at the first taste of warm human blood on her lips.

By some sorcery, they managed to get from the Slaughterhouse to Jude's new room. All she knew was that she'd been tossed onto a comforter like a cloud and a mattress that sank down around her.

"Wow. You're right. This is a better bed."

He crawled onto the bed to join her, and she tucked herself closer, peering over his face now that she could see him in the light.

"I went to 360° at your request, but are you really *here* of your own volition?" he asked.

Katelyn nodded.

"What changed?"

"I had a basis for comparison."

"And?"

"And I concluded that most of what I feel for you isn't forced. What is, I'm not sure you can help that. I just don't know how to distinguish between what's me and what's familiar."

"If it makes you feel any better, love, I don't know, either." Jude slowly untangled her new blonde hair, knotted from the way he'd held it as he'd fucked her. "I can't tell what part of my affection is for you as my familiar and what is for *you*. All I can do is feel what I feel and hope that it's true." He draped the rest of her hair over her shoulder and ran his fingertips down over her breast to the dip of her waist. "I do know that other vampires don't love their familiars as I do you. I'll sometimes err, and master I must be, but I'll give you whatever chains you desire until the day when you can choose without bias. I'm afraid I'm more selfish than I'd like to admit."

She covered his mouth with two fingers. "Jude?"

"Yes?"

"You talk too much."

He reached behind him to turn the lamp down low and drown them in dark amber light. She rested over his chest, her thigh brushing his erection, but he didn't need her again, just accepted her into his arms and held her.

Master. Familiar. She was here, but how much of that was really her? Did it matter?

It was a long time before she could sleep.

Want to see more from this author?
Here's a taster for you to enjoy!

Meridian: Avarice & Creed
Aurelia T. Evans

Coming Fall 2024

Excerpt

"Have you accepted Jesus Christ into your heart as your Lord, savior and friend?"

Ana Molina handed out the pamphlets to everyone who walked the path where she and the rest of her Zacchaeus Tree small group had gathered for their weekly evangelism push. She knew most of the pamphlets would end up farther down the path—in the trash or, for the more eco-conscious, paper recycling bins—but she'd stopped being discouraged by people's indifference late in her freshman year.

If Zacchaeus handed out a hundred flyers and even one inspired someone to join their small group or one of the dozens available through the interdenominational department, that made every eyeroll and sneer of disdain worth the thorn prick in her chest and behind her eyes. As Jesus had said in Luke, angels rejoiced if even one sinner repented…and so did she. It wasn't Zacchaeus' job to change minds or souls, merely to plant seeds that God could tend and grow according to His will.

Ana was a student, too. She was one of them. She knew how easy it was to believe that nothing bad could ever happen to them, that the cradle of University of Texas-Meridian was a mini-Mount Olympus of bacchanalian gods.

That's why she didn't take it personally that most people didn't accept a pamphlet or even acknowledge their existence with basic eye contact. Nor did she take it personally when a Cro-Magnon with his other dudebros spat something that smelled suspiciously alcoholic on her shirt when she tried to hand him a pamphlet, as well. The boy laughed and slapped his bros' backs as they headed down the path, while Ana wrung her shirt and tried not to think about where his mouth had been.

Freddie came up from behind her and kissed the crown of her head near where her ponytail began. "Are you okay?"

"He won't remember it five minutes from now. Neither should I." Ana continued to hold out pamphlets without hesitation.

Some in Zacchaeus claimed she was fearless. They thought she couldn't hear them whisper about how easy it seemed for her to stand in the middle of university grounds in one of the most selfish cities in the country, speaking the Lord's truth to people who dismissed her like any street-corner soapbox preacher when there were much more interesting prostitutes on the other side of the street.

But Freddie knew better than anyone where her conviction came from.

"I know it seems easy and fun to go to these parties and fraternities, but I promise you, you may not live to regret it, but you'll die with that regret like ash on your lips," Ana said as more groups passed by—with women wearing short skirts and midriff tops, sometimes little more than bras, and guys in shirts and jeans designed to display lanky length of limb or curve of carefully cultivated muscle. Courting like birds of paradise, beautiful and flashy, but birds didn't have marriage or strictures about how courtship should reach its inevitable conclusion.

"Go get fucked," some guy yelled from within the group. "No, really, get fucked. Sounds like you need it."

"It's not sin that will be your downfall. All of us sin, every one of us, including me," Ana said, barely blinking. It helped to stare into the darkness rather than focus on any one face. That way, everyone thought she was talking to them, and she didn't have to see their contempt too clearly.

"I'll bet you do." It could have been the same guy…or someone close to him. She couldn't tell.

"There's not one on this earth who does not sin. There was only Jesus Christ, who died on the cross to save you from those sins. I'm not saying that if you sin, you go to hell. I'm not the person to tell you that. But without Jesus…that's hell *and* the handbasket that takes you there."

"Which direction is that going now? Could that be 'going down', maybe?"

Snickering surrounded her like hallucinations, but she forced herself to continue. She usually didn't get this kind of attention, but when she did, it went little worse than beer spit on her shirt.

"If you accept Jesus and His truth, you won't need the sin like you think you do, like the world tells you that you do—the 'college experience', just young people having fun, getting their wild out. They *lie* to you. They say that so they don't have to blame themselves for their failure, so they can turn a blind eye to the terrible things you're doing to yourself, because that's easier than trying to save you from the same mistakes they made."

"Oh my God, get a hobby...or a job. Don't you have anything better to do?" An eyeroll strode by her with two textbooks under her arm. "Like an actual Religious Studies class?"

"The danger here isn't the devil. It isn't sex, drugs or rock 'n' roll. It's moral relativity. Do you know the humanities produce more atheists than STEM majors?" Ana shouted after the girl to be heard over the crush of the last evening classes headed toward the Student Center. "But none of them teach you the truth. They teach you theories that they call facts, as though something ancient and rich and magical has to be wrong."

"If I'd wanted to go to school in seventeenth-century Salem, I would have sent my application somewhere that has actual autumn," the girl replied without looking over her shoulder.

Sometimes, any response at all meant that she'd strummed someone's soul, thrown a pebble in their pond for a round of ripples to spread. If they weren't just flinging sexual innuendos at her, she'd caught their attention, and if she'd caught their attention, the words that God gave her to reach them wouldn't be so easily forgotten. Even an antagonistic response was an acknowledgment of the conversation.

"I'm not judging. I'm begging," Ana continued.

The girl who'd passed her stopped on the other side of the group, hugging her books. She looked out of patience, but she'd *stopped*.

"*I'll* make you beg," someone muttered.

Ana ignored him. "I'm begging you to see that you're not going to find love anywhere here—only lust that leaves you empty."

"*I'll* leave you empty."

"For God's sake, shut up," Freddie snapped.

Ana reached behind her to rest her hand on Freddie's arm. "You might find success, with accolades or financial compensation, false acrylic idols. Those are the things you *think* you want, what the world tells you you're supposed to want. Sex, money and power—the devil's Trinity."

"You must be so fun at parties." The girl shook her head. "Go touch grass or drink a lemonade or something—anything to let the helium out of your head and get you out of heaven back to the ground where the air isn't as thin. Life's a lot better when you stop looking at everything like a cosmic battle. Sometimes a Friday night is just a Friday night."

"And sometimes a Friday night is your last night," Ana said. "If it is, are you sure where your immortal soul is going? Look... I don't care if you're the blackest heart on campus, if you've done coke or meth or murdered your mother and got away with it."

The girl's eyebrows rose, her lips curving in an involuntary grin.

"Believe in Jesus as God's Son who died for your sins, and heaven is guaranteed. That's all. That's it. It's really that easy." Ana wove between the groups, most of whom were finally drifting away since Ana refused to take the lascivious bait. She held out the pamphlet to the girl.

"Yeah. It would be nice if it were that easy." The girl took the pamphlet. "It's people that make it so damn hard."

"I'll tell you who's damn hard." The guy congratulated himself with braying laughter and hand slaps among his friends.

Freddie finally put himself between Ana and their group. If anyone else had taken a more aggressive stand on her behalf, it probably would have prompted a macho, manly man-war among the frontal-lobe developmentally stunted. But Freddie was a big guy, over six feet and broad as well as heavy, so significantly bigger than even the average fit athlete on campus. She'd always called him the Viking, even though he wasn't positive he had any Scandinavian ancestry, much less an impulse to pillage and plunder. Even if someone thought he wasn't very fast, there was no question that he was a sledgehammer of a person.

"Hey, man, it was just a joke. Fuck, no one can take a joke these days." The boy backed away with his friends, and he wasn't so enamored of the subject of his 'jokes' that he leered at her as he left.

"If you want to learn more, contact me at that university email," Ana said to the girl. "Or even better, come our small group meetings on Sunday and Wednesday evenings. At the very least, it's one of the few get-togethers that doesn't expect you to study, get drunk or take your clothes off."

"More's the pity." The girl tucked the pamphlet into one of her textbooks but lifted her face back up with apology in her eyes. "I'm pagan as fuck, though. Other than celebrating the holidays that Christians stole from us first, I don't really do small groups with people who tend to imagine stoning me to death."

"We accept everyone, even witches. Everyone is in danger, so everyone has a chance to pull themselves out of the mire."

"Doesn't sound very welcoming to me," the girl said.

"I never said we'd agree with you or not challenge you," Ana replied in concession. "Just that you'd be welcome. Admit it, though. If you came to an evangelistic small group, you'd probably be disappointed if it was too agreeable. Cookie?"

When in doubt, offer snacks. Free food was irresistible to college students. She was surprised that more unscrupulous characters didn't swoop into the UTM with canapes. The devil himself could purchase souls wholesale if he gave away cake.

The girl accepted the cookie with a smile that bordered on genuine. "Not supposed to take baked goods from strangers."

"There's nothing but strange around here."

"You're not wrong." The girl saluted her with the cookie, then took a bite before leaving the dispersing crowd and the far more persistent Zacchaeus.

Ana thought they might see the girl within a month, although it was hard to anticipate how deeply curiosity would root.

"Never forget that you're amazing," Freddie whispered, then gathered her into his heat and encompassing arms. No one made her feel as safe and loved as he did. When he encouraged her, she felt the Spirit's presence through his words—far more cogent than tongues, but no less powerful.

"Shut the door. Keep out the devil," she said, not quite under her breath. An old mantra rather than a rebuke.

"Keep the devil in the night," he finished for her.

But she'd already stepped out of his arms to approach the next wave of people on the path. Her stomach clenched and growled in hunger, especially so close to fresh-baked cookies that drew enough people within their reach. God came first, all other needs second. There was too much at stake. Ana knew better than most what happened when people chose wrong.

* * * *

Later that night, Ana lay on Freddie's couch with her head on his lap as they watched new episodes of one of their current TV shows of choice. Some people might have been surprised by what she and Freddie enjoyed watching, especially its occasionally risqué or violent content. They tended to assume that because she was concerned with the state of immortal souls, she must be some homeschooled zealot with hemlines below the knees who wasn't allowed to watch anything above a kid's rating.

She did prefer a certain amount of modesty in the public eye, but that was personal rather than moral. In the privacy of her boyfriend's apartment, she shrugged off the light jacket and just wore the loose tank top and bralette underneath, which exposed the edges of her back tattoo and wrists wrapped with crystal beads that sometimes got her confused for Neopagan, especially since she didn't always wear a cross around her neck.

The crystals were relics of her childhood from visits with her mother to Book & Candle, a place that in itself was neither good nor bad. God had made the rocks before He made man, and spells of protection were neutral, whether the protected was a witch or not.

Beneath his shirt, Freddie had tattoos as well, some of which matched hers. There were a few other students on campus with the same back tattoo she and Freddie shared, members of a brotherhood deeper than a Bible study group—people who knew that the darker

Bible stories were more than just metaphor. Freddie was one of the few who hadn't experienced the darker side of the city for himself, but he believed those who told their tales. More specifically, he believed Ana.

She hadn't told him *everything*. There were things she didn't want to think about, didn't want to remember. But she'd told him enough, and he was there when she needed to share something new—like cutting open a vein all over again, weakening the walls, even as she built up scar tissue.

He stroked her loose blonde hair, and she turned her bracelets over her wrists, feeling over the beads like a rosary, a prayer—sometimes the same one—for each sphere. Slightly more effective than wishing on a star, even if only idle. Her slice of birthday cake stood lonely on its plate on the coffee table in front of her. Every time she thought about sitting up to eat it, Freddie stroked her hair again.

"No reason not to celebrate, even if you don't like your birthday—*especially* if you don't like your birthday. Any occasion for cake and presents," Freddie had said. He was always the one who made her celebrate holidays—personal, federal and spiritual—but he was gentle about it. No balloons. No candles. No card, except for the one on her dormitory desk that would be trashed unopened when she could stomach touching it.

But she liked cake, and she liked presents, and if Freddie happened to give them to her on a day that coincided with her birthday, that was just a happy accident.

Her present gleamed on the middle finger of her right hand. They'd talked about marriage, but neither of them were ready for that until after she graduated, so this wasn't that kind of ring. The silver was real, but the stone was glass—a promise of a promise. Not his first—and she hoped not his last.

He loved her, loved every wary fiber of her heart. She loved him enough to shed her layers and show the anxiety that the rest of Zacchaeus didn't believe she had.

At the start of the next episode, Ana convinced herself upright to pick up her cake. Her taste buds thanked her, and at least when she was finished, she felt less ambivalent about it.

"I'm only going to say this once, babe." Freddie brought her against him in a bear hug, making her giggle. "Happy birthday."

"Make a wish," a new voice said.

Ana nearly slipped off the couch in her instinctive response to get as far away from that voice as possible.

Freddie swelled to his feet to tower over the woman who had entered his apartment without invitation.

Ana's mother was not intimidated. Instead, she looked like she'd run into Ana by accident at the grocery or a bookstore. She tapped her purse with her immaculate nails, bit her lipsticked lips in what Ana recognized as a performance of nervousness.

That didn't mean her mother wasn't nervous about seeing Ana again for the first time since Ana had fled home for college. Ana just couldn't trust the way her mother *looked*, not when she could be the most two-faced bitch this side of the Atlantic. Most people would never believe it—in her delicately tailored, hand-stitched suit made to her specifications, every line marking her enviable shape at its most flattering. Although she was forty-five years old, most people wouldn't clock her past thirty-five at the oldest.

Occasionally, someone asked who she'd killed to have a figure and skin like she did. When Ana had been a little girl, strangers had gotten a kick out of her saying that her mom had made a deal with the devil.

"You look so good, darling." Her mother held the purse like a shield, as though Ana were the dangerous one here. "I swear, when you left, you were just a child. Look at you now, all grown up."

"Yeah, only a few years behind you." Ana got up from the couch but kept the coffee table between them.

She could count on one hand the number of times her parents had hurt her. But the ones she could list on those five fingers… They'd made an impression, three of them literal scars.

"Get out of here. This is *my* home, and you're trespassing. Get *out*!" When Freddie bellowed like that, it usually brought to atavistic mind a grizzly bear. Star football players considered voiding their bladder.

Her mother barely blinked.

"I don't think it's asking for much to spend time with my only daughter on her twenty-first birthday. I would have trespassed in her home, but she wasn't there." Her mother slowly set down her purse in an attempt to make herself approachable. And most people found her beauty eminently so.

But there was a reason why Ana wore looser, more neutral clothing and didn't use makeup or hair products beyond basic shampoo and conditioner. Her mother hadn't met a hair mousse she didn't like, while Ana balked from a hair dryer.

Everything her mother was, Ana made a point not to be.

"Not just grown up. You might have actually grown a little. I swear I didn't have to look up at you before in these heels. But maybe I'm confusing you with one of our friends' daughters. It would help if I'd seen you these last four years instead of just your tuition statements."

Ana's mother was prim, proper and perfect. Those who didn't know her well would assume that Ana was a typical selfish post-teenager, a spoiled brat who dismissed her elders out of hand just because they were older—not that gray dared to creep into her mother's coif, nor lines from the corners of her eyes.

"I thought we had an acceptable arrangement," Ana said, crossing her arms.

"Get *out*!" Freddie pointed emphatically at the door.

Her mother waved his shouting away like it was an annoying mosquito buzzing in her ear and stepped around the coffee table to approach.

Freddie kicked the coffee table to the side and gathered Ana against him to protect her. "I'm calling the police."

"So this is your charming prince. Is that the best ring he could find? He didn't even size your finger beforehand. Oh, honey, you can do so much better."

"You have no idea what you're talking about…on so many levels." Ana let herself be held, gave herself over to the calming effect of Freddie's natural heat.

"I know that you're beautiful. I know that you're my daughter. I birthed you myself." Her mother laughed a little. "If I'd known what you would become, I would have been even more excited. And you've almost graduated, too. It's impressive, Ana, what you've managed to do on your own."

"Great. Glad we had this little chat. You've seen your daughter. Now you leave," Freddie snapped.

"My daughter, who took nine hours of hard labor, back contractions and a scar that no amount of bowing and praying can fully get rid of. My daughter, who I helped with homework, from reading to math. My daughter, who doesn't want to even talk to her family on her birthday. You're just here, doing hell knows what with hell knows whom. I get to imagine all kinds of rebellious scenarios in my spare time, with no way to anticipate or prevent whatever insidious ideology takes hold—Calvinism, paganism, veganism..."

"If all you wanted was to see me, Mom, you can go now. I'm not interested in digging fence posts or mending bad fences. When I said I didn't want to see you again, I wasn't kidding."

"That is no way to speak to your mother."

Ana broke away from Freddie to advance on her. This time, the prim, pretty woman exhibited some surprise, possibly even a little fear, because this Ana was not the same Ana that her parents had deposited on the university's doorstep.

"We had an arrangement," Ana said. "You pay my tuition and housing bills because you're the ones who wanted me to come here. And I don't come home on break, I don't answer your calls or texts, I don't write back to your emails or snail mail, I don't acknowledge your smoke signals. And I don't go to the police about what you and your friends do at three in the morning on the high unholy days. That was the agreement."

"We're just exercising our right to freedom of religion," her mother said mildly, gesturing her blood red nails with uncanny grace.

"I don't think your sacrifices would agree." Ana shrugged her shoulder on the side of her body where old scars were pearly and knotted on her back.

"You never did understand the concept of sacrifice."

"I understood it fine. You just always ensured it was someone else's sacrifice."

"Not always."

"What do you *want*?"

"I wanted to spend some time with my only daughter. Is that such a crime?"

"It is when you do it. Look... Our arrangement's almost at an end. Then not even school will tie you to me anymore. You shouldn't get so much as a piece of junk mail in my name. We'll be strangers who happen to be related." With each step Ana took forward, her mother stepped back, the doll-like perfection of her face cracking with uncertainty, but Ana couldn't even trust that. "Now, you were never invited into Freddie's home. You are trespassing. This is Texas. If he weren't a pacifist, he could kill you."

"The door was unlocked." Her mother indicated the open deadbolt and the undone lock latch.

"The hell it was," Freddie snarled behind Ana. "You're the reason I lock it every time."

This wasn't the first time her mother had tried to worm her way back into Ana's life, and it certainly wasn't the first time she'd tried to do it in a legally fuzzy way.

"The best of us forget now and then. Just let me look at you, Ana. Please." When she touched Ana's face, Ana twitched, but her mother stayed gentle, so Ana tentatively allowed the intrusion.

She'd had therapy session after therapy session about her parents—albeit abridged, even with a Meridian psychologist. The general consensus within those sessions was that she owed her parents nothing—not blood, sinew, approval or love. Her parents had brought a living, breathing autonomous human into the world of their own volition. It was their basic human duty to feed, clothe, shelter and educate her within their means. More than that might have warranted a smidgeon of gratitude, but anything more that they'd done had been offset by blood- and tear-collecting, even organ-stealing. The least they could do in exchange for bodily fluids and a vestigial organ or two was pay for four years of college, and the least she could do for herself was take advantage of it.

Her therapist had also said that she was allowed to feel any way about her parents, including conflicted. She just didn't have to give those feelings any greater credence than the knowledge that her parents had hurt her in unforgivable ways—graver than grounding her, taking away her phone or detaching the door from her bedroom to make sure she never got with boys or girls in her teen years. They'd never actually done any of *those* things to her.

Her friends had always envied her because her parents let her do whatever she wanted. Except once Ana had realized who her parents were, she hadn't wanted to do any of those things they let her do anymore.

Yet she also remembered her mother singing lullabies when Ana was sick, sometimes standing over her bed after reading a chapter to her and touching her face just like this, as though trying to memorize her. She remembered her mother holding her when she cried, putting bandages on skinned knees—even though sometimes she'd tucked the tissue used to clean her daughter's blood in her pocket rather than throwing it away. She remembered her parents cheering at soccer games, when she received good grades for a semester and at her high school graduation, well after she'd stopped begging for their approval.

For all the terrible things they had done, they'd also done these other things that they hadn't necessarily needed to do as parents or even just people.

Was that enough to give her mother another chance? Ana knew that it wasn't.

But at the center of it all, she missed her family, mourned what she dreamed her family could have been—if her parents weren't raging psychopaths in the privacy of their own coven. Ana wished they were only witches.

"So beautiful," her mother muttered, framing her face. "You look just like my sister at this age—so grown-up, but with the natural bloom of youth, before the relentless battle against gravity."

"She's sharp as a tack with a flair for memorization, too," Freddie said. "But I guess substance doesn't matter much with you people."

"Oh, it matters very much. Just not with what we need her for." Her mother reached behind her to open the door.

Men in hoods swarmed the apartment. Their attire wasn't as costume-y as robes, just nondescript sweatshirts and jackets that obscured their faces, some of which had been further hidden behind rubber masks that mimicked human features.

Ana tried to run, but it was a third-floor apartment. There was nowhere to escape, nowhere to hide where they wouldn't find her in two seconds. Freddie tried to fight, and he managed to do a little better than she did on that front, pacifist or not. When he walloped three of them with one swing of his arm to push them away from her, she dared to imagine that he could grab her from the cultists, throw her over his shoulder and plunge through the crowd like a boulder rolling through a river.

But a strong enough river could move a boulder instead, and all a man needed against another man was a well-placed syringe.

Another well-placed syringe knocked Ana out before Freddie even hit the ground.

About the Author

Aurelia T. Evans is an up-and-coming erotica author with a penchant for horror and the supernatural.

She's the twisted mind behind the werewolf/shifter Sanctuary trilogy, demonic circus series Arcanium, and vampire serial Bloodbound. She's also had short stories featured in various erotic anthologies.

Aurelia presently lives in Dallas, Texas (although she doesn't ride horses or wear hats). She loves cats and enjoys baking as much as she dislikes cooking. She's a walker, not a runner, and she writes outside as often as possible.

Aurelia loves to hear from readers. You can find her contact information, website details and author profile page at https://www.totallybound.com

TOTALLY
BOUND
Home of Erotic Romance

www.ingramcontent.com/pod-product-compliance
Lightning Source LLC
LaVergne TN
LVHW091029080826
845145LV00002B/420

9781802505900